The Fall Collection

Books by Geneviève Antoine Dariaux:

THE FALL COLLECTION
ACCENT ON ELEGANCE
THE MEN IN YOUR LIFE
ENTERTAINING WITH ELEGANCE
ELEGANCE

The

Fall Collection

Geneviève Antoine Dariaux
Translated by Helen Eustis

Doubleday & Company, Inc.
Garden City   New York   1973

*To Dominique
with the unconditional love of a mother*

The Fall Collection

Chapter I

With a swish and a bang, the curtains were opened and the shutters thrown back. July light flowed into the room, and the occupant of the bed, of whom nothing could be seen at first but a mass of blond hair because she was sleeping on her stomach, turned over with a groan. Carefully she opened one eye toward the French doors leading onto a terrace. The view was due south from the sixth floor of a newish apartment house on the Quai de Béthune, by the Seine. Simultaneously Popoff, the pale beige cocker, stretched and groaned on his cushion, in exactly the same way as had his owner.

Thérèse, Madame de Forval's cook and housemaid, waited near the bed for her mistress to sit up so that she could slide a second pillow behind her back and place a tray on her knees. With eyes still puffy from sleep, Marie-Victoire smiled and said in a slightly hoarse voice:

"Good morning, Thérèse, haven't you fixed any breakfast for Mademoiselle?"

"Mademoiselle Clothilde has already gone out."

1

Though she offered this information in a carefully neutral tone, Marie-Victoire knew quite well that Thérèse, who had been in her service for twenty years, was reproaching her once again for not being concerned enough with her daughter, for devoting herself to business matters. "As if a Baussigue lady needed to sell dresses . . . !" she had once heard her say.

"Already out at eight twenty-five?" This after a quick glance at the little lapis-lazuli clock from Cartier. Thérèse didn't even answer, and her mistress, angry at being made to feel guilty, barely refrained from sticking her tongue out as she used to do when she was ten years old. . . . She exudes hostility from every pore, Marie-Victoire said to herself; if she were a squid the carpet would be soaked in ink.

"Thérèse, I asked you a question!"

"Madame knows very well that Mademoiselle goes out every morning at about eight-ten; I even get up a quarter of an hour early so she won't leave the house with an empty stomach, poor lamb!"

Thérèse had grown up in Baussigue, Marie-Victoire's family's ancestral home in Provence, and she had never known any other "masters," as she would have put it. She was completely devoted to the family. In return, she felt herself part of it, and entitled to open criticism of anything that displeased her.

"That was perfectly natural when she was studying for her exams, but now that she's passed them, she could sleep until noon if she liked!"

"So it seems she'd rather be elsewhere!"

"Really, Thérèse, say what is on your mind instead of dropping these dire hints!"

"It's all very well to be one of the greatest *couturières* in Paris, but if you have to sacrifice everything else—your

2

husband and your child—to do it, well, I'd rather be Thérèse Tripouille and earn my daily bread in the Midi!"

"In spite of the fact that you were there and know what happened, are you going to be like my in-laws and say I drove my husband to commit suicide?"

And, as always when the fatal word suicide was pronounced, she could not keep herself from rerunning the dreadful scene in her mind: blood everywhere, the white hand gripping the black revolver, the accusing looks of the entire Forval family, the hatred of the faithful secretary revealed at last, the whispering at the funeral. She still felt the poisonous glances of all those people trying to peer at her face through her widow's veil. She told herself for the hundredth time: They could not help shrugging their shoulders when they saw me sobbing.

"Madame knows very well what I think about that. Poor Monsieur, he was a weakling. I'm well aware of how he wasn't capable even of choosing a tie or deciding whether he should take along an umbrella. It seems impossible he ever found the courage to kill himself. . . ."

Marie-Victoire shuddered. Had the telephone rung in his quiet office at just the crucial moment? The doctors who had been treating him for his chronic mental depressions had concluded that Jérôme must have been playing with the idea of a death like this for a long time; must have placed the barrel of the revolver in his mouth without really having intended to fire, when perhaps the abrupt sound of the telephone surprised him, and out of pure reflex, he pulled the trigger without meaning to. Marie-Victoire had tried to phone him at just that time and had received no answer. It haunted her that she herself might have been the innocent spark that had exploded the dynamite. In effect, then, she *had* killed her husband.

"But no, there is certainly nothing to reproach Madame with unless it's the working," Thérèse went on, characteristi-

3

cally shifting her attack. "It isn't easy for a man to see his wife being more successful than he is, to see her decorated with the Legion of Honor before he is! My father wouldn't have liked that either!"

"My poor Thérèse, even in the country things have changed these days and women no longer wait until their lord and master has finished his meal before they sit down at the table!"

"Well, it was all very unfortunate, but it wasn't all Madame's fault. . . ."

"Thanks so much."

". . . but what *was* her fault was not remarrying and giving Clothilde a father!"

"Really, I've raised her very well by myself! She's going to get her degree in chemistry, and soon she'll be able to run my perfume plant. She speaks English and Spanish fluently; she knows how to behave in company and which fork to use; she doesn't say 'pardon me'; she knows how to dress; she swims; she skis; she rides horseback; she has traveled; she can tell Bach from Mozart, and Botticelli from Rembrandt. Pretty as she is, and with such an education, she could marry anyone at all, a prince of the blood, an English duke, or whom she pleases!"

"Oh, she can't complain about having beautiful clothes and going to all the balls, but maybe she would rather have stayed home and talked!"

"But Thérèse, don't you remember how we used to spend all those Sundays together, and how we used to laugh and chatter when she came to have breakfast in bed with me? She's the one who has gone away, not I!"

Thérèse looked at her employer pityingly. It was true what she had just said, and raising children wasn't easy. But her "ewe lamb," as she called Clothilde, was always right, and if she wasn't happy, the fault must be her mother's! Now she

4

heard the concierge ringing the bell, shrugged her shoulders, and went to get the mail.

Marie-Victoire, as she sipped her enormous cup of tea, scolded herself for showing weakness. Popoff, seeing that her mind was elsewhere, jumped on the bed, out of reach of the hand that knew so well how to scratch behind his ears, but that was also quick to deliver a slap.

"Get down, you bad dog, that's not allowed!"

He flattened himself humbly on the covers, his eyes pleading deceitfully, his brow furrowed.

"Down, I said!" and she pushed him with her foot. Resentfully, he went to lift a leg on the rosebushes on the terrace. So sulk, old boy, I don't care in the least; no biscuits for you, that's all.

She frequently held long conversations with the cocker, her constant companion. He even looked like her—at least his hair did, for it was exactly the same color as hers.

Marie-Victoire was an eternal optimist. She was capable of seeing the bright side of her most painful memories and her bitterest remorse. As usual, when she thought of the breakdown of her marriage, she looked around for comfort to the luxurious setting she had managed to provide for herself. For the past ten years, this setting and her success in fashion had taken the place of a lover. Once again she counted her treasures: the white linen bedspread embroidered with a Louis XIII design of many-colored flowers; the sleeping alcove bordered in the same pattern; the authentic paneling, copied in the two big wardrobes framing the alcove; the pink-and-white antique Venetian glass chandelier hanging in one corner of the room over a Louis XIII game table on whose ivory and ebony chessboard stood a collection of antique bottles; the magnificent ivory and tortoise-shell cabinet, also Louis XIII, on the opposite wall; the white carpeting scattered with antique

5

rugs in faded colors; the 1904 Picasso, the only picture; the green-veined white marble bathroom with its malachite and gilded bronze taps, with carpeting and towels in the same green.

. . . Yes, she might well be pleased with herself; all this was well worth a few business worries!

Thérèse arrived with *Le Figaro* and some letters. Marie-Victoire looked through them.

. . . Bills, bills. Good heavens, an ad from the travel agency —2,000 francs for a week in New York—her air fare alone had cost more than that! A letter from friends in Kansas City, a color postcard of Greece from a former mannequin who was still dazzled by her rich marriage, poor baby, she should learn that colored postcards are only for intimate friends; she must have written a handful of them and the dressing room would be plastered with sunsets over the Acropolis. Really, I wonder if the Queen of England gets some postcards too? Come, don't exaggerate, you're hardly the Queen of England! But admit that you are rather a snob. Remember that tomorrow is the wedding of one of Philippe's seamstresses, luckily the ceremony will be short. Marriage, what madness! I certainly won't push Clothilde into marrying, unless she's cooking up some mischief, really, she is so distant these days and she looks at me as if she saw me in some new dimension. . . .

The telephone interrupted her musing.

"Hello, darling, it's Mitzi."

"How are you?" Before her eyes the picture of Mitzi appeared as if she were seeing it on television: a beautiful creature who worked hard at being one of the Beautiful People and who, at the moment, was probably languidly stretched out between pink sheets with cream on her face.

"I just spent a wild week with Dédé at Deauville and I won the golf cup last Sunday."

6

"Congratulations, but who is Dédé?"

"Really, darling, the Duke of Décarlie."

"That upstart!"

"He's very rich and he married the Cadillac girl."

"As you know, I'm not so familiar with nobility other than the French. . . ."

"That's a mistake; they aren't very good customers. How's your collection coming along?"

"It's divine, darling, absolutely divine. Adrien is in top form and we have so many marvelous things that the workrooms will be going full blast until October. And then, you know, I have Princess Herminie's wedding with eighteen dresses to make for the fifteenth of September. Are you invited?"

"Not yet."

"Would you like to have me ask Count de Waverlink, the chief of protocol, to put you on the list?"

"Terribly nice of you, but I don't think I could go anyway because Elias had asked me to sail on his yacht in September. Besides, these royal weddings are really a bore."

"Then you must go sailing of course, because if I know you, you must have bought some dazzling yachting costumes."

"You know I adore Valentino and I went to Rome on purpose."

"I hope he didn't sell you the same ones Suzy bought. She adored them too."

"I'm quite aware of that, we have the same saleswoman. By the way, will you do me a favor and ask Madame Sophie to fix my orange coat? The lining is torn. That lining doesn't wear well; you should tell your supplier."

"Mm. Solidity isn't the primary objective of haute couture. I'll make a note of it, though the workrooms are working overtime on the collection and I can't promise you to have it done before next week."

"That's impossible. You know very well that I'm leaving for Dorothy's in three days and one needs a coat in the evenings sometimes on Cap Martin. Thanks, darling. I'm counting on you."

"Hmmm, have a good time"—and, hanging up—What a bother! And anyway, Mitzi would rather die than be seen on Cap Martin in a city coat when she owns twenty-five scarves, capes, and ponchos more suitable to that resort. And she'll take advantage of our so-called friendship not to pay for the repairs! Why do I waste my time on these idiots?

She had just put back the receiver when the bell rang again.

"Marie-Victoire, Paul Malet here."

"Oh, Paul, how nice of you to call! It's lovely to hear your voice when I was afraid that it would be another horrible woman. How's Jacqueline?"

"Fine. She is in Dinard with the children and the weather has been good; I go down every weekend. She asked me to find out how things are going with you; she knows that you haven't time to write. She's worried about the collection too. Is everything going as you had hoped it would?"

"What a dear she is! Thank God for childhood friends! If you knew how hateful women generally are! I just had one on the telephone I could have cheerfully strangled! My dear Paul, tell her that as usual there are plenty of difficulties, but I'm hoping to survive them."

"You're sure I can't do anything for you?"

"Oh dear, if it were only a matter of organization! But one also has to please the reporters, they appreciate a kind of lecherous eccentricity more than elegance, and one must adapt or die, as our dear friends the Russians would say."

"I hope you know that you can count on us. Have you decided about Big Mills of Indiana? I just had an answer from my American correspondent. You needn't worry, it's a very solid outfit and their offer is fair. I think you should decide to sell your business to them."

"I'll never resign myself to seeing my name on blue jeans. What's more, once the business is theirs, I'll have absolutely no control and they can use my name on anything. You know, they have a cosmetics business as well as a big mail-order operation."

"Remember, that much capital well invested would assure you a very luxurious life."

"I can't see myself playing bridge in the afternoon to kill time. Horrible! And all my staff? Let down all those people who trusted me? I couldn't look them in the eye. What would become of them? There are fewer and fewer jobs in couture. Poor Adrien! To think that *Women's Wear Daily* once called him the designer of the century! Soon I'll be the only one who appreciates his gowns. And I'm already wondering if I don't prefer the ones his assistant, Jean-Loup, has designed, much as I hate this type of tough casualness—like Alain Delon in a gangster movie! I'm waiting to see Oliver Mayer again before deciding. I'd like to persuade him to go in with me on a luxury boutique instead of continuing this constant anxiety of haute couture."

"When will he be here? I want to get some information about him too."

"Good. He should be here any day now, but if he's not a millionaire several times over, either I'm much more gullible than I think or he's a marvelous swindler! How's my god-child? Not too disappointed at failing his exams?"

"No, he's all right. At sixteen and a half it's not such a tragedy, and he's having a romance with a fourteen-year-old girl which keeps him busy."

"Lord, soon they'll start in the cradle!"

"And Clothilde?"

9

"I don't see much of her, but she seems to be getting on. You're a love to call me! Kiss Jacqueline for me and tell her I miss her."

"If you want to come to Dinard, we'll be delighted. Anyway, keep me informed about Big Mills of Indiana and this Mr. Mayer."

"Thanks, Paul dear, I won't forget."

Marie-Victoire didn't like thinking that her childhood friend was leading the bourgeois life that she would have had if her marriage had not been a disaster. Of course nothing very exciting ever happened to Paul and Jacqueline—if the latter ever saw her picture in a paper it was on the local news page in Dinard for having won a golf cup! Usually, all Marie-Victoire had to do was to think of her past successes to feel deliciously superior. But this morning that talisman was no good, fame had lost its magic. She began to think about her friends' happy tranquillity, of their affection, of their two non-problem children: the boy wasn't on drugs; the girl wasn't a nymphomaniac; they weren't even quarrelsome. The kind of children nobody had any more. And Paul, a nice fellow, a good position, perhaps a little too dictatorial, his wife couldn't buy a dress without asking his advice. And was that what happiness was for seventy-five per cent of all women? Drowning in submission as in whipped cream! In her rare moments of self-examination, Marie-Victoire was obliged to recognize that she had succeeded in business to make up for the failure of her emotional life. If her precious label went sour, too, she would be a total failure. The idea was too much to bear. Since she had chosen success, she must hold onto it. Selling her name would be too easy. No, she must find a way to save the business by giving up haute couture, which nobody seemed interested in any more. Make ready-to-wear clothing like everybody else? Of course, after all, there is not much difference between the two.

The creation is the same. It becomes haute couture if it's made to order with three fittings, or boutique if it's made in advance in standardized sizes. But what then? Adrien Lecouture, her designer, always insisted on an all-round collection. The huntress, Diana, could find her culotte and hunting jacket in it, the ambassadress her evening gown and one for her daughter's first ball. There were tailored suits, bridal gowns, raincoats, and furs. Even more than the lengthy fittings and the outmoded setup, it was the lack of specialization which cost them so dear. To expect to dress a woman from morning till night for every occasion in her life was insane. As insane as to sell 5,000-franc shorts. Women went to Ungaro or Courrèges for a well-cut coat or a pants suit. Days when they felt like being amused, they went to Saint-Germain-des-Prés to buy a crazy outfit. But when they married their daughter or when they were meeting their husband's boss for the first time, they wanted to be sure of what they were wearing. A serious house, but up-to-date: an heir to Balmain and Saint Laurent that would be sure success. Where you could find embroidered hostess gowns from Hong Kong and the perfect outfit for the doctor's wife from Lyon who is going to the radiologists' convention for the first time, all under 2,000 francs.

To do that, one would have to have a factory and branches in the provinces: the same setup as Cardin or Saint Laurent, but more specialized. In America, almost all the manufacturers were highly specialized, and the one who only made blouses between twenty and forty dollars would have no idea of how to turn one out at ten dollars, or of matching it with a skirt. One might as well begin by copying America; in the long run one ended up doing what they did, but ten years later.

Thinking of America meant thinking of financial backing,

11

and at this point, Marie-Victoire's thoughts turned quite naturally to Oliver Mayer.

She had met him in Dallas, among a number of other businessmen. But one day, after her return to Paris, he had telephoned her, had taken her out several times, then had suggested a little cruise on the yacht he had rented at Cannes. She had not asked if there would be other guests, much too afraid that he would say *no* and that she would have to admit to herself that she was going off with a lover. It was much easier to pretend to be surprised, to be the perfect lady carried away against her principles. That was a year ago. Business was poor and she made the excuse to herself that this American, who already owned cosmetic companies, TV stations, and other properties, might perhaps want to add a prestigious Parisian name to his Texas kingdom. She had planned it all, but she had left out of account his charm and authority. She had planned to manipulate him, but it was he who pulled all the strings. He had said neither yes nor no about the purchase of the maison de couture, or capitalizing a new business. All he wanted was to enjoy the sun, herself, her beauty; he had listened to her seriously, yet he also knew how to laugh, to swim, to enjoy good food; he was an ideal lover but not yet a silent partner.

For the first time in her life Marie-Victoire had found herself in the arms of a man who was able to dominate her entirely and she was ashamed of the pleasure it gave her. She sometimes said to herself: "Admit it, my girl, you're enjoying a great roll in the hay just like all the other females you've always made fun of." Since that time he had come to Paris fairly often and their relationship remained unchanged. He listened to her laments about the troubles of haute couture, the ideas she had for setting up another kind of business, which were each time a little different, but never said: "OK, here's X-million." Her inability to make him commit himself, plus the acceleration of her pulse when she thought of him, made her furious.

To break the trance the mere thought of Oliver plunged her into, she began abruptly to open her mail.

. . . Let's look at these bills. Two thousand francs for repairing the Directoire chairs in the dining room . . . much too expensive, but necessary, fat Lydia smashed one completely the other evening . . .

. . . And this, what can this be? I've never bought anything at Bazar de l'Hôtel-de-Ville . . . a receipted bill, for heavens sake! A mattress and box spring, a blanket, a comforter, two pairs of sheets, three saucepans, two kitchen stools and a small refrigerator, delivered to Rue de la Huchette to a Monsieur Feuillot and paid by check number 6281 on the National City Bank . . . but that's Clothilde's account. This is unbelievable, she's set up housekeeping with some tramp. She'll have to give me an explanation of this! She's going to be furious that I opened this bill, but the envelope was addressed to me . . . what luck, it really wasn't my fault!

In her everyday life, Marie-Victoire dealt with many difficult problems and was always decisive. Unfortunately, now that her daughter was grown up, she never knew how to approach her for fear of hurting her feelings. She readily admitted that she was a poor psychologist, and that she missed the presence of a man most of all in matters concerning Clothilde.

. . . What a shame, she thought, that my father has become old and frail. Once upon a time, he would have told me what to do. Let's see . . . if I went to Rue de la Huchette to see who this Monsieur Feuillot is? If Clothilde found out about it she'd kill me, because I can't really deceive myself, I know perfectly well that it's not some old man she's picked

13

up but probably some bearded revolutionary student. Anyway it would be more dignified to ask her directly. But where is she anyway? A girl of twenty . . . it's awful . . . what a responsibility. I want a good life for her so much. One really can't do much for one's children. Although one dreams of being the good fairy for them, with a magic wand in hand, in reality they have to find their own magicians. She sighed. Though I don't envy them I admire the fathers of olden times who banished their children from the house at the least lapse of conduct. The worst thing that could possibly happen to me would be not seeing my daughter again, and I'll be any kind of coward to avoid it. Letting her do as she pleases may not be the best way to make her happy . . . my God, I really don't know which way to turn. Besides, with all the things I have to do! I'll look at this bank statement at my office. Now I must get up . . .

Marie-Victoire threw back her covers and went to breathe the morning air on her terrace. The Seine looked like silver foil—and was probably about the same consistency from pollution. The bulk of Notre Dame offered reassurance to troubled souls. The rosebushes on the terrace were dry, and that damned Popoff had lifted his leg on them . . . quick, a little water. She spattered her hand-embroidered white linen gown, said "Damn," and went to shut herself in the bathroom, a refuge where she could usually melt away all care in a warm bath. But today it was no use that her bath was a perfect temperature, that the bath bubbles tickled her skin, no good to be steeping in warm water like tea leaves in a pot. She could not make herself feel as optimistic as usual.

The profit and loss figures from her manager, Chavanaux, swarmed over the barricades in her head like so many 1914 soldiers armed with bayonets. Couture was operating at a

14

loss, as usual. Perfume made up for just a part of that loss and it was only the salary she gave herself as President-General Manager which assured Marie-Victoire's way of life. Of course her elegant wardrobe was tax-deductible, as was her car and any entertaining, but in spite of that fact, it was absolutely necessary that the next season be profitable. If the sale of perfume leveled off, couture must have a smaller loss, and the success of the collection would be the determining factor.

Marie-Victoire told herself for the hundredth time that she needed customers to keep her workrooms busy. But the management of haute couture was so anachronistic that a traditional house, with a big overhead, a high-salaried designer, a manager, a publicity man, a doorman, secretaries, stock girls, delivery boys, two collections a year, costing a total of two hundred thousand dollars, not counting a dozen mannequins, would lose between forty and sixty thousand dollars a year if she made only made-to-order costumes, even at top production. Besides, since couture was maintained just to keep the connected business of perfume, ready-to-wear, etc., going on its publicity, managers of haute couture complexes now expected to lose money in the couture department. It wasn't unusual to hear a designer say: "I can indulge in a loss of X-thousands a season." But she wasn't selling any ready-to-wear.

So the only hope of making a little money in the couture department was by having a lot of buyers for paper patterns.

Marie-Victoire tried to remember the most salable models. Let's see, she counted, there must be ten of them, that's not enough.

The "paper pattern" brought in some money to the house when it was sold to couturiers from the French provinces and at a higher price to the other European houses. This was an important factor in the returns on the collection. In fact, it was the French, German, Belgian, English, Swedish, and Dutch buyers who kept a house going, much more than the Americans, who did not buy paper patterns but the *toiles,* or even the model in its original fabric, which was much more expensive to make.

She thought of the Italians again. Some of them had a special position among the buyers. Many of them resold the patterns "as is" to other professionals, although the very principle of this transaction was prohibited in haute couture. So they were asked to make a very significant minimum purchase, or were forbidden admission to the house by giving an "exclusive" to only one of them.

. . . I wonder if I chose the best house to give my exclusive to . . . all the same it's annoying to think that half the buyers go to Italy to get French models at a quarter of the Paris price! And that way it's much easier for them to choose from the cream of the crop than to have to decide for themselves which model will be successful out of ten collections of a hundred or two hundred models each. If it wasn't for that, those lousy Italians have so much charm that I've never been able to resist them . . .

A good collection should first of all, then, please journalists so that buyers would come to see it. But they (the buyers) talked a lot among themselves and also trusted their commission agents. There were a dozen commission houses in Paris who shared all the buyers, took care of all complaints, consignments, and the piles of documents required by customs. For example: to sell in the Arab countries, it must be sworn on oath that the garment was free of any Israeli materials. Very often the commission agents, who did not pay for admission, came to the second showing to get information for

16

their clients, and they drew a great deal of flattering attention from the saleswomen.

Running over these details, all necessary to the welfare of a maison de couture, Marie-Victoire wondered if she had forgotten anything.

Just then the telephone rang again. She opened the bathroom door and called: "Answer it, Thérèse. I'm late, so if it isn't important say I've already left."

"It's Monsieur Chavanaux, madame. He says it's urgent."

"All right, I'm coming."

She wrapped herself in a big green towel and took off her shower cap. Her hair fell on her shoulders and she tossed it back with a youthful gesture.

"Chavanaux, what's wrong this time?"

She had hired him when the business began sliding, and instead of accomplishing the miracles she had vaguely expected, he always seemed to bring up new insoluble problems. In spite of his youth—he was only twenty-eight—he took everything very seriously, including himself; he dressed dismally and thought couture was an insane occupation.

"The fabric for the bridal gown has finally come, but the salesman has orders from the company not to leave it unless we pay cash, and we only have enough to pay the workroom salaries here."

"How much is the bill?"

"Seven hundred and eighty-six francs."

"Just a minute! I'm going to see if I have it here."

She ran to open her bag and found only three hundred-franc notes there.

"The salesman will have to wait until I can get to the bank. I don't have enough with me. Tell him not to come around to us again: I don't do business this way. If it weren't so late, I'd tell Monsieur Adrien to find another fabric, but

17

at this point, I can't do that to him. I'll be there in a half an hour. See you then." And she hung up abruptly.

It was easy to see that Adrien didn't have to worry about bills, she said to herself. He could just as well have chosen something on approval which would have given us ninety days to pay the bill. All designers live in dreams of grandeur; they get their salary every month and their noses are out of joint if they aren't allowed to buy whatever fabric they want at whatever price. There are miles of fabric in the studio, lent by merchants who would lick our feet to get us to use it. And Monsieur can only make his bridal gown out of fabric from a Swiss house we've always avoided because they're so demanding about payments! Really, he's exaggerating, there's no reason to pay the money out of my own pocket. Didn't Paul tell me not to do that? Should I call him back? It would be a miracle if a customer happened to pay for her dress this morning. Still, we can't show the collection without a bridal gown. Unless we bluffed, said that Princess Herminie had seen it the day before the collection and refused to hear of having any other so we couldn't show the gown publicly. Yes, but when her chief of protocol read the story he would be furious, and the princess might cancel her order. This isn't the moment to lose her. What a mess!

Although these days she told customers that a gown for 5,000 francs or $1,000 was a bargain, the fact of having to lay out 786 francs from her own purse for fabric suddenly seemed an unbearable blow. Popoff, with his infallible instinct, felt that this was the moment for a grand reconciliation and he came to lick her leg below the big towel.

"You're tickling me. . . ."

And she took him in her arms, enabling him to give her a big lick on the nose.

18

"You're lucky my face isn't made up, you little pig. You love me, anyway!"

And putting him back on the floor, she scratched his rear end, which made him groan with pleasure and wiggle all over.

"Thérèse, hurry and cook me two hard-boiled eggs and give me some biscuits for Popoff; there's nothing left for him to eat at Place Vendôme."

When she didn't want to go out to lunch, she often brought a little something to the office with her, but she was careful to have a collection of beautiful bags, marked MVF, intended for costly perfumes rather than hard-boiled eggs. One day a customer, one of the most pretentious and slowest to pay (faults which often went together), while beating a hasty retreat, knocked over Marie-Victoire's little bag and two hard-boiled eggs rolled out.

"Good Lord, what's that?" she had yelped in an English accent painfully acquired in Marseilles.

"Two hard-boiled eggs, obviously, my dear. They won't bite you, that's my lunch box."

"Your what?"

"My lunch box, just like my apprentices. Haven't you ever noticed all those people with little brown bags in New York at the lunch hour? Well, I do the same thing. If my customers paid their bills, I'd eat at the Ritz every day."

The next day, the customer had sent a check directly to Marie-Victoire at Quai de Béthune enclosing her card on which she had written angrily: "Good for a few lunches at the Ritz." She had also told all her friends that Marie-Victoire was "so miserly, my dear, that she eats in her office to save money—she's basically bourgeois. Her father has one of those small provincial titles, he's one of those country squires, you know." Afterward she had stayed away sulking for six months,

19

but she had not been able to resist the temptation of coming back when Marie-Victoire made news by creating the trousseau for the bride of a reigning king.

In fifteen minutes, Marie-Victoire was all ready. She got her little beige and black Austin out of the garage and drove along the Rue de Rivoli to the Place Vendôme where the doorman would park the car while she went to the bank.

Chapter II

Maurice, the doorman, had just come back that morning from Agadir where he had spent his vacation at the Club Mediterranée. He was very tanned and clearly knew that he was the best-looking doorman on the Place Vendôme, where there were a good many handsome ones, what with the Ritz and the great jewelry shops. He was dressed in a brown frock coat with a red vest and MVF embroidered in red on his cap. He loved pretty women, who returned the compliment, and he had taken more than one mannequin to tourist nightclubs where he once had worked and was given a discount. At Agadir, he had told all his conquests that he was the president of an import-export business, and his acquaintance with American buyers and rich clients helped him considerably to pose as a man of means. What secretary would have been suspicious enough to doubt a gentleman who knew that Madame Derval, the owner of the Folies-Bergère, had a Rolls, who knew that this actress drove her own Ferrari, and who spoke knowingly about

21

the Marie-Victoire Forval dresses that he had bought for his lady friend?

Now, at the sight of the little black and beige Austin, the *soi-disant* man of the world hurriedly removed his cap and helped his employer out of her car almost tenderly. Popoff, whom he walked several times a day, said good morning to him in his own way, happy to see an understanding human being again who would allow him to smell all the delicious odors on the street lamps around the square. Maurice was handsome and Popoff liked him very much: these were two qualities which, in Marie-Victoire's eyes, made for a model doorman. And as she hadn't seen him for a month, she stopped for a moment to ask him how his vacation had been and to give him a wink.

"How many victims, Maurice?"

"Oh, madame, women are crazy!"

Marie-Victoire admitted that she loved her business with an almost physical love. It was her own creation and there wasn't a day when she did not feel a wild joy at seeing her name shining in the sunlight of the Place Vendôme. She only rented the three-story building, but she sometimes felt that the whole square belonged to her. If fact, in certain moments of objectivity when she could joke about her chauvinism, she admitted that she regarded all of France, Paris, and especially Provence, home of her father's family, as her personal property. Each time she entered her little entry hall with its black and white marble tiles, where in one stark show window a single enormous flagon of her perfume, "Ah!" was displayed, and when she climbed the steps of the wide Louis XV staircase, she relived the stages of her fantastic career. She let the memory of it melt in her mind as a delicious mousse covers the taste buds.

Must this fairy tale she had retold herself so many times come to an end? It seemed that each step of the big staircase gave her a little more strength, and she arrived on the second-floor landing girded for battle. This landing opened on the entrances to the two large salons and was brightly lit by two high windows giving on the Place Vendôme. A regal Italian Renaissance table reduced the hall to a narrow passage, for it was placed in a manner which would have seemed odd to a decorator not acquainted with the exigencies of haute couture.

The reception desk of a couture house is an important position; its occupant must have a wide knowledge of people and even be something of a psychologist. Almost every manufacturer had an elegant wife who did not hesitate to order an expensive garment so as to steal ideas, not to mention fashionable women who brought a "friend" to view the collection. The friend often turned out to be none other than their little seamstress. And there are also some royal highnesses incognito, who look like chambermaids but whom one had better not treat as such.

During the eight hours of the day that the salons are open, there is always an employee seated behind this table. Maurice, the doorman, would admit anyone who was decently dressed. But, once in front of the big table, the customer must give her last name, first name, address, and submit to "questioning."

Has she been to the house before? Is she sure she had never received an invitation?—very suspect, that!—ah, she has forgotten her invitation! Would she remember the name of her saleswoman then? No, how annoying! Hasn't she a friend who has her clothes made here? Madame Durand? Which one? The one from Avenue Foch? No, she thinks she lives in Boulogne. That's really very vague, and also the only Madame Durand one could know is the one who lives on Avenue Foch.

The tone becomes more and more condescending, and the

unhappy customer, if she doesn't have a purse filled with five hundred-franc bills, feels so snubbed that she would give anything to find herself back on the sidewalk of the Place Vendôme.

Finally, since "Madame" is entirely unknown, she will be given a saleswoman "for the tour." A big register is opened and several lists are consulted. There is the regular tour for French-speaking customers, then the English tour, the German, or the Spanish, according to the linguistic ability of the saleswomen. Certain women don't want to say that they have already come four or five times, and when another big register is consulted, it becomes clear that on each visit they have a new saleswoman. So this "tour" is like a lottery: for every serious customer there are twenty window-shoppers.

After 1946, haute couture collections had become such a show that numerous travel agencies and convention bureaus began to include a visit to the principal houses along with the Eiffel Tower and dinner at the Lido. The Chambre Syndicale became concerned with this state of affairs and demanded that the groups pay a contribution, to be turned over to the funds of the schools for couture apprenticeship. But this did not prevent housewives from coming to entertain themselves for an hour before going to have a cup of tea. Each day they lined up on the grand staircase. It had become practically impossible to separate the wheat from the chaff; so when the visitor looked altogether too shabby she was told in a barely polite way that the salons were full.

The couturiers, like Dior, whose salons were over a boutique could reasonably hope that a certain percentage of the window-shoppers would buy a lipstick when they came down, but the others really got no benefit at all from this less and less elegant crowd, and the very rich customers began to object to the com-

24

pany at the afternoon showings. Some of them even demanded that gowns be shown to them at home!

In addition, some women gave themselves a treat by trying on models they had no intention of buying, asking the price, and saying that they would talk it over with their husbands. It was a way of playing at being rich. To pay for these happy hours, they had to put up with aggressive telephone calls from the saleswoman. A minority were honest enough to say that their husband thought the price was too high. Most invented some more elegant excuse like: "My husband has just bought a Rolls," "We've had to put new central heating in the château," or worse, "I found almost the same coat at So-and-So for five hundred francs less." In this case, the saleswoman felt herself personally injured by the high prices of her house and went to complain to the management, never doubting the veracity of what her "dear customer" had said.

When Marie-Victoire glanced at the crowd sitting in her salons and when she observed the furtive departure of women who had come in with so much assurance but suddenly panicked when the bridal gown announced the end of the showing and the arrival of the saleswoman, she would say aloud, "I see the rain has stopped," and she regretted not having Cardin's commercial power; since 1970, he had demanded a hundred francs from visitors the first month of the collection and thirty francs after that, to be applied against an eventual order.

To take care of this unpleasant task of reception and also of the tours, Marie-Victoire had engaged a remarkable woman. She was a real Italian princess who had undergone financial reverses and various other catastrophes, most of which had certainly been the result of her own poor judgment. However, she had known how to make capital of her knowledge of the world of fashion and of four languages. Tall, emaciated, very dark, she resembled an El Greco figure, and the sight of her had dis-

25

couraged more than one little housewife who would have very much liked to look at the collection so as to give her seamstress some ideas. Marie-Victoire thought her not quite bright. She had sacrificed her entire fortune to get her husband, one of Mussolini's former ministers and a skirt-chaser and otherwise disreputable character, out of prison after the liberation when, if she had remained a French citizen, she could have divorced him! But she was very fond of her just the same, for she was perfect at her job, giving the house that stamp of high snobbism which distinguishes a haute couture house from a boutique, even an extremely elegant one. Besides, she was still invited into the best society; it was even thanks to her that the house was going to make Princess Herminie's trousseau. Besides the two dresses she made for her each season, Marie-Victoire let her borrow all the coats and the dresses she liked, for society reporters always mentioned her and the house profited from the free publicity.

Her great name and her aristocratic air had created a problem when she first came. Was she to be called Madame Elizabeth, like the saleswomen and the forewomen of the workroom, or Princess? The haute couture world having a passion for titles, Marie-Victoire had decided that everyone else would call her Princess, while she herself always addressed her as "My dear."

"Good morning, my dear, I see that the painters have finished the staircase. Have they started on the big salon?"

"Yes, madame, I think they'll be through this afternoon and the cleaners are working on the chair seats. Don't go in, the odor is unbearable. Look, even Popoff is sneezing."

Twice a year the couture house was cleaned this way. The Princess went on:

"Madame Arène is waiting for you to give her the color scheme of the floral decorations. Do you want to call her yourself or do you want me to do it? Potel and Chabot are also waiting for the usual catering order to be confirmed; they say they have a new chicken canapé that is delicious."

"I'll call Madame Arène when I've asked Monsieur Lecouture if he still thinks we should use shades of orange. And you can tell Potel and Chabot to do as they like, but that I don't want it to be any more expensive than usual. Remember to tell them no black currant brandy; it makes indelible spots on the carpet, and last year there was no iced coffee. Let me know when the new saleswoman comes. I'll introduce her to the other ladies myself."

And she went up a flight to her office, also called a "studio" as a token of her former activities as a designer. She called in Chavanaux at once.

"Here is the money for the fabric for the bridal gown. It must go to the workroom right away. If it doesn't, the gown won't be finished by Thursday."

"It was taken care of a half hour ago. Alan Harside happened to be there during the discussion with the salesman and gave him the money."

Marie-Victoire was quite surprised, but did not show it. Like all good public-relations men, Alan must have had some idea in the back of his mind; he never did anything for nothing.

"Good, I'll be seeing him shortly. Nothing else?"

"No, except for the company we always rent the chairs from. They're insisting on being paid in advance."

"Really! The process is catching. Well, tell them we'll do it this time, but that we'll deal with their competitor next season."

As she said this she instinctively touched wood; would there be another season?

To raise their morale, alcoholics take to the bottle. Marie-Victoire's solace was her book of press clippings. This large red leather book, printed with her initials, was kept in a drawer of

27

her desk. Only articles which were about her personally were in it, since if it had included all those which had come out about her collections it would have been much too large. She knew all the clippings by heart, especially the first ones. In her moments of truth she admitted that she gazed into them like Narcissus into his pool, to admire herself.

Women's Wear Daily, July 1949: "We've found the designer of those Vichy grey dresses which were so successful this summer in Jacques Fath's boutique. She is a gorgeous young woman who received us in her very amusing studio with a grass-green carpet. She had just moved in and had barely finished hanging mobiles à la Calder from the ceiling. Felt-covered screens and curtains serve as fitting rooms. The visitor receives a welcome (which may or may not be warm, she says) from her black cocker, who deigned to approve of us. Madame Forval told us that she has always designed all her own clothes. At fourteen, she began to work with a seamstress who came in by the day. She said that at that time every bourgeois family had one of these queens of the foot-pedal sewing machine. Lucky French . . . they disappeared from America long ago! Jacques Fath is her first customer and she has endless admiration for him . . ."

. . . How not? she sighed now, more than twenty years later. He was as handsome as a movie star, he had exquisite ideas, a sense of color and detail that dazzled you. Sewing nutshells on jute—who else would have thought of it! And he gave marvelous parties, that "Crazy Years" party at his château at Corbeville, what fun it was! And that charming act he put on for me at my first visit! It was the first time that a man had looked me over from top to toe like a collector of 1830 opalines examining a Louis XV commode. Even if he didn't start calling me "my pink rabbit" that time, I still felt that I was fully admitted to the category of "chic" women that he liked.

She went back to reading *Women's Wear*: ". . . very modestly, Madame Forval tells us she would never have dreamed of showing her designs to a couturier if one of her friends had not persuaded her. She still seems overwhelmed by the sophisticated world of haute couture, to which she is so well suited. In her, Jacques Fath has discovered a talent we'll be seeing more of. We look forward to seeing the most unexpected fabrics made into charming gowns. Madame Forval showed us those she will be taking to the Midi for herself: they are all made of mattress ticking, butcher linen and sateen! She didn't want to unveil her secrets for next season, but we saw scraps of felt on her table . . . ! Could it be that Marie-Victoire Forval is going to turn us into billiard tables? This is a young woman to watch."

The second magazine to recognize her existence was French:

Elle, October '49: *"Women are terrific.* We visited Marie-Victoire Forval, the very young woman who turned us all into schoolgirls in Vichy grey this summer. This winter she has concocted marvelous skirts and coats in felt. We adored her studio. On page 43 you'll find all the clever and inexpensive tricks she used to decorate it.

"We asked about her education and whether her background, or her husband or her family had influenced her in the creative role which seems to suit her so well. She told us that it would be harder to find anyone further removed from the business world than she is. Her father, Nicolas de Baussigue, presides over the court of assizes of the Seine province and her mother is the daughter of General de Ploermel. In fact, she laughed, 'War and Justice brought forth the infant Hermes.' She graduated from college like anyone else and although she has always designed her own dresses, she never dreamed that a genius (her word) like Jacques Fath would notice them.

"She admits that when he ordered twelve Vichy grey dresses

29

from her, she had no idea that she would have to enroll in the Registry of Commerce to be able to make them for him! 'My husband was marvelous, he taught me everything, from taxes to Social Security. Even though he wasn't very happy about it. When I came from my first interview with Jacques Fath I was on such a pink cloud that I burned the roast . . . even the pan was charred!' "

Rereading this, Marie-Victoire could smell the horrible odor and thick smoke bellowing from the kitchen. Poor Jérôme, he seemed so eager to teach me all those things! Why did he lose interest when everything began to run smoothly? Couldn't he stand my not needing him any more? How many centuries will it be before men stop feeling frustrated when they don't have to protect women any more? It's stupid! A woman bursts with pride when her man succeeds, but the reverse is rare indeed!

Someone knocked on the door. Marie-Victoire covered the clipping book with an open copy of *Women's Wear Daily*. She did not want to be caught *in flagrante delicto* admiring herself. It was one of her saleswomen.

"May I speak to you about Madame Durand?"

"You know I hate to be interrupted this way. Why don't you use the telephone?"

"I'm sorry, madame, but it's important. Mr. Harside says that there is no seat for Madame Durand. She's leaving the day after the showing and wants to place her order at once."

"Very well, I'll take care of it, but don't expect me to put her in the front row, she's really too dowdy!"

"If only they were all dowdy like her, at 100,000 francs a season!"

"A year is more like it; you exaggerate, but never mind, I'll take care of it."

30

The saleswoman left in a huff, and Marie-Victoire went back to her book.

. . . Goodness, this article in German! I don't remember what it says any more, but the photograph is nice. This must have been the year of Dior's "tulip." What a becoming style! I had given up gimmicks—that was real couture. And this is Clothilde's first appearance in a fashion magazine . . .

Modes et Tricots, October '51: "We asked Marie-Victoire Forval to describe her baby's layette for us. This elegant young woman has chosen the prettiest accessories for her first-born, and her layette is carefully planned. We were surprised to find jackets, sweaters and bootees in pale yellow wool. We hadn't imagined that this unusual color could be so attractive. Dressed all in yellow, little Clothilde looked like an adorable newly-hatched chick. Besides, adds Madame Forval, this way she avoided the usual blue layette for a boy or pink for a girl, which betrays the mother's disappointment when the baby's sex isn't as expected. Far from being disappointed with her little girl, this young mother is bursting with pride. 'A hand-stitched baby!' she told us."

Heavens! A hand-stitched baby! How could I have said such a thing! How must Mother's face have looked when she read that! Reporters will write anything. Oh, well, it wasn't too bad, but yellow still wasn't accepted for layettes until the Princess of Monaco used it. What a blessed period! Jérôme was thrilled by the miracle of the child and finally seemed happy. My parents glowed with joy and idolized their granddaughter. The styles were marvelous. There were so many buyers that I could hardly keep up with them. We felt we had finally come out of a five-year tunnel of misery and horror. Women were thirsty for beauty and elegance, they weren't yet blasé the way they are today. Maybe they weren't happy with only a bar of chocolate or soap the way they were in '44, but it still amazed them to be able to take a plane to New York or to give a ball! Young people didn't yet need to take refuge in drugs; they were still reveling in all the things they had been deprived of. If people can only be happy after a war, it's a depressing prospect. Never had couture achieved such prestige, there was a line standing in front of Dior every day, the saleswomen had to work at night to take care of the buyers. And the sumptuous receptions that Suzanne Lulling, the manager, gave were constantly in the gossip columns . . . the world's clothing manufacturers knew that all they had to do was buy Paris models twice a year to coin money hand over fist. The maisons de couture were temples, the couturiers were high priests of taste. The moment she entered their portals a woman felt more beautiful. In spite of the fact that her torso was squeezed into a wasp waist, her breasts were pushed up and her dress with its petticoats weighed at least five kilos . . . the more she suffered the happier she was! Then too, that was the period when "ready-made," once a synonym for shoddy fabrics, dull colors and utilitarian cut, suddenly learned all the tricks of haute couture and adopted the more flattering name of "ready-to-wear." And haute couture, by selling its ideas and techniques, had lived off "ready-to-wear" for twenty years. But now that the pupil has learned everything, it pretends that its master is dead and that ideas can be found in the street! It may be true of Saint Laurent, but it isn't of Grès or Givenchy . . .

She continued to leaf through the big book:

"The stunning Marie-Victoire Forval in gold lamé at the first of the de Cuevas 'ballets.'"

"The elegant Madame Forval asks the Aga Khan for a tip on the next race. Her enormous hat shades her from the sun and even showers."

Photos followed; here was her favorite:

"One of the queens of the Century Ball, Marie-Victoire Forval in a sumptuous Dogess's gown, arrives at Bestegui Palace. She is accompanied by her new designer, Adrien Lecouture, a name to watch!"

Then the article in *France-Soir* two years later: *"A unique event in the annals of haute couture.* Couturiers are not noted for their kindness to one another and are not likely to visit each other's collections. Today, they were all united in the Place Vendôme to wish their new colleague, Marie-Victoire Forval, luck. Here she is, radiant with joy, centered between, left to right, Hubert de Givenchy, Jean Dessès, Pierre Balmain, and Christian Dior. At the extreme right, Adrien Lecouture, her designer, who is adored by all the women reporters." Anyway the pair of them must have bewitched old Mademoiselle Eva, who had owned the house since 1920, because the rumor spread that she did not ask any money for the lease on the only condition that all her old workers, saleswomen and all, would stay in the new house.

. . . The peak of our success, it lasted four years. Here are all the American clippings, this time I was given a double-page spread in *Women's Wear*. Radio, television, overnight stardom, they worship success so . . . it was marvelous. Yes it would really have been heaven if Jérôme had shared my joy! The fearful scene when he refused to go to Venice with me. While I was gone he moved his bed to the study, he never opened his mouth at meals, I hardly saw him any more. When I was home, he would spend hours in the bathroom. But I tried everything, of course I hadn't much time, he ought to have understood! I had to fight with all those saleswomen my predecessor had left me. Things were going well enough, but it was a job to deal with ten females inherited with the premises, each one a hundred and ten if she was a day, with thin hair dyed mahogany and a little diamond pin attached to her left lapel. And I was used to doing my own selling! Well, I finally got rid of half of them. And all those trips we made to show the collection abroad, six mannequins, our good Suzanne for a dresser, and myself. It's true that Jérôme was left alone during these periods, and from Paris, these trips may have looked like fairyland: embassies, bouquets tied with tricolor ribbons, television, newspapers! But then there was the packing and unpacking, a hundred costumes with accessories, arguments with hotels, mannequins who disappeared with a boy friend or ones who tried to sneak a transistor or a camera through customs. And Madame Suzanne's "souvenirs"! She didn't miss a one—a Manneken-Pis from Brussels, a Tyrolean hat, beer steins from Munich, and the little seal from Oslo! Dear Suzanne, how could anyone have such a big heart and such bad taste? Still, those were good times! We felt we were French taste incarnate! . . . now it's something else again.

While Marie-Victoire was reliving her successes, the Princess, seated behind her big table, had written the instructions for Tuesday's buffet on a pad.

The two big registers where the entries for customers were written, one with the name of the saleswoman and the other with fittings, were closed. The Princess had already begun a new page with: Autumn-Winter Collection.

Hidden in a drawer to which only she had the key lay the big "tour" register. She had learned to her cost that this book could prove a package of dynamite, and she never forgot to lock its drawer.

There were eight saleswomen in the house, including the new one who would arrive today: five who had passed retirement age, left over from the former management, and three who were younger and had come from other houses.

They all hated each other and spied on each other ceaselessly, accusing each other of "swiping" clients. They inhabited a room opening on the landing, to the left of the big table.

Each locked her address book (into which the Social Register was practically transcribed) into a little school desk. They brandished them, clucking like furious hens, whenever an important person who was not yet assigned climbed the staircase.

They received a minimum fixed salary and a commission of 3 per cent on all sales. But this system was relatively recent, for ten years ago they received 10 per cent from any customers they brought into the house and only 2 per cent from those assigned to them from the "tours."

The atmosphere, already charged with suspicion, was completely unbreathable during that time, for each saleswoman turned into a genealogist or a police detective to prove that the Countess X had come because her mother-in-law, the Duchess Z—"*My* customer . . . I sold her her bridal gown in 1936 at Paquin!"—had told her to ask for Madame Germaine, but she had forgotten the name and it was a scandal that Madame Suzy had got her . . . etc. . . . etc.! The habits of that period were still deeply rooted, and the eldest saleswomen still wrote "Personal Customer" with a flourish on their order sheets.

Everyone had tried to buy the favors of the Princess to get the best tours assigned to them, without realizing that in her previous grandeur she would have made them come in by the service entrance.

Even after years of poverty, the Princess was absolutely immune to their intrigues, their underhandedness, and to the persecution mania from which they all suffered to one degree or another.

She listened to their constant jeremiads. She helped them out, when needed, with their clumsy conversations in English, Spanish, Italian, or German. She also gave them lessons in etiquette when they made blunders that were too dreadful;

for example she had made a list of certain aristocratic names, like the Broglies, which is pronounced "Breuille"; but she had finally given up trying to make them understand that there were ordinary Smiths and those who were Smythe.

Thanks to all her accomplishments, she had succeeded in making herself unanimously detested. Marie-Victoire even had to warn the saleswomen that she would listen to no more of their complaints against the Princess. They had gone so far as to accuse her when a number of thefts were perpetrated by a maid who was finally caught with her hand in someone's purse. The idea of having the "tours" assigned to them by someone who earned less money than they did but who was invited to all the royal weddings could easily have driven them to commit crimes, if they had had more courage.

This morning, they were waiting with prurient curiosity for the arrival of the new saleswoman. And the two young women, who had arrived last, remembering the tortures they had undergone during their first weeks, joined forces against the old guard who, huddled at the end of the room, were plotting dark schemes against the newcomer. The number of regular haute couture customers in the entire world is never more than two or three thousand women, and among them, there is only a tiny minority that is faithful to one house. These are branded, ticketed, inventoried, ambushed, and wooed by some 150 to 200 saleswomen in Paris haute couture. For example, when the Aga Khan is to marry, his fiancée, unknown until then, will receive an avalanche of invitations. However, no house could live on this clientele alone, for it is also so demanding that workrooms always lose money on fittings and retouching.

In the end, it had to be recognized that the rich bourgeoises, at whom they sneered when they came in to buy an impeccable outfit for some special event without quibbling over the price,

36

were in much larger supply. They were also much less difficult to satisfy—the label was enough to please them.

The new saleswoman appeared at the bottom of the staircase, dressed in black linen, her face youthful in spite of her short white hair. She climbed the stairs, looking quite calm, but inside she was dying of apprehension. She greeted the Princess and introduced herself.

"I am Madame Annie, the new saleswoman. I suppose that you are the Princess Carminola; I am delighted to meet you."

At last, one with some poise, thought the Princess. It's plain that she's been with Balenciaga and Givenchy. Smiling, she picked up the telephone.

"Madame, Madame Annie is here. Shall I send her up to you?"

"Good, I'll bring her back down again."

The Princess made a sign to her pink-cheeked seventeen-year-old assistant: "Accompany Madame Annie to Madame's office." Good, Annie said to herself, she's to be called just plain Madame. Marie-Victoire got up when the new employee entered the studio. It was a large white room which she had just done over entirely in avant-garde style, with windows opening on the Place Vendôme, like an amusing anachronism.

"I welcome you to our house and I hope our ladies won't give you too hard a time."

This frank welcome helped Madame Annie (who admitted to herself that she was terrified) relax a bit. She had spent twelve years with Balenciaga before the house closed; then four with Givenchy which she decided to leave only because the manager showed undisguised hostility toward her.

"My dear, you must submit to the formality of having your address book inspected. The Princess will take care of it, you can trust her completely, she's the sword of justice in person. All the customers who already have a saleswoman in the house will remain with her, of course, unless they haven't bought anything in the past five years and you bring them back here. Otherwise, you mustn't solicit them; it annoys women to receive three invitations from three different saleswomen. Also, I don't like to have them pestered on the telephone; you may call one to tell her that there is a gown in the collection which would be just right for her, but I've noticed that by and large they hate being pursued. Besides, if the collection has good notices, they come running, and stay at home if it hasn't. And, finally, if one of them prefers you to her usual saleswoman, you must split the commission with her for a year. Come now, we'll go down to the lions' den. I think that you will get along well with Madame Sylvette, who came to us from Dior and with Mademoiselle Estelle, who spent ten years with Balmain."

And as she opened the door for her to pass through first, Marie-Victoire added: "You must ask my permission to lower a price. I know that there are women who will only buy if they believe one is doing them a favor, and you are surely aware enough of this little mania to raise the price as much as you'll ask me to reduce it. As for the commission agents, you have been assigned to a new house which has just started; I hope for your sake that it has lots of customers."

The magic word *customers* was pronounced just as they entered the saleswomen's room. All of them were silent, their ears pricked as though they were a pack of terriers hearing the prey break cover.

"Mesdames, here is our new saleswoman, Madame Annie. I'm sure that you are going to give her a warm welcome and help her over the rough spots. I believe that Madame Sylvette has decided on this desk for her; I see that she has put a bouquet of flowers on it. That's a very kind gesture, and I thank her. I'm sorry I haven't the time to make the introductions my-

38

self, so be kind enough to make them yourselves. I'm depending on all of you to be at the general rehearsal, Monday at four-thirty, as usual."

When she spoke to the saleswomen as a group, Marie-Victoire knew she always sounded haughty and cold, although she could be charming with each individually. Some of them said this was shyness, but, in fact, it was scorn, for she believed that none of them knew how to sell as well as she did herself and she hated having to depend on them for such an important part of her business. Twice a year she repeated to them that she preferred losing an order to meeting an ill-dressed customer in society. Old Madame Nicole (she had called herself Nicolette until the day when Marie-Victoire called her into her studio and said that at her age it would be more becoming to leave off the final "ette" which was a bit girlish) still trembled with malice at the memory an incident that had taken place five years ago. She had sold a plain crepe dress to the wife of a rich deputy. The customer, who loved flowered fabric, had asked to have it in a print. Without mentioning it to Marie-Victoire, Madame Nicole had had an assortment of silk prints in blues, greens, and oranges brought in on consignment from different houses for the customer to choose from. Of course the woman had chosen the worst and most ordinary of them, which was hastily approved by Madame Nicole. Up to that point everything had gone smoothly, since Marie-Victoire would have known nothing about it had not the deputy, who had accepted a post as minister, been photographed for *Paris-Match* with his wife opening a flower show. White with rage at seeing her dress distorted in this way and thinking of the chortling of her competitors when they saw this horror bearing her label, Marie-Victoire had telephoned the customer herself. Marie-Victoire was very dissatisfied with the dress, she was taking it back, would Madame be kind enough to come to try another which would be ready for her in a week?

Marie-Victoire had even added slyly: "And for this one, I'll personally supervise the fittings."

The good woman was totally confused by the attention accorded her and, plagued by an inferiority complex about her appearance, instead of replying to the impertinent lady: "My dress suits me very well and I have confidence in my saleswoman who has assured me that I am the height of elegance in it"—thanked her for taking so much trouble. She arrived that afternoon with the dress, which was sent to the clearance rack within the hour, where its ample proportions made some Belgian tourist happy.

Marie-Victoire, who up to that time had never spoken to this anonymous customer, immediately decided to see if an elegant woman could be made out of this honest housewife, whose open and reassuring face and lack of chic had been responsible for a good many of the feminine votes which had elected her husband deputy. In less than an hour she had appointments with a doctor who made her lose twenty pounds, with a hairdresser who made her look ten years younger with a good coloring job, and with a shoemaker who made her elegant shoes that were even comfortable, unlike the gunboats she had always worn. Finally, at great expense, she bought a whole new wardrobe, including accessories, under Marie-Victoire's watchful eye. A great friendship grew between the two women, and Marie-Victoire practically ran the ministry, ordering dinners, flowers, and even indicating to her new friend, who happened to be quite intelligent, which guests she ought to invite. Grateful for these services, the minister gave her the Legion of Honor on the Fourteenth of July of the following year. Meanwhile Madame Nicole, with rage in her heart, had to be satisfied with her commission and running to fetch samples for them.

The day after the photograph had appeared, a memo had been circulated in the house: no order that involved changing a model in the collection in any way at all could be put through without the signature of Marie-Victoire or that of the designer, Adrien Lecouture.

Satisfied that she had dispatched her chore of introduction, Marie-Victoire gave the Princess a friendly little pat on the arm as she passed and went directly to Adrien's quarters. There a feverish atmosphere reigned in the two rooms which served as a studio for Adrien and his assistant. Three salesmen were waiting in the first room to show jewels, buttons, and belts, which had arrived at the last moment. Four mannequins wearing wrappers and accompanied by the designer's first assistant, waited for Adrien to check the last fittings. Bolts of unused fabrics were piled to the ceiling or lay on the floor, and everyone spoke in a low voice.

Marie-Victoire greeted the group in a friendly manner and stopped a moment near Lucienne, the head of the studio. A tidy woman with gray hair and very blue eyes, she was dressed in a white smock as were all the workers in the studio (a custom Adrien had picked up when he worked at Dior). Madame Lucienne jokingly called herself the midwife of the collection. And in fact she presided over the birth of each model, making out a numbered card for it which first went to the manager, where the amount of material required was noted along with all the findings to be used: buttons, thread, zippers, lining, facing, etc. The package of materials, with its order attached, was sent to the workroom which had executed the muslin model from a pattern made by the designer. The day the garment was finished, the card went to the files, and the number,

41

which would be matched to a name eventually, was written on a tape sewn to the inside of the garment.

"Good morning, Lucienne, not too rushed, I hope."

"A bit, madame. Monsieur Lecouture and Madame Alphonsine have just decided to do a new gown in this velvet. Fortunately it's black, so we have all the trimmings in stock. If we'd had to have them dyed we couldn't have had them by Tuesday."

"Have you enough help, Alphonsine?"

"Yes, madame, we'll manage."

"Good luck."

She went into the back of the studio, a sanctuary forbidden to almost everyone else. White shades with black fringes were pulled down over the windows that opened on the Place Vendôme. One day, someone had seen that certain buyers, using powerful binoculars, were spying on the fittings from a window of the Ritz. They weren't the only house spied on this way. For several seasons Balenciaga, famous enough to do without publicity, had refused to receive the press until a month after the opening of his collection. But he was obliged to live with all his shutters closed on the Avenue George V because *Women's Wear Daily,* not wanting to admit defeat, set up an observation post in the apartment opposite.

Daphne, the mannequin who had been with the house the longest, was standing in front of a very large mirror where Adrien and Philippe, the tailor, were studying her. "Turn a little," said Adrien. Slowly she turned in place and in passing gave Marie-Victoire a vague smile. "Good morning, madame." Adrien and Philippe, without taking their eyes off the hem, also said: "Good morning, madame," at the same moment.

42

"The hem droops in front, but don't touch it, I'd rather lift the whole thing a little."

Philippe put two or three pins at the top of the armhole and, as if by a miracle, the soft tweed coat, instead of hanging limp, flared away from the legs and began to come alive.

"Much better," said Marie-Victoire. "Philippe, you're a genius!" and she gave Adrien a wink as if to say: I know who the real genius is, but he loves to be flattered.

Daphne quickly got out of the coat which Philippe covered with a sheet. For a second she exposed her flat little body in brassiere and girdle, but was almost aseptically decent in spite of that, then she put on her white smock and left without a glance at anyone.

"What's the matter with her?" Marie-Victoire asked Adrien.

"She's exasperating. This morning, at eight o'clock, she rang me up to beg me to change Amalia's red dress for that blue crepe she hates."

"Just between us, I think she's right. Day before yesterday she looked like a waif in it. Anyhow, she looks like a stick in bias cuts. My dear, if you bring bias lines back in fashion, you must use mannequins who are a bit rounder and less like consumptive little boys. But you know she adores you, poor baby, so don't be too mean to her."

"You actually come to her defense though she seethes with jealousy every time she sees you!"

"Come now, Adrien, this is no time to get irritable."

She bit her lip, she had almost called him Adrienne. His reactions were sometimes so blatantly feminine that she was still surprised by them after ten years. She refrained from shrugging her shoulders and told herself for the nth time that one really had to be stupid to fall in love with a homosexual. People had often teased her about her friendship with Adrien, and she had always replied with a smile: "He's my best

43

girl friend. At least he isn't jealous of my clothes, since he designs them, and then I really enjoy the company of homosexuals. In France, most women are so futile. At least these boys like me for my manly qualities. They know that they don't need to pretend to be courting me and that I don't expect any special attentions from them. Besides, I like their feminine qualities, their finesse, their taste in decoration, the way they are interested in all our problems, from clothes to diets, the way they love gossip. They have women's good qualities without the inconveniences. It's true they grow old ungracefully and are even sillier than aging women with hair ribbons when they try to play baby-doll with jowls and a paunch. Adrien is never really ridiculous. I've seen him at Port-Grimaud. He wore color combinations that were a little far out, but he didn't get himself up in the latest chichi from the Saint-Tropez boutiques."

Actually, it would have been hard to find a man who looked more virile than Adrien. Even in his white smock, which might have made him look like a well-dressed cook, he managed to look more like an atomic scientist or an eminent surgeon. He admitted to being forty-five. Actually, one day when he had his passport renewed, a clerk in the passport office with ornate handwriting had written the 0 in his birth date, 1920, with a sort of a tail above it which the next clerk transformed into 6 without questioning it—nor did Adrien. Since then he often left his passport lying about in plain view. Six years off his age without even having to tell a lie was a bit of luck he couldn't pass up. He was so used to the false date of birth now that he no longer believed he was any older. Anyhow, he didn't even look forty-five for he religiously kept up his morning exercises, counted calories, had massages, manicures, pedicures, and went to the hairdresser every week. He passed hours at Lanvin choosing the material for his suits, shirts, ties, socks, and handkerchiefs, which always had to blend subtly without matching too perfectly. He went in for a rather formal look, very "Quai d'Orsay," and despised nothing more than the "roaring queens" doused in perfume and wearing jackets lined with orange-dotted chestnut silk.

He was seen at all the receptions, all the balls, all the charity fêtes, surrounded and greeted intimately by the prettiest women of the jet set. To see him lording it over the salons one might have thought him a Don Juan incarnate, but it was soon obvious that the only person who aroused any passion in him was himself. He was only interested in his lady friends' external appearance, in their hairdressing, in problems of precedence at table, or in their costumes if some millionaire was giving a masked ball in Venice or Acapulco. He was as gossipy as they were and spent hours chattering on the telephone. Husbands liked him, too, because he had a knack of listening with apparent enthusiasm to their dullest stories and besides, they had nothing to lose to him except the big bills for their wives' dresses, which, for the most part, were not a problem.

It was well known that he had lived for years with a talented decorator and antiquarian named Hubert Mezac. They shared a small house at Neuilly and another at Port-Grimaud. As they were both excellent company, cultivated, amusing, and entertained well, they were received in the most snobbish circles in Paris and New York.

So when Adrien fell for a little twenty-three-year-old ready-to-wear designer who stopped off in Saint-Tropez looking for a softer bed than his own (which was often no more than a beach mattress), he created a juicy gossip item for a few weeks.

"My dear, are you going to *invite* that little climber? I know

45

he's terribly good-looking, but I don't like the idea of having to count my spoons after he leaves."

"That poor Hubert, what an expression he had on his face! It seems Adrien has persuaded Marie-Victoire to hire the boy as an assistant."

"That's nice. How will he dress us?"

"His name is Jean-Loup, I believe. It certainly suits him because he has remarkably sharp teeth. Let's hope Adrien doesn't lose too many of his feathers."

"Well, I'll invite him to the house in Saint-Tropez, but certainly not in Paris."

"That's a very good idea, my dear. Even these days there are some limits. But I'm really surprised at poor Adrien; you know what an egoist he is—now all he can think of is pleasing that boy." Excited by the idea of introducing him to Italy, Spain, and the pleasures of skiing, Adrien went on more and more trips with this young man who had never had enough money to leave France. In Italy, Jean-Loup yawned at Florence but woke up in Capri, where his looks earned him a number of flattering propositions. Poor Adrien, tired of playing chaperone, had to cut their stay short. There was a very rich German on the island, in his sixties but still handsome, who had even offered Jean-Loup a sort of contract to stay with him for a year. At the end of this time, he would pay him ten million lires and give him his freedom. In any other circumstances, Jean-Loup would have jumped at the offer, but he wanted to have a go at being a couturier and so refused.

In Spain, the Prado left him cold, but he had to be snatched away from Torremolinos where he had managed to escape for a few hours with a magnificent beach boy, whom he remembered far more fondly than the Alhambra. Finally, in Switzerland, where the mountaineers had healthier tastes, he turned his attention to a bunch of Pigalle-type hangers-on he met in a bar, whose vulgarity and resemblance to Marseilles pimps made Adrien sick.

Adrien was to say later: "There are more people one can never really help than there are those one can render some service to." And this bitter realization ultimately confirmed him in his natural egocentricity.

Eleven-thirty. Jean-Loup entered the studio and Marie-Victoire looked at her watch pointedly. He stared at her insolently, caroling: "Good morning, everybody!" He was dressed in blue jeans that hung low on his hips and were so form-fitting that it was impossible to ignore the size of his genital equipment. With the jeans he wore a pink shirt with a plum-colored scarf at the neck. He had long hair, black and curly, and his eyes were blue, thickly fringed with lashes which would have been the joy of any woman. Above all he possessed that nonchalance which is to actual elegance what good grooming was to yesterday's splendors. Adrien, checking an evening gown on Amalia, turned a bright smile toward him: "Good morning, baby. Sleep well?" This was more than Marie-Victoire could take; if she had been a cat she would have had her claws out, her teeth bared, and her fur on end. She turned her back on him and directed her attention to the big bulletin board where all the models, each represented by a little square of fabric, were pinned in a row under the name of each mannequin in approximately the order in which they were to appear. After studying it a moment, she said to Adrien:

"At the rehearsal, we might try grouping the reds and the blacks together. That would catch the reporters' eyes. If we move Arlette, we can do it."

Adrien trusted her to organize the mannequin parade because he knew she had more sense of show business than he did. A well-presented collection could have a dazzling success though the same models taken individually might have only limited interest. It was the triumph of the stage director over the author. Some young couturiers understood this so well that they presented their collections to music, with dancers for mannequins. But Marie-Victoire thought this undignified, and, though she recognized the importance of the order in which the models were shown, she refused to turn her collection into a music-hall performance.

"You and I can decide at the four o'clock rehearsal. I would prefer to have the saleswomen see the collection in the best possible order on Monday."

She had emphasized the "you and I," and when Jean-Loup thumbed his nose in her direction, the first assistant and the mannequin pretended to have seen nothing, and Adrien said:

"Please don't be childish!"

Lucienne stuck her head in the doorway. "Monsieur Vermont has brought the gold-embroidered gown himself. He says it is so beautiful that he wants to show it to you right away."

"Bring him in. I'm eager to see it."

The young embroiderer opened the box and with pride brought out a real museum piece.

Adrien exclaimed: "It's a miracle. Call Madame Julie so that she can finish it. Jean-Guy, you're a genius!"

The couturiers, fabric merchants, embroiderers, and jewelers were on excellent terms with each other, a little like members of the same club. Haute couture not only meant large sums of money to its suppliers, but even more than that, a fantastic promotional vehicle. The big specialty magazines had half their pages paid for by these manufacturers. When a house as important as Du Pont de Nemours wanted to introduce a new fiber, it began by giving the fabric to the couturiers to make into a dress. Then the company would buy the dress, photograph it, and publicize it all over the world. Parisian haute couture's reputation for caution was an unequaled guarantee of quality. Sometimes it took a certain grandeur of soul for the couturiers to refuse to make a model in a fabric that they did not consider up to the standard of the house in spite of the temptation of a large sum of money. The manufacturers of traditional fabrics also tried to defend their products, and the Wool Bureau, for example, bought dozens of models to use in promotions all over the world.

For a respite, Marie-Victoire went to see her press agent, who was also in charge of public relations, and for whom she had a soft spot. Alan Harside was in his thirties, American, rather unpredictable, almost aggressively elegant, impertinent but winning, with his ready smile. He welcomed each important journalist like a special friend, and the Americans whom he took to fashionable night clubs and restaurants adored him. However, he was far from enjoying this kind of flattering popularity in Maison Forval, for not only did he think that publicity was more important than any other part of the business, but he was gauche enough to say so. He had made a particular enemy of the manager who found his expense accounts exorbitant. Acting on the principle that haute couture is a luxury profession, he could not imagine taking a journalist any place but Maxim's. Unfortunately, he often extended invitations to people who had nothing to offer in return. For some time, the manager had been asking Marie-Victoire to replace him with a woman who would be less flamboyant and extravagant. Up to now she had always found excuses not to, but she was beginning to realize that the era of great entertainment was over and journalists could no longer be bought with dinners. The new snobbism consisted of discovering a craftsman in some hidden corner of Menilmontant who used a forge, preferably a Louis XIII one, to make dresses out of old pans cut up into discs—until one stumbled onto another talented jack-of-all-trades who molded

49

them out of plastic. Up to now, humanity had been divided into two kinds of civilization: the draped and the sewn. Soon it would be necessary to add a third, the welded. And Alan Harside, haute couture, and the refinements of a decadent society would play no part in this revolution. This season, Chavanaux had offered Marie-Victoire a choice: either Alan Harside stopped wasting the firm's money on useless entertaining or he, Chavanaux, would leave to work in some less insane business.

Being the only two real males in the firm, it was natural that they should hate each other. Also, Chavanaux was full of jealousy. He had married a nice, insignificant little housewife after completing a respectable commercial course, and lived in a big apartment complex in Boulogne. He played tennis on Sundays, bridge on Thursday evenings, and went to the movies every Saturday. Always dressed in an oxford gray suit with a maroon tie, he was a typical petit bourgeois, as removed from haute couture and its ambiance as Mars is from earth.

Alan looked like Warren Beatty. He lived in a garden apartment behind the Place de Furstemberg. He painted in his spare time and he always had twenty stunning women who asked nothing better than to share his bed because he was so dashing. Moreover, he never forgot his former girl friends and represented a sort of unemployment insurance to them. Everyone also knew that he was heir to a large American tire firm and that one day he would have to go back to Akron, Ohio, his home town. But for the moment he was delaying this eventuality as long as possible; he adored Paris and the life he lived there.

It was five years ago, after his graduation from Harvard, that his father had given him a first-class airplane ticket along with a respectable number of traveler's checks and had suggested that he travel around the world for six months before coming to work at the factory. But this healthy child of the Middle West, raised on steaks and Coca-Cola, who had been told that in France the only people one met were waiters and prostitutes, was introduced, through a chance meeting on the plane, into the best society as soon as he arrived, and soon discovered all the refinements of an old civilization. In the end, he traveled no farther than Versailles, sold his return ticket, and wrote a long letter to his father explaining that he wanted to live and work in Paris. His mother, who rushed to Paris to plead with him to come home, not only did not succeed in changing his mind but was also quickly introduced to all kinds of delights reserved for true lovers of Paris. She gave him the money necessary for his move into Place de Furstemberg, and promised to come to visit him often. Alan told how she had remained unmoved before the Louvre, Versailles, and the Tuileries, at Maxim's and at Dior's, but that one morning she had inexplicably melted at the sight of the Eiffel Tower, which, she had said, reminded her of a friendly giraffe nibbling a pretty little round cloud as white and plump as a baby's backside.

After a few months of working in a fabric firm, he was taken on at Forval and soon became very friendly with Marie-Victoire and her daughter. He considered the latter a good pal with whom to go to the movies or dancing until one day when she expressed some outrageous opinions about America, which she had just heard from a leftist student. Although he preferred living in Paris, he was not one of those Americans who saluted the Viet Cong flag instead of the Stars and Stripes. But, inexplicably, instead of answering her sharply, he argued with her, and for the first time he began to desire her. The more unacceptable the things she said to him, the more he wanted to possess her, and that night he even dreamed of seeing her as a good little wife and president of a women's club in Akron. To obtain what he wanted, he put himself out to do her a thousand services and had even let Marie-Victoire know that he might very well invest capital in the business. Which was why he had paid for the fabric that morning.

When Marie-Victoire entered the publicity office, he was on the telephone impatiently explaining to some unimportant journalist that there were no more seats for Tuesday. The first showing of a collection is always reserved for the press and for celebrities, but with the number of reporters for the press and television swelling each year, it was necessary to establish a hierarchy among them—a hierarchy which might have surprised a non-initiate. While *Vogue* and *Harper's Bazaar* each had the right to fifteen seats in the first salon, *Family Weekly,* which is read by nine million people, was relegated to the second row in the second salon. The manager often called Marie-Victoire's attention to the absurdity of these methods. For every *Vogue* reader who ordered a dress, there were thousands of readers of *Family Weekly* who might buy a bottle of perfume.

Alan hung up, looking exasperated, but seeing Marie-Victoire he calmed down like a pot of boiling milk taken off the fire, and came to kiss her hand. "What a wonderful idea to put that red scarf on that chestnut-colored dress. You're glowing."

"Thank you, Alan, you're a terrible flatterer. In fact I'm dying of fright."

"Why? They're fighting to get seats. I've refused at least thirty people this morning."

"Have the saleswomen told you which customers are coming to the press showing? I had to accept Mother Durand."

"Good, we'll stick her in the second row. . . . I put Estée Lauder beside *Vogue* and the duchess, there," and he showed her the chart of the salons pinned on the wall. "Here's the ambassadress' corner, as usual."

"Very good. Thanks for paying for the fabric this morning. Here's the exact amount," and she put the bills on his desk.

"You could have paid me at the end of the month, I'm in no hurry."

"No use confusing the accounts."

"After the collection I want to have a serious talk with you. I have several ideas for changing the house."

"Good, we'll see. For the moment, what we need is a success."

The telephone rang again, and one of the assistants called him with a harried look: "The Kansas City *Star* . . . !"

Marie-Victoire threw them a "Keep your chin up!" and left, feeling that she had upset them more than she had helped. She looked at her watch. One o'clock. It was time to go to her studio and eat her hard-boiled eggs in peace.

Popoff, lying on a handsome red cushion, his head turned toward the door, jumped up wagging his tail and welcomed her as if he hadn't seen her for a week.

"Yes, my Popoff, you're beautiful and I love you. We'll call your friend Maurice, so he doesn't go to lunch before you have your walk. And then these two hard-boiled eggs. It's really too sad! What would you think of a nice little orange tart and some coffee from la Quetsche? You can bring them back to me."

Like all women when they feel low and out of sorts, Marie-Victoire comforted herself with sweets. When she caught herself buying chocolate, which she adored, she knew she wasn't entirely happy. It was hot. She took off her big red stole and stretched out on the white leather couch, her hard-boiled eggs on an antique porcelain plate, the last of a service of eighteen settings which had belonged to her grandmother Baussigue. Out of a drawer in her desk she took a white paper napkin with her initials in gold—a friend had sent her a package of them from

53

Bergdorf Goodman. I'll feel better soon, she told herself. I'm just hungry. She knew perfectly well that this hollow in her stomach was much more from anxiety than from hunger, but that was something she still could not admit. To let herself be carried away by unhappy memories like a bit of wood on the dark waters of a Canadian river would have been, to her, the equivalent of suicide.

On the other side of the partition, Adrien, too, was lying down during the hour when everybody else was at lunch. Normally, he would have taken advantage of the beautiful sunshine to go to the Tuileries and under the chestnut trees eat a runny fried egg and a little round cake welded in a pleated paper collar like a mummy in its shroud. To his friends who were surprised to see him, gourmet that he was, eating by the kiosk that sold sweets, he answered: "An hour of fresh air and simplicity is as necessary in my profession as a glass of water after a sweet dessert." And finally all those who wanted to pay court came to lunch with him. To satisfy such an elegant clientele, the owners of the kiosk added cold meats, salad, cheeses and ices to their menus. So all summer long one could see elegant ladies carefully dusting off the iron chairs before timidly settling buttocks covered in some admirably cut dress which would have been more at home in the Elysée gardens or the British embassy. *Women's Wear,* always abreast of the latest fashionable spot, even printed a little note in its "Eye" column, and the Tuileries kiosk became a serious rival to the Relais Plaza!

But today Adrien did not want to see anyone at all and he even told Jean-Loup that he wanted to be alone for a bit. The sketches of the collection were piled on his desk in the approximate order of their appearance. Some had already been given names, while others were still waiting to be christened. He began to separate the finished models from the ones he had only seen fitted once or twice. The pile of the latter was certainly the thicker. With the collection four days away, this often happened, but it seemed to him that this season it was worse than usual. Chavanaux was going to howl, he told himself, for they would have to work overtime Saturday and Sunday, which would cost a fortune. He wondered if it was worth the trouble of finishing them all. There would be plenty of time after the press showing. Anyway, these weren't models for the press. They were customers' dresses. He could even drop one or two of them. He picked up all the sketches again one by one. Certainly not this suit, nor this coat. Ah, Daphne's famous bias gown! It was true that she looked awful in it; it wasn't worth the trouble. Actually, he hated this kind of fabric, it always looked like a nightgown; no one since Vionnet had known how to use it properly, but then it was in style—and he hated the style.

He had never gotten used to all these costumey get-ups. He did not like the new classics, either, and he was sick to death of the cleverly cut things that had made his reputation—so what was left? You're getting old, my boy, he said to himself, and anxiety dug an enormous hole in his stomach.

There wasn't a thing he was really proud of in this collection. Ah yes! The little suits are charming. It's ridiculous that Jean-Loup wouldn't show his designs. If Marie-Victoire knew that! He'd been very weak with Jean-Loup, who'd cut his throat one of these days. He'd do better to get rid of him . . . New hole in his stomach. Good God, how handsome he'd been this morning! He had a sense of color, the bastard, that pink and plum, that was divine.

He looked at the sketches again: If there were time to start over, he'd throw them all in the waste basket . . . and dreamily he began to sketch a marvelous cape, sweeping, theatrical, haute couture, by God! That's not bad, he thought, and a cape makes up quickly. There's a fabric of Carlotto's that would do very well. And he got up, much cheered by his creation, still capable of enthusiasm for his miraculous profession. He hunted through the bolts, found a length. Luckily there was enough; quick, put it on Lucienne's table to go to Philippe. We won't make it up in muslin, that won't be necessary. No! He'd cut it himself! He spread the fabric on the carpet, and, on all fours, as in the old days, pins in his mouth and big scissors in his hand, he got busy with the cloth which in half an hour became a cape: the cape that reconciled him with life!

Monsieur Philippe's workroom was very quiet. All the designs were almost finished. Since his workroom always had the most orders for paper patterns from the buyers, he had decided that the first assistants would check them right after lunch. The second assistants would finish lining the jackets and coats.

Several seamstresses had spread a cloth on the table where they worked and were eating lunch and chatting. There was cold chicken, ham, a sandwich for the youngest, and all of them shared a bag of peaches they had bought together. Sometimes some of them went as far as the Tuileries gardens to bask in the early sun. Others went to the neighboring cafés to have coffee and cake, while some used the sewing machines in their free time and, with the help of a colleague, fitted the dresses they were making for themselves.

Young Marinette was going to be married tomorrow. She was standing on the table dressed in a beautiful white faille gown, offered by the house, while three of her friends turned up the hem. Many rich girls would have envied her such an outfit, copied directly from an evening gown of the previous season. In principle, the workers were forbidden to copy a model from the collection, but in fact they did, and many of them could have given lessons in elegance to some of their customers. Most, however, in spite of the pretty things they saw all day, had dreadful taste. The maids of honor, checking out the last details of each other's costumes, were striking examples. They wore a nauseating assortment of too-shiny silks in pastel tones. They would wear these dresses again on Saint Catherine's Day, the twenty-fifth of November, with gold shoes and carnations tied with ribbons of green and yellow, the saint's colors, pinned to their left shoulders.

As his second assistant in the workroom, Monsieur Philippe had Madame Hilda. She had been in the house the longest of any of the seamstresses and she had followed all the steps of its rise. She had begun work with a couturier in Stuttgart, her birthplace. She had married a young metal worker at Renault, a forced laborer she had met there, and they returned to Paris at the end of the war. She was a taciturn woman with a strong German accent and a pronounced taste for discipline and hierarchy. She was not much liked by the women she supervised. Madame Hilda never wasted time, and after swallowing some potato salad and sausages from her lunch box, although she had half an hour left to relax in, she began to put together the pattern of a gray flannel jacket with a white mink collar. The second assistants in the workrooms were always chosen from among the best-organized and most serious workers, for they were the ones who took over for the tailor or the first assistant, who were often away from the workroom for fittings in the salons. Sometimes a chance to become the first assistant in the workroom was offered to the most able, and it was the only hope of promotion for a seamstress.

After a while, all the others went out to take a walk in the sun. Madame Hilda, alone now in the workroom, continued to busy herself efficiently. All instructions were written on a piece of heavy paper, cut in as many pieces as the jacket: the proper thread, the seams, the buttonholes, the darts, the pockets, where it should be gathered or eased. A great part of the final look of a haute couture garment comes from the way it is pressed and cannot be done properly on mass-produced garments. Also, the pattern is always made and delivered in a "model" size, that is, very small. In haute couture, where work is always done to specific measurements no one knows how to enlarge in standard sizes, so it is up to the buyer to do his best to adapt his pattern to the exigencies of ready-to-wear.

Monsieur Philippe was among the first to return to the workroom. "My poor Hilda, we aren't that far behind! That could wait."

"I won't be relaxed until they are all done. This afternoon I'm going to do the checked coat. That's the most difficult because the checks must match."

He approved with a grunt. It's curious, he thought, how little energy and discipline are appreciated in France. This girl is a model of order, devotion, punctuality, but in spite of these rare qualities, she isn't very well liked.

Amalia stuck her head in the door. "Are you ready for my fitting?"

"Yes, love, come in."

Beside a big cutting table, higher than the one where the seamstresses worked, there was a long mirror before which the tailor fitted garments on the mannequins. A coat-dress had been finished, and Monsieur Philippe, looking at it on Amalia, found nothing to be changed. His eye on the mirror, he had her turn slowly so that he could check all sides. "Do you like it?" he asked her.

"It's super!"

It was the latest fashionable adjective. She could also have used "terrific," "divine," "fantastic," or even, if she were very young, "out of sight," when in fact it was simply pretty and very well cut. To the saleswomen it would be "good," or "easy," and to the buyers, "a great little dress." Now, sealed with the approval of this laudatory adjective, it could be shown to Monsieur Lecouture. Amalia, wrapped in a big muslin cape which entirely covered her dress, went with Philippe to the studio. At once, the tone of the conversations in the workroom rose. But Madame Hilda tapped on the table with her yardstick and called the workers to order, particularly the two little apprentices who, like girls all over the world, burst into giggles they tried to conceal with their hands.

Instead of the usual babble, silence reigned in the mannequins' dressing room. Daphne, seated in front of her mirror and her cosmetics, was drinking a cup of very strong tea in little sips. Before coming to work at this house, she had gone to England for a year to learn English and had brought back a passion for tea. She was deep in a beginner's bridge book, for she hoped that Adrien, an enthusiastic player, would ask her to make a fourth some time. It was seven years since Adrien had met her in the Tuileries and had asked her, almost as a joke, if she wouldn't like to be a mannequin. She had just started work as a salesgirl at Smith, the English bookshop on the Rue de Rivoli, and she had liked it very much.

"Me, a mannequin!" she said in the tone she would have used if she had lifted a stone and discovered the treasures of Ali Baba under it. "Are you joking?"

"Not at all, come tomorrow at noon to Marie-Victoire Forval, Place Vendôme."

The next day, she was first dressed in a suit, then in an evening gown, and sent into the salon before Marie-Victoire and Adrien, who sat in the middle of the room.

"Of course she doesn't know how to walk," said Marie-

Victoire, "but she has a sort of innate grace which is even rarer, and I like the way she carries her head. If you wish, my dear, something could be made of her. Those round cheeks will have to go, but in this profession that happens fast."

"Yes, I like her because, thank God, she has no bosom," he said, like a housewife selecting a piece of beef without too much fat.

That was enough to make the poor child lose her poise. She had always been a little ashamed of her flat chest, and suddenly it was her greatest asset.

Adrien asked what her first name was.

"Simone, Monsieur."

"Dreadful!" And after a few moments of thought he decided, "You'll be called Daphne. That's prettier, isn't it?"

In a dream, she signed a starvation contract with Chavanaux. For once he'd found a beginner who didn't know going wages; he must take advantage of it! He did not realize that for a look from Adrien she would have cleaned the floor with her tongue. No, he thought that like the rest she already took herself for another Jean Shrimpton or Penelope Tree. Also he told her of all the trips that five mannequins and part of the collection took each year: Cannes, Biarritz, and Beirut, plus Tokyo, Hong Kong, and Bangkok. This last trip all of them fought to go on, of course, but if she was good, if she would model for the buyers . . .

"What does that mean?" she interrupted, vaguely disturbed.

"Don't worry, little one, nothing bad, only a bit tiresome. The garments ordered by the buyers are fitted on you, that's all."

"Oh, well."

She did not see how such a minor service should earn her a lovely trip . . . but this world of haute couture was so complicated.

"Then in a year you'll be entitled to your 'advance dress,' that is, a garment you'll return the following year for reduced sale, and to another for which you'll furnish the fabric and which will belong to you. Of course, if you're invited to a big gala, you may borrow evening clothes, but don't take advantage of us to borrow a gown on Saturday evening to go dancing with your boy friend!"

"I haven't got a boy friend."

"You will."

And for once he thought, "I don't know why I don't sleep with this pet; it wouldn't cost me more than a promise of a trip to Teheran or Oslo. All the other managers take advantage. I'm really a fool." Feeling an overflow of tenderness at this new idea, he took her arm gently.

"Go to the dressing room, little girl. Madame Suzanne will tell you anything else you need to know, and if something's wrong, come tell me about it."

"Everything will be fine, monsieur." Suddenly, all she wanted was to get out of his office.

In the next seven years she remained impervious to Chavanaux's winks and came back in the place only four or five times to ask for a raise. Today she was earning much less than the temporary mannequins who moved from house to house showing the ready-to-wear collections, or went to Brussels or Geneva to show the collections to buyers who had liked them in Paris, and who posed for magazine photos.

Though Daphne was a marvelous mannequin in the salon, unfortunately she was not photogenic and had no hope of earning extra money by posing for magazines. But all she really wanted was to be on hand when Adrien needed her, and she refused to think of the future as hopeless. Little by little she grew bold enough to express her preferences to him and now he often asked her advice. Sometimes he took her to the movies or even invited her to dinner at his house with Hubert when a lady dropped out at the last moment. On such occasions he chose her dress himself and she believed she had a special place in his life.

She told herself that some day he would decide to settle down, and she even hinted from time to time that married people paid less taxes than single ones. She couldn't imagine that a man capable of draping fabric on her body with so much love could feel no desire for her. She did not understand that a dress designer was not quite like the ordinary homosexual who, his mother excepted, wouldn't have noticed if a sudden epidemic had exterminated all the women on earth. He admired a woman's chic, and he needed her for inspiration. It could even be said that he loved women, in so far as they gave him an outlet for self-expression, but if their bodies had been wax or a robot could have been made to move with as much grace as a human being, he would have welcomed its invention with joy.

Adrien complacently accepted the homage Daphne gave him. After all, it is not unpleasant to play absolute monarch and from time to time throw a few crumbs to an attentive slave.

But lately he had found that the slave was becoming an encumbrance. She criticized certain dresses openly, even refused to wear them, dared to make scenes with him, and could barely conceal her hatred for Jean-Loup. Her unconditional love was becoming tiresome; he had neither asked anything of this girl, nor promised her anything. In a word, she was a drag. Why couldn't she take a lover like everybody else instead of lavishing all her affection on him and on her dove, Crou-croune, which was allowed to fly around in her tiny apartment?

The poor girl was quite aware that she annoyed him. But is there a lover in the world able to accept the idea that she is poisoning her idol's life with her attentions? Of course not. So, in traditional style, one day she would bring him a rose, another she would make a cake which he had said he liked, but when she felt rejected she would stage a big scene with twisted handkerchief and sound effects of groans, sighs, and desperate sobbing. She had tried to console herself with religion, and had gone to mass every morning for a while. But it seemed that even the Lord had no time for her, and now, four days before the collection was to be shown, she was trying to learn the answer to a demand bid of four no trump.

Madame Suzanne, head of the dressing room, was putting a pile of gloves in order, though they were scarcely worn any more. The day before, she had sold all last year's shoes to her "girls" (that was what she called the mannequins) at ridiculously low prices, and she thought nostalgically of the good old days when almost all the gowns were shown with black satin high-heeled pumps whose shape didn't change every six months.

Because she ate candy all day she was almost as wide as she was high, but her hair was as blond as a Viking's. Madame Suzanne was probably the nicest person in the house. She had spent her whole life in the dressing room. In 1928, at fifteen, she had begun with Chanel under Madame Julie, who was a real policeman in skirts. She had taught the prettiest mannequins in the world their trade (all of them had passed through Paris at one time or another). Instead of being jealous of these lovely creatures, she had always considered herself a mother to them and had never thought of anything but how she could help them. She always had handy one or two good addresses of accommodating midwives, which was very useful before the era of the pill. She frequently lent a little money to this girl or that to tide her over to the end of the month—money which was not always repaid. Once in a while, a girl who was a little less of an ingrate than the rest would bring her a little present, and when one of them got married or had a baby, she was always the first to be told. She had known enough of love affairs to fill the pages of all the confession magazines in the world.

She saw to it that the collection was always impeccable—besides ironing and sewing buttons, hems, or tapes that worked loose, she knew how to take out all kinds of spots and said truthfully that she could have earned much more money as a dry cleaner. She was unequaled at getting rid of the black marks from Popoff's wet but affectionate paws. Popoff, in spite of his links with haute couture, did not distinguish between yellow gabardine and brown tweed. So Marie-Victoire often came to see Madame Suzanne and chat in her slip while she busied herself over a spot with her mysterious powders and lotions. She was an island of calm in a sea of nerves and an oasis of kindness in a desert of feminine bitcheries.

Now she was watching Ingara, who, her eyes closed, was stretched on a chaise longue, her feet up on her dressing table.

"Shall I massage your neck, sweetheart? What's the trouble?"

The beautiful Swedish girl opened her lavender-blue, almost violet eyes, full of sadness, and said in her harsh accent: "No thanks, M'dame Suzanne, just a little headache. It will pass."

"You're sure you don't want to tell me what's the matter? You don't look much like a girl who is about to get her marriage license! You can't kid old Suzanne, my baby. I'm sure something's bothering you, and there are no troubles you can't work out, take it from me!"

The big, rangy blonde only smiled a little and closed her eyes again, but a few seconds later she surreptitiously dried two tears as they slid gently toward her ears. Madame Suzanne shook her head: what could be the matter? She remembered two weeks ago, when Ingara had come to announce the news of her engagement to a photographer, the squealing of the other mannequins, and the particular interest of one of the American temporaries when she heard the name of the fiancé.

"But, honey," this girl had said, "he's one of the biggest photographers in New York—he gets fabulous prices for his work even though he's so young, you're really in luck! I'll leave you my address in New York and when you come I can introduce you to lots of interesting people."

Ingara would have loved her photographer in the same way if he had been a street cleaner, and she had not realized that by marrying him she would hit success with a "capital" S—she did not know either that in the States it's only success that's worshiped, so she was ecstatic with the offer. America, her lover's country, sounded more and more like Eden to her. That day she felt as if, while having her fittings, she was floating a foot off the ground, on a cloud of happiness, and everybody said she glowed like those horrible statuettes of the Virgin lighted from the inside sold at Lourdes!

Adelaide came back from her fitting with Philippe and said to Ingara: "Go up to Monsieur Adrien right away; he's just cut a terrific cape and he says it's made for you."

Daphne descended from the heights of a "six-spade demand bid" to cast a venomous look at Ingara, fond of her though she was. Ah! If only she, Daphne, could show the whole collection! She took it as a personal injury if a model worn by another mannequin was a success.

"A cape," she said. "Well, that's something new!"

"Yes, love," answered Adelaide. "You don't know everything that goes on in the house; your darling had a stroke of genius during lunch hour."

Adelaide was Jean-Loup's favorite mannequin, and for that reason, Daphne's mortal enemy.

Suzanne interrupted: "Come, come girls, simmer down! Go on up quickly, Ingara, it will cheer you up . . ."

Marie-Victoire, resting on her big white couch, was roused by the ringing of the telephone.

"London calling, madame."

"Good, put them on."

"Marie-Victoire—it's Oliver."

Immediately, she was completely awake. "Hello, my dear, I didn't know you were in London."

"I'll be in Paris this evening at eight forty-five. If you'll come get me at Orly, we can go straight to Maxim's for dinner."

"What a good idea, that will raise my spirits, you always know what I need. But now that I think of it, it's Friday, and black tie is a must."

"I do enough business there so that I don't have to worry about that. Besides, no one will have eyes for anyone except you. I have an important meeting in London at five and if I have to go change at the Ritz, it will be too late. I've reserved the table for nine-thirty. OK?"

"OK," Marie-Victoire answered.

"So I'll be seeing you."

"Until then."

Click. He hung up. It makes me mad that he's so sure of me . . . he didn't even ask if I were free. I must leave Quai de Béthune at seven-thirty and it won't be easy to choose the right thing to wear for both Orly and Maxim's. If anyone else had asked me so casually, I would surely have pretended to have an engagement. As usual, when she was facing any new situation, Marie-Victoire imagined herself dressed for the occasion. She even had a dress laid away in a drawer for her burial. If she had not always been thinking in terms of clothing, she would have never succeeded in couture. So instead of anticipating her lover's caresses, she first thought about what she would wear for him.

. . . Zut, everyone will stare at me. Still, I'd like very much to wear the black mousseline which is so becoming, shoes with jeweled heels, it's easy to change those in the car. I'm going to look in the sale merchandise and see if there's a wrap there to wear over my dress, I may die of the heat, but . . .

All of a sudden, the remainder of the day seemed interminable. I'll leave about five, I'll just have time to wash my hair and put on special make-up. . . .

Her imagination spun on. She saw herself dressed in black mousseline at Maxim's beside Oliver. The lighting was flattering, he was looking at her, listening to her. She was persuasive, she had found the right formula for rejuvenating haute couture, the businessman was enthusiastic, the lover was ecstatic, she was triumphant, he took out his check book, kissed her hand, she had won all around. . . .

She took hold of herself and sighed: "You're dreaming, my poor fool. . . ." But this time, some solution must really be found: either sell to Big Mills or persuade Oliver to gamble on her. Even if by some miracle all the other couturiers created horrors and *Women's Wear Daily* decided that Adrien was the only good designer left in the whole world, even if they sold as many patterns as they had in 1960, the problem would come up again in six months. No, better to deal with it now.

She telephoned Adrien. "Will we be able to have the rehearsal by three-thirty? I have to leave at five o'clock."

"Not much will be ready, but I've just cut a marvelous cape. Do you want to come and see it before we take the basting out? I'm just trying it on Ingara."

"I'm on my way."

Chapter III

At about eleven-thirty that morning, on Rue de la Huchette, in an old building with no elevator, where brown paint had scaled away to dirty plaster in spots, a girl with her arms full of packages slowly climbed a staircase. She stopped to catch her breath on the third floor. She was dressed simply, but a connoisseur would immediately have noticed her Mexican tote bag, Jourdan shoes, and a little cotton dress that might have come from Galeries Lafayette but that was circled by a Hermès belt which had cost five times as much. The girl had straight blond hair to her shoulders, a golden tan, and big green eyes. She was the image of Marie-Victoire Forval, only a bit taller, a bit thinner, a bit more modern. And there was nothing surprising about that, for the girl was Clothilde.

Arriving at the fourth floor, she put all her burdens down and searched feverishly for the key to the tiny apartment which was painted white and had a big window filled with geraniums. She rushed at once to the bathroom where, seized with violent nausea, she leaned over the toilet. She recovered quickly, wiped the sweat from her forehead, sat on the edge of the seat for a moment to catch her breath, and then went to get the packages she had left on the landing.

She was pregnant, beyond a doubt. How could she keep it from her mother—and especially from Thérèse—for any length of time? And she dreaded Marie-Victoire's reaction to the idea of having a son-in-law like Pierre. After all the things that had been in the papers, she must imagine that he ate a bourgeois for breakfast every morning. Her mother certainly would have preferred Alan, the rich American tire manufacturer. But, Clothilde told herself logically, to be her mother's son-in-law, the boy would have to want to marry her. First things first. The news must be told the happy papa. This called for a festive lunch, and she put a bottle of champagne she had brought in the refrigerator. That would surely help cushion the shock. . . .

While she was busy preparing the rest of the meal and making toast for the smoked salmon, the three past years of her life passed before her eyes like an old newsreel.

Because she was an only child, it wasn't until May of '68, at the time of the student revolt, that she discovered the intoxication of "sharing"—from a sandwich to editing a manifesto. She had never known such an exciting world, a world of commitment, of enthusiasm aroused for the defense of a common cause, of spontaneous camaraderie, a romantic, disheveled world, with a streak of madness in it. When at sixteen she emerged from the reassuring doze of her Catholic school and the well-organized household where Thérèse still washed her hair while Clothilde was in her bath, she was a little horrified to find herself associating with boys and girls who, at twenty, had already tried and rejected the theories and practice of Marxism, had broken with any and all systems of logic, and manipulated dialectic with the mastery of the old sharks of the

Third Republic. Many of them talked a lot of nonsense, but Clothilde, whose mother had taught her how to tell who had class (she called it "grace"), was taken in tow by a splinter group called the "22nd of March," which seemed to her to have clearer ideas than the rest. Exclusivity and mistrust were totally foreign to them and their only tenet of belief was: "It is forbidden to forbid."

Clothilde still remembered her mother's incredulous and forlorn look when she saw her leave the Quai de Béthune dressed in old jeans and sneakers, carrying an enormous basket loaded with food, sweaters, and even toilet paper. At that moment she had felt a pang of pity for the older generation and had gone back to kiss her mother. In a flash of comprehension (which soon evaporated), she had even recognized that Marie-Victoire was not indifferent and that she was both more open-minded and less rigid than most of the so called elite. But her indifference to politics in any form, her world in which one was either vulgar or distinguished, now seemed to Clothilde as distant and dated as the century of Louis XIV.

She never forgot her first meeting with Pierre. He was quite handsome with his auburn beard. His skin was pale and his eyes hazel. He was tall, well built, and spoke French with the pure accent of the Loire country. For two years he had been working feverishly for a doctorate in law, looking forward to becoming a defender of the oppressed. Money didn't interest him; he lived with two comrades in a miserable furnished room without a bath. He considered love quite a useless complication in the life of an incarnation of the Great Redeemer, which he was convinced he was. When he felt like it, he went to bed with girls who offered themselves—in exactly the way that he ate a roll if he felt hungry.

As for Clothilde, she was the unknown soldier saluting her general, and it was several days before he noticed her. He carried heavy responsibilities. He gave orders and advice at the Sorbonne; tore up streets; formed little groups which he led into striking factories to effect an impossible union between the intellectuals and workers; tried to be everywhere at once, carrying the good word.

During quiet times, or during the long hours when the two camps agreed to a truce, Clothilde watched Pierre with fascination. He seemed the epitome of the new generation which wanted to be avenging angels without being fanatics, and devoted themselves body and soul to their chosen Utopias. She drank his words, and early one morning, when the gray dawn was breaking over a riot-torn neighborhood, they went off hand in hand to look for comrades who had been taken off during the night after being wounded by grenades.

When the Sorbonne fell, one Sunday morning in June, Clothilde left to go home to take a bath. That's how she escaped being arrested, and when she came back, she learned that Pierre had been taken with the rest of the occupants.

Held at Beaujon, allegedly for verification of his papers of identity, Pierre was released in return for a promise to dissolve his movement and leave Paris for a while. Clothilde could still see him at the exit of police headquarters at Beaujon, near the Étoile, a district as distant from them as the moon from earth. He was pale and thin, but most of all, bitter. The exaltation that had sustained him had also kept him from seeing the reality of a system re-establishing itself after having been turned upside down for several weeks. When he realized that everything was going on just as before, his enthusiasm left him and he found himself once more naked and shivering like a castaway on a beach, or, less romantically, like a car out of gas. She would always remember how gray, dirty, and pitiful he had looked and how her heart had melted, and she had wanted to comfort and console him.

71

But it is impossible to console someone who is waking from a Utopian dream to a hopeless reality. He had pushed her aside, exasperated by this pretty girl who did not seem to understand how crushed he felt, how humiliated, how betrayed.

"Yes, betrayed!" he had exploded. "We are nothing but poor dreamers who have waked up in a world of small-time hedonists. The sight of these snails who have come out of their shells after their moment of fear and are parading up and down the Champs Élysées with their horns waving in the sunshine makes me sick! Not to mention all the comrades who are recuperating in comfortable surroundings, taking their sacred vacations with families who are only too happy to find their sons and heirs free and in one piece. No really, it's disgusting. Anyway, I have a ticket for Cuba on a student charter and I'm leaving tomorrow."

Clothilde wrote him twice without receiving any answer, and for the first time, refused to leave for the annual trip to Baussigue. She told her patient mother that she would rather go camping in Brittany with her friend Agnès. It was the last straw that her child should prefer camping and Brittany to the château in Provence, her most precious possession; Marie-Victoire could just manage to understand a revolution, but not camping in the rain at Locronan.

When he came back, Pierre was enraged to find that his draft deferment had been canceled and he was to leave for military service. The army took care to disperse the more disturbing elements, and he wound up in Corsica.

Clothilde did not see Pierre again until the beginning of '72. One day she spied him on the Boulevard Saint-Michel, ran to meet him, but had to remind him that she had been a member of his group during May '68. He was about to walk on, but she delayed him, asked where he lived, and if he would like to come to a party at her house—she would invite the people who had shared those crazy times with them.

For two and a half years she had thought of nothing but him, had gone to the big balls like an outsider, only because her mother wanted her to, and had worn the prettiest dresses without being aware of them. She had gotten herself a solid reputation as a wet blanket with the in-group of the sixteenth Arondissement, as she called them. And if she had not been so pretty, so well dressed, if she hadn't received an absolutely smashing MG for her eighteenth birthday, it wouldn't have been long before the whole Lycée Janson crowd would have dropped her. But there was always some boy who was a climber and thought he might get into bed with her, and at last, it began to amuse her to have a string of suitors and to dazzle the bourgeoisie.

"Say, old girl, you've got quite a pad here," and "What a neat-o place," were the kindest remarks the first guests made, while one or two girls pursed their lips and said nothing. As the stereo poured forth their favorite tunes, they settled down, whiskey in hand, to their fond memories.

Pierre arrived rather late and showed no surprise at the establishment; this was the kind of boy who wouldn't distinguish between the Grand Trianon and a coal cellar. He went his own way and the only thing he really enjoyed was holding an attentive audience under his spell. Seated at his feet, Clothilde drank in his words, and he stroked her neck exactly as he would have scratched under a dog's collar. He felt fine and did not even consider that he was in a capitalist stronghold of the worst kind and that he was drinking, in the form of whiskey, the sweat of miserable underpaid workers. If the fourteen months of military service had done him a great deal of good physically, he was still fuming at the loss of time, the villainy of the noncoms, and the "shit" the officers handed out. On the plus side, he said, a dozen good men had come around to his way of thinking, which meant some strong muscle on the right side. Demobilized now, he no longer knew exactly what he wanted to do: whether to go into politics at once and fight for the P.S.U., that extreme left movement, or continue his studies; or do both at once. He was sleeping a week here and a week there, with whichever of his comrades had room: it didn't bother him in the least to carry his suitcase from one end of Paris to the other. His family sent him barely five hundred francs a month and he never asked for a penny more. For the moment he was living in a young newspaper-woman's room, which she had lent to him for two months while she was doing an important report on the condition of women in Africa.

Clothilde told him that she would come to get him for lunch the next day, and he accepted as a matter of course. She arrived at half-past twelve with a little picnic meal, in memory, she reminded him, of her former contributions to the mess. She had washed her hair and soaked a good half hour in a bubble bath, just as her mother would have done, but she would have been furious if anyone had pointed that out.

After lunch, which he had gobbled without comment, Pierre quite naturally pulled her onto the bed with him as if they had been married for ten years. She allowed it to happen without saying anything; hadn't she come for that? She tried as hard as she could not to seem awkward. She managed not to cry out when he entered her very quickly, but could not stop two large tears from running out of her eyes.

Still panting, he said to her: "You might at least have warned me. We look like some allegorical painting of 'The Virgin and the Revolutionary' but since you want to learn, let's get on with the lesson."

74

This boy was a born pedagogue and evening was falling by the time they parted.

He had gone back to his law studies, and after their respective classes they met every day. She always brought something, three flowers for a cracked vase, an extra turntable she had, she said, when in fact she had just bought it, big hunks of chocolate, cigarettes she "left" on the table. She sewed on buttons for him, took a garment to the cleaner, or said she would take the wash to a laundry on the corner, so he wouldn't have to pay. Even the most violent revolutionaries are susceptible to the comfort of having a woman around who is docile, has soft skin, and poses no feeding problem. Moreover, she knew how to listen religiously, always agreed with him, and had made great strides in bed.

When spring came and with it the irresistible budding of the nesting instinct, Clothilde realized that when the newspaperwoman got back from Africa, Pierre would have to pack up and leave and that, if she didn't begin looking out for a lodging herself, he certainly wouldn't do it. She finally found a room, with a shower and a kitchen in a cupboard, in a very old house in the Rue de la Huchette. The place was to be torn down soon, so the rent was very reasonable. She persuaded her man to move in. She told him that she had furniture and he made no attempt to find out otherwise. She had the tags and tickets of the Bazar de l'Hôtel-de-Ville removed before delivery so he wouldn't notice that everything was new.

Delighted to play lady of the house, Clothilde dreamed of carpets, pillows, hangings, and even a television. Without quite realizing what she was doing, she wove a net of solid bourgeois ties around Pierre to attach him to these reassuring comforts. He accepted it unconsciously, his head in the clouds, not even noticing that his feet were sinking into a soft carpet.

Two perfectly happy months passed this way, during which

75

they studied together quietly and passed their examinations. Their friends often came to talk, delighted to find nourishing spaghetti in addition to spiritual provender. Clothilde, playing both Mary and Martha, bloomed. She got home very late at night and passed more and more weekends "in the country where there was no telephone." In June, she began to smear her skin with beauty products designed to tan without exposure to the sun so that her outdoor cover story would sound more probable.

Marie-Victoire had broken off from her in-laws after Jérôme's death, but had not been able to prevent their seeing their granddaughter from time to time. Actually, Clothilde got on quite well with her grandfather. A professor of surgery, he dreamed of her marrying one of his students and was delighted that she was doing so well in her studies. She liked the Forval ladies less, sensing that they were jealous, and she had special difficulty in getting along with an elderly aunt. She made her mother laugh by remarking that her Aunt Forval had hands which hung from her arms like dust rags. In fact, this lady, instead of letting her arms drop like everybody else in the world, thought it more graceful to carry them at right angles, with hands softly dangling.

The Forval aunt, who had never forgiven Marie-Victoire for her beauty and success, waited patiently for Clothilde to be old enough to feel her father's tragedy in depth. Then one day she revealed his suicide to her. She told Clothilde that he had not been able to bear his wife's arrogant success. Her version was that Jérôme had been an affectionate lad, a bit shy, adoring his wife, suffering silently while she went to parties with homosexuals. She insinuated that if Marie-Victoire had been a good wife, she would have noticed his depression and had him treated.

"Everyone has nervous depressions these days. With a little

affection they pass quickly, but your mother was much too busy with her couture and Baron de R.'s next ball to pay attention to her husband."

If Clothilde didn't entirely believe the calumnies her aunt poured out, and refused, much to the other's disgust, to discuss her mother's conduct further, all the same she was horrified to learn that her father had killed himself. She could only remember him vaguely. She did remember that he had been taciturn and had only rarely played with her, but on the other hand he had always talked very seriously to her, as if she were a grownup. Now she remembered how she had loved that feeling of importance he had given her. She would have to have had a heart as dry as the Sahara not to be moved by such a desperate act, and Clothilde wept over the loneliness of a father who had not been able to find enough affection in his home to make him want to live.

Just as her mother had never spoken to anyone of her conjugal disappointments, Clothilde was incapable of telling even Pierre of her discovery, much less Marie-Victoire. It seemed to her that a great wall had grown up between the two of them and she could barely stand to kiss her mother. The world Marie-Victoire inhabited seemed to her more than ever impossibly frivolous. Her mother's bright biting wit seemed to her a sign of total egocentricity and overnight she lost her admiration of her and even began to criticize her.

These discoveries intensified her submission to her lover, and shortly afterward, she became pregnant. When she realized it, she was almost happy. She told herself that Pierre would marry her in time, that Marie-Victoire, after the first disappointment was over, would accept him and that a child would make everything right.

When Pierre came in this day, he seemed surprised at the unusual spread she had laid out, so she told him that they had an occasion for celebration and that she would tell him what it was over dessert. Feeling euphoric with the champagne, Pierre outlined a marvelous world in which man was to make up for God's injustices. He had come to the point where all the hotels on the Côte d'Azur were turned over to senior citizens, those on the Atlantic coast to children, and a compensation allowance would be paid for ugliness and stupidity —flagrant injustices on the part of nature—when she interrupted gently.

"Charity well organized begins at home. Please, let's talk about us."

Slightly annoyed at being interrupted, he said, "What's there to say? Everything is all right, isn't it?"

"It's so all right that we're going to have a baby."

"A baby?"

It seemed the word he had just pronounced was Chinese and he couldn't understand it.

"A child, if you like that better, a child of our own. Isn't that wonderful? We'll have to get married as soon as possible."

"Get married!" he choked. "Why?"

"So that your child will have a legal father."

"As if he couldn't get along without a legal father! I thought you'd gotten over being so middle-class! Anyway, there's no use your insisting, I'll never get married."

"Then I don't want this child. Don't forget that I'm still a minor, and my mother, not to mention Grandfather Baussigue, won't be very happy about having a bastard in the family."

"It won't be the first time there's been a bastard in a noble family. Just remember the taking of the Bastille."

"To hell with the Bastille! I love you, I'm carrying your child, I want you to be its father forever, and for everyone to know. There's nothing old-fashioned or middle-class about

78

that, I assure you. Normal men are usually quite happy when this happens to them."

"Then I must not be normal because I don't accept this biological necessity. In modern society this kind of idea of paternity is grotesque. Women should be able to raise their children by themselves. They should be adopted by the community and belong to everyone."

"My baby belong to everyone? You're crazy, that's horrible! If that's how it is and you're already living in the year 2000, I'd rather get rid of it while there's still time."

"That's something I won't agree to at all. A woman should know how to shoulder her responsibilities, not run like a rabbit at the slightest complication. If you get rid of this child I won't see you again, and besides, no one has the right to kill a living being."

"But you're out of your mind! Now you're talking like a priest!" And she began to sob.

The young man's generous views of the future of humanity did not extend to consoling women in tears. He went out, slamming the door on his final words: "Think about it."

She remained prostrate for most of the afternoon. By turns she imagined him changing his mind and saying "yes" in front of the mayor (in her wildest imaginings she did not go so far as to expect a priest) or, at worst, putting her in the hands of some friend who was a medical student. However, she knew very well where the truth lay and that he would never give in.

In the evening he came back at the usual time and said: "I hope you changed your mind."

"I was going to say the same thing to you."

"Absolutely not. Either you keep this child, work to bring it up, and we stay together, or we each go our own way, and the two aren't likely to meet."

79

"You don't love me even a little bit?"

He thought about it, as if for the first time. "Yes, I love you, but not to the point of sacrificing my convictions to you. While life is such a mess, I'll go it alone. Good-by, Clothilde. You are good and beautiful, but you belong to the past."

Now that he had assumed this admirable pose, she told herself, he'd never be able to back down. He must be overwhelmed by the enormity of his sacrifice. So with great dignity, in silence, she packed the eternal little suitcase for the "Prophet of Tomorrow." Unconsciously or not, she forgot to give him the ticket from the laundry where half his clothing would not be ready for two days.

When he had left, she looked around at all the poor little treasures she had collected to please him. Mechanically she watered the lupins, which were beginning to droop, plumped up a cushion, and, with tears in her eyes, and great fear in her heart, went to find her friend Agnès.

She knew that Agnès had had an abortion during the previous year and that she had the address of a relatively competent practitioner. She found her friend at the usual table in her favorite café and in the process of planning to hitchhike to Saint-Tropez with her boy friend. Clothilde asked her if she could talk to her in private and the boy teased:

"OK, girl-talk time, I'll go buy cigarettes."

"Can you give me the address of the woman who did your abortion last year?"

"Of course. She's a seamstress who used to be a hospital aide. Have you got four hundred francs to give her? That's her price, and I can tell you it's not much fun. When I think that there are lucky girls who can go to England, or Sweden, or now New York and have it done with anesthesia . . . When the pill is bad for one, what else? You have to say that Agnès

80

sent you; all she'll ask is your first name so she'll recognize any patients you send her later. You'll see, it's kind of funny: she takes her calendar and she checks off the name of the saint. You can see by the check marks that except for Saint Cunegonda, almost all the holy ladies have already been there. Anyway, all you'd really have to say would be that you came from Suzanne to be sure that she had already helped a half a dozen by that name, but you don't know that until afterward."

As she spoke, she scribbled the address on a piece of paper. "Go as soon as possible, especially if you're getting sick mornings—and really, you don't look very well. If you want me to, I'll stop in to see you afterward. It's better not to be alone. What does the great man think about it?"

"He doesn't agree."

"What a bastard! He's really out of it, that cat."

"Thanks, darling, you've been very nice."

"*Ciao,* take it easy!"

With the paper in her pocket and her fate decided, Clothilde suddenly wondered if it wouldn't be comforting to be with her mother. With a hope growing in her heart, she went into a café to telephone her.

"Hello, Thérèse, is my mother in?"

"Oh, Mademoiselle, Madame just went out. I think she's left for Orly to pick up her American gentleman. She washed her hair and primped and she put on her black mousseline dress and her evening shoes with the rhinestone heels. She mentioned dinner at Maxim's and she certainly won't be home early."

In spite of her disappointment, Clothilde smiled to think of Marie-Victoire's fury if she could have heard her faithful maid describing her romantic preparations with southern flipness.

"Thanks, Thérèse, I'll try to meet her later."

"If Mademoiselle wants to come home for dinner, I can

81

easily stay. I have some chicken with mushrooms left over, and I could make crêpes."

"Thanks very much, I'm going to the country until Wednesday or Thursday. Leave mother a note so that she won't worry. Good night, Thérèse." And she hung up before Thérèse had time to ask for more details.

The less she sees me, she told herself, the better it will be; she is good as gold, but she pries into everything. In Baussigue, wearing her Parisian glamour like a halo, she probably holds regular press conferences in the kitchen, and the lowest gardener must know about everything I say or do. There's nothing to do but go back to Rue de la Huchette and try to call my mother tomorrow early.

Marie-Victoire arrived at Orly with three quarters of an hour to spare. She sat in her car for a few minutes. Then, because a swarthy man who looked like the late Nasser was staring at her, she got out and wrapped a black jersey cape around her mousseline dress. She threw such a disdainful look at the unhappy Middle Easterner that he choked and began to cough.

Everyone was turning to look as she passed, so to hide her face, Marie-Victoire bought a magazine at the newsstand, sat down, and buried herself in it.

If I were dressed in satin hoopskirts like Scarlett O'Hara or in hot pants like that girl over there, no one would look at me. Elegance has become so rare today that a well-cut black jersey cape makes heads turn. It isn't chic to be chic any more! All the magazines may write now that clothes are "civilized" or "ritzy" again, but they should never had given their seal of approval to hippie style. That was what gave a fatal blow to the old notion of elegance. Maybe something newer than pleated shirt dresses will come out of the chaos and it would

82

be most exciting if I were to find the formula! Though, if I'm honest, I'm as bored with tough chic as I am with camp. Well, old girl, you'd better think of arguments for winning Oliver over to back you instead of thinking how your profession is finished. If you did less daydreaming, you'd probably have come up with the right thing to do before now. And when you get right down to it, you really don't know what you want. Actually, the only solution is the one Cardin found: using his designs for his own ready-to-wear line. You must admit that was inspired! What I need is a designer like that. Poor Adrien would do better to retire like Balenciaga. Here's the London flight at last, Gate 36. Good.

A crowd of tanned people in shorts and beach clothes with bare sandaled feet appeared at the customs office.

That had to be a chartered flight from Barcelona. How could anyone travel in such get-ups? They must still have their bathing suits on underneath, and where are they going to hang those enormous Mexican hats in their little efficiency flats? And that horrible smell of sun oil mixed with sand and sweat!

With the look of Phaedra visiting the Zulus, she drew back to let this jolly crew pass. A dignified gentleman in a bowler, rolled umbrella over his arm, and proudly holding a British passport signified the arrival of the London plane. Oliver Mayer appeared at last from behind a red-haired giant. Oliver was tall, too, but the giant could have hidden a whole Rugby team behind him.

The anxiety one feels when an expected traveler does not immediately appear left Marie-Victoire. A warm wave made her cheeks pink. Oliver smiled at her from a distance as he settled his passport in his pocket, after convincing the customs man that he was carrying only business papers in his briefcase.

"That red-haired hippopotamus completely hid you. I was afraid you'd missed your plane." She said hippopotamus in

English, but pronounced it as if it were French, with emphasis on each syllable.

"Hi, my dear, you're more amusing than ever. How nice to see you." And to warm the banality of his greeting, he leaned over to kiss her lips lightly. "I only have one bag, we'll leave it in your car."

He preceded her on the escalator and turned to take her hand. He was a step below her so that their faces were at the same level.

"I see black must be back in style since you're wearing it. It's wonderfully becoming to you."

"Some men hate it."

"I don't hate any color unless it's used badly. My last cosmetics packages were green and yellow. They looked cheerful and sales went up 2 per cent."

"That wouldn't do in France. Those are St. Catherine's colors."

"St. Catherine?"

"Yes, the patron saint of couture. On the twenty-fifth of November, all the twenty-five-year-old girls who are still unmarried wear a St. Catherine's Day hat trimmed in green and yellow. It's the big holiday for couture. We drink champagne and dance. Once there were great shows put on for the staff, but now that's too expensive. I still get lots of flowers, but it's not as gay as it used to be."

In a flash she realized how difficult it is to make oneself understood by a foreigner. All through his childhood on Allhallows Eve he must have dressed up as a ghost like a good little American imp, and blackmailed the neighbors with "trick or treat," while she was getting ready to go to the cemetery to pray for her ancestors' souls the next day. And to have to explain who St. Catherine is!

Oliver, as though he had been criticized, shrugged and said:

84

"If St. Catherine is as popular as that in France I don't see why her colors wouldn't be fashionable. The French are really very strange people."

"I couldn't agree more!"

And to comfort him, in case she had offended him a little, she took his arm. A superb Vuitton bag appeared on the moving platform at the baggage gate. I'll bet that's his, Marie-Victoire thought, he can't resist the trademarks of opulence. There seems to be a regular Vuitton club among American travelers; they almost greet each other when they meet! That kind of weakness for expensive things is very useful to luxury businesses. Too bad it's considered more elegant to look poor here!

When they got to the Austin, he suggested that he drive.

"I won't make you put up with that. You have to shift gears all the time and Americans have forgotten how—and then I know the way better. I hope you won't be frightened to death, I'm not a bad driver."

In the Rue Royale, in front of Maxim's, he hesitated to leave his briefcase in the car.

"Give it to Paulette, you never know."

Paulette was the cloakroom attendant at Maxim's and any with-it Parisian needed her seal of recognition. She had a big, overfed dachshund who watched the world's celebrities pass before his blasé gaze, and although Paulette never gave anyone a number, she never made a mistake in returning an overcoat.

Roger, the maître d' who had replaced the famous Albert ten years ago, immediately recognized Oliver and Marie-Victoire and hurried to welcome them.

"Sorry about the black tie, but I just got off the plane."

"Oh, Monsieur Mayer, you don't have to worry about that."

He went ahead and pointed out a table at the left-hand

banquette in the big room. Marie-Victoire was delighted; it was the place reserved for crowned heads. On certain evenings it was necessary to give it up to them if they were too numerous, but today there was no one in the room who was a real celebrity, and most were foreigners. Marie-Victoire buried her nose in the menu after she had looked around without recognizing a soul.

"Who are those people with all the diamonds who are giving you such big smiles?" she asked Oliver.

"The ones who bought the fake pictures in Dallas."

"They look as if they hadn't much minded being ridiculous. A Japanese would have committed hara-kiri for less."

"Don't forget that it may have been very good business for them, my dear. After they had given all their paintings to a museum, they got a tax deduction a lot bigger than the amount they paid for the pictures. Anyway ridicule isn't fatal and by now after five years everyone has forgotten the story. Mrs. Jones would be a good customer for you; would you like to meet her?"

"There's plenty of time; we couldn't get rid of them afterward, and I'd rather be alone with you."

He nodded a little, smiling. Either she was more devious than he thought she might be or else she was not as good a businesswoman as he had supposed, he said to himself. An American "lady executive" would have jumped at the chance.

"You still like Dom Perignon?" he asked.

"That's one of the few things one goes on liking all one's life."

She watched him order the dinner and the wine with the ease and authority the long habit of wealth combined with a deep feeling of inner security brings. She remembered poor Jérôme's fumblings—he always wound up ordering the same

86

dishes she did and wishing he'd had the ones he saw being served on nearby tables.

When the headwaiter had approved the order, they both leaned back against the red banquette.

"Are you satisfied with your collection?" Oliver inquired.

"No, not terribly. Adrien seems to have lost his confidence in his kind of couture, but realizes that he doesn't know how to adapt to anything else. The trend back to elegance in the last two years really wasn't effective. It's just too hard to make either the word or the idea fashionable again. It's like asking today's women to wear the five or six undergarments and corsets that their grandmothers would have felt like women of easy virtue to be without. Anyway, women today dream of being women of easy virtue, or at least looking like them. But elegance and sexuality don't really mix. Elegance is always a bit puritanical. When sex is reduced to mechanics with numbers pinned up on a board, it may be useful to know about, but I can't imagine trying Position No. 3 just because I'd read that it gave so much pleasure. Though they seem to have very little relation to couture, attitudes toward love and fashion are utterly inseparable: fashions are always the reflections of a state of mind and the customs of the times."

"How well said, darling. You have a future giving lectures in town halls! Let's be serious. So this is a good time to sell to Big Mills of Indiana. Their offer is fair."

"How do you know?"

"I have business dealings with Monsieur Lefebvre, their representative in Paris."

"If I sold the business to them, I'd feel as if I were cutting off my right arm. Besides, I think selling a prestige name to a firm which would use it to manufacture God knows what is dishonorable. I admit that haute couture is no longer profitable, but the luxury boutiques, like Lanvin, for example, are

87

doing very well. Of course they need a good deal of capital at the beginning."

"My dear, do be logical. Why would I give your business a new lease on life when I want you just for myself, as Mrs. Oliver Mayer? I know very well that so long as *Marie-Victoire Forval, Place Vendôme,* is in existence, I don't stand a chance."

"But you've never said that before!"

"Since my divorce, I've never really missed a woman when I was away from her. I've missed you—terribly!"

"Oliver, I think of you a good deal and I've missed you too."

"Well, that makes it simple. . . ." and he took her hand.

"But not as simple as you think! At twenty when one has scarcely any past, it's easy to say 'yes' to a man with a completely foreign background and to follow him to the ends of the earth, leaving behind all one's habits, friends, family. But at double that age, however little one has accomplished, if a few dozen people depend on you, leaving isn't high adventure but a cowardly flight."

"Unless you're very much in love."

"Come, come, we must look at things squarely. For example, would you retire to my father's château in Provence?"

"The life that I'm offering you in Dallas is not like being buried in the country, and besides, I travel almost six months a year."

"Darling, I know you won't believe me, but if I married you it would be in spite of the easy life you're offering me and not because of it. What I love about you is not your millions, but the authority and control you have over me. It's really very simple, every time I think of you I feel myself melting."

She blushed as she said this, and thought, luckily he hasn't a Frenchman's evil mind.

"It's not very clever to tell you that," she went on. "No other man has ever had this effect on me. . . . This champagne must really have made me forget all my feminine wiles and even my common sense."

"Since we're baring our hearts, I'll tell you that your frankness is what I like most about you. In the beginning of our relationship, I think you saw me only as an eventual source of funds to save your firm. But I must tell you that you aren't cut out to be a golddigger, dear; you don't know how to lie and you lay it on too thick or too thin."

Marie-Victoire raised her eyebrows but said nothing. Funny that that I don't like having him tell me I'm no good at playing the whore! she thought.

"When we were on the boat to the Balearics and I watched you forgetting your rags a little more every day and thinking more about love, I was amazed to find a real woman emerging from the asexual monster of chic that you tried to be."

"You're the only one who ever made me drop my façade. When my husband returned from prison camp, I was ready to devote myself to him as I had when we were engaged, but he had lost the key and the password. That was when I put on my armor, when I began to want success. I've always loved clothes, of course, but if I had been a satisfied woman, I would certainly have been content with Vogue patterns and an occasional Balenciaga original on sale."

"You see how you prove my point. You don't need your façade with me; it doesn't protect you any more anyhow. Throw it away and come with me!"

"What a lovely temptation! It would be as sweet as floating on calm water. Give me a little time to pull myself together.

89

If I say 'yes' this evening, much as I'd like to, I'll surely regret it tomorrow. Come on, let's dance."

At midnight, when they were back in front of the big door at Quai de Béthune, he asked if he could come up, and, gravely, she said yes.

They went directly to her room, where he had never been. Popoff, who was waiting like a good dog, clearly disapproved. He sniffed the cuffs of Oliver's trousers and then went to his bed to lie down sulkily. Although this was the first time it happened in his life, he immediately understood that he could not hope for any attention from his mistress and that it was the fault of this stranger.

The mousseline dress fell in a heap on the carpet. Marie-Victoire stood naked as Oliver admired her. Then he kissed her breasts and quickly shed his own clothing. From old habit, he took the telephone off the hook. They fell on the bed together and she gave herself to him with an absence of shyness, an ardor that she would not have believed possible.

At about six in the morning he left before she could speak. At ten o'clock, thirty-six Baccara roses were delivered with a little note. What a shame he couldn't think of anything more original, she thought. He must have ordered them by phone. Well, be glad they weren't gladiolas! She hated those stiff flowers which looked as if they belonged in a concierge's office, or worse, on the rear desk of some nouveau riche yacht.

Let's see what he writes: "My darling, you made me forget everything and I didn't tell you that I'm leaving for a weekend in Deauville—an important business meeting. I'll be back Monday. I adore you. Oliver. P.S.: Don't think too much."

Well, he's gone already and I'll be alone Sunday. . . . Like all single women, she had a horror of having nothing to do that day.

During Clothilde's childhood, she had jealously kept the day for the two of them. This was when they tried out new recipes, when they opened a bottle of champagne, when they didn't get dressed all day, and when they listened to the new records they'd bought just for the occasion. Or else they would go on an expedition to the Jardin des Plantes, or to the Louvre to "play tourist" and have lunch in a good bistro. But in the past year or two, Marie-Victoire had felt her little parties were beginning to seem forced to Clothilde and she no longer dared suggest them. Since she didn't like losing face, she continued to pretend that Sunday was a private holiday when she chose to see no one, but she often gave in to the temptation of a bridge game or a film which would make the solitary day pass more quickly. She did not realize that her daughter was behaving just as she did in wanting to keep one day of the week when she could do just what her fancy dictated at the last moment.

Fighting back anger, Marie-Victoire got up without noticing that the telephone was still off the hook and tried, without succeeding, to forget her disappointment in a bath. Does he want to teach me a lesson and show me he won't play the submissive lover while I wait my pleasure? He is really much stronger than I.

Finding no answers in the warm water, she dried herself and went to look absently through her wardrobe. What to wear? She had to go to work, and also to attend the wedding of Philippe's seamstress, and then it was raining. Dress reflects the state of mind, and today instead of being the elegant Madame Forval, she would have liked to lie on a chaise longue in a pink negligee, with her hair down, waiting for her master's return. She let her mind play with this picture for a moment; then other more distinct ones came back to her. . . . What a fool I've been to spend all this time without a lover, it's the only real thing!

She chose a navy blue coat dress. With a jewel it would look quite appropriate at the wedding.

How funny it is the way a dress changes a woman, she thought, that must be why we love clothes so much. Last evening I felt like a *Playboy* cover and my dress said "sex" at every step. This morning all I need is spectacles and an order book in my hand to be the perfect successful businesswoman. At the word *success,* which she had only thought, she leaned over and touched the back of a chair; it was the only superstition she had inherited from her mother, a woman from Brittany who divided her devotions between the Virgin Mary and Morgan la Fée. Seeing her touch wood so often, someone once asked her why and she had answered: "I don't want to admit everything is going well for fear that God will remember me and strike me down."

But that morning, wood must have lost its magic power; God or Fate had some real trials in store for her.

Chapter IV

After her futile call to Quai de Béthune, Clothilde felt that the whole world had deserted her. She reproached herself for not having accepted Thérèse's offer; at least chicken crêpes would have been better than the sandwich she was swallowing. But after saying she was leaving for the weekend, she couldn't go back and sleep in her pretty room. She had seen all the good films in the neighborhood, so she finally decided to go to a little theatre where Harold Lloyd's old movies were playing, but she found even them depressing. She left. There was nothing to do but go back to Rue de la Huchette alone. It seemed that all the lovers in the Quartier Latin had decided to meet that evening and punctuate her path with embraces. It was plain that everyone in the world was half a couple except herself. She suddenly remembered the childhood game of musical chairs, when there was always one chair less than there were people to sit in them. She felt useless and rejected, like an indivisible number after the decimal point in division that finally is dropped.

And if Pierre were back at Rue de la Huchette? She hurried. No, the window was a black void. And if he were asleep? Her heart in her throat from climbing the four flights so quickly, she lit the only lamp in the room to reveal—emptiness. Then she threw herself on the bed and sobbed like a baby until sleep overcame despair.

Saturday morning she woke up at nine quite calm, and decided to call her mother again. From the little café where she always telephoned, she tried for a half hour to reach Quai de Béthune. Even the operator, whom she finally dialed, confirmed that the number was busy. Feeling that there was nothing else to do, Clothilde paid for her three espressos and hailed the first passing taxi.

". . . Rue des Pyrénées."

"All right, little lady, but I hope you're not in a hurry, because it's a long drive."

"I have no idea where the place is."

"Well, I was born in Rue des Pyrénées so I know what I'm talking about; it's the longest street in Paris."

"So much the better."

Lord, let him not talk during the whole trip. She pretended to be interested in the cross streets.

"Here we are, little lady," the driver said with a smile.

"Thank you. That wasn't so far."

The hall, painted brown, was dark and cool after the sunshine in the street, but a smell of cabbage and onions lingered there, obviously coming from the concierge's office. To save herself trouble, that good woman had pinned up all the names of her tenants on the flowered curtain covering the glass panes of her door. Clothilde took a few minutes to find the right name. She heard her heart beat like those in TV doctor shows. She climbed the four flights slowly. On the first landing, a baby howled and she winced. On the second, a radio announcer

94

fed incessant commercials sugar-coated with easy jokes to locked-in housewives. On the third, someone was plucking a guitar doggedly, playing the same phrase over and over, trying to speed the tempo. On the fourth, all one heard was the machine-gun rattle of an old sewing machine, and Clothilde, before ringing, waited a full five minutes for heaven to send some sign that would tell her to turn and run away.

But the Almighty, no doubt, was busy elsewhere with wars, crimes, and injustices committed in His name. So she finally made up her mind. A big, mannish woman with short, bristling gray hair and a tape measure around her neck opened the door, looked her up and down, and said:

"Mademoiselle?"

"Agnès sent me."

"All right. Come this way."

She closed the door of the landing behind her carefully and showed Clothilde into a room whose door she also closed. It was light enough to perceive a couch covered in wine-colored velours, in front of which stretched a hideous rug displaying a dying doe whose throat was seized by a hound straight from hell. It was enough to finish one with the canine species forever. Above the couch were some flimsy bookshelves. A big mirrored wardrobe occupied the end of the room and the sewing machine was in front of the window. A size 42 mannequin stood on a wood pedestal. It was half covered in loud print fabric, while the other half had been strategically stuffed with rags to imitate the customer's curves.

Without asking Clothilde to sit down, the seamstress said:

"So, we have the same trouble as little Agnès. I remember her very well. She's the only one I've had by that name. I hope she told you what the price was."

Seeing Clothilde open her pretty bag and noting her well-cut Forval suit which she recognized from having copied it from a photograph in *Elle,* she added quickly: "It's six hundred francs this year, and you pay in advance."

"Here is six hundred francs."

Smiling smugly, the seamstress counted the bills and put them in her pocket, saying: "Come this way, I'm going to wash up and get you settled."

"This way" led into the Henri II dining room typical of any petit-bourgeois French home at the turn of the century. The seamstress must have inherited the furnishings. It was plain that she ate there only on feast days, when the liquor cabinet on the buffet would ceremoniously be opened and the tiny silver goblets filled with Cherry Rocher or Benedictine.

Clothilde, who was expecting a white-tiled room like her dentist's, stood frozen. She started when the woman asked her matter-of-factly to help put in the extensions of the table. Then she told Clothilde to take off her skirt and underpants and stretch out on the table, putting her legs up on two chairs.

Tears rose to Clothilde's eyes as she faced the cracked ceiling above her. The woman opened the sideboard and took a silver metal speculum which had been standing in liquid in a glass jar along with a long steel tube. She covered the speculum with vaseline and with no adjustment plunged it into Clothilde's vagina, making her shiver and stiffen at the contact of the cold metal. The woman moved a lamp near.

"Can't see anything there."

Quickly, she opened the sides of the instrument. Clothilde, tears pouring from her eyes, murmured: "That hurts a lot."

"Hold on, little one, it isn't over."

Having seen enough, she introduced the probe and tried to open the neck of the womb. Clothilde cringed and could not help groaning.

"Be quiet, the neighbors mustn't hear anything. Relax. Otherwise, I'll never get anywhere."

96

In spite of this advice, Clothilde shrieked when the probe pierced her. The pseudo-midwife withdrew the instrument hastily. Had she pierced the uterus? Anyway, she could do no more. Now all that was left was to get rid of this patient, who had suddenly become an encumbrance.

"Come now, it's all over. The effect isn't as pleasant as the cause. If you girls would use your head first, you'd make fewer mistakes. Come, sit up, you can get dressed." And she helped her down from the table.

"What will happen to me now?"

"Go home, but walk as much as you can to help get rid of the foetus. Don't panic, examine what you pass, and if your temperature goes much over normal, take antibiotics. What is your first name?"

"Clothilde."

"Well, you and your girl friend certainly don't have ordinary names. When is your saintday?"

She carefully marked the day on the calendar.

"There now, don't worry. . . ."

She opened the outer door, and seeing the tenant from the fifth floor coming down, said loudly: "I promise you'll have your dress next week so you can wear it while the weather is still nice. Good-by, mademoiselle."

Clothilde held fast to the railing so as not to fall. The staircase seemed to her a bottomless black pit. In the street the sun blinded her and she put on her big dark glasses. She went to the corner, praying, Let there be a taxi in this miserable place! Luckily she did not have to wait long; one came and she was driven to the Rue de la Huchette.

As if in a dream, she set a bottle of water, a glass, and a big package of cotton beside the bed, swallowed two aspirins, and lay down, her abdomen hurting terribly and her ears buzzing. As soon as she closed her eyes she saw that terrible furniture again, that humiliating position, that hideous and pitiless slattern, and she began to hallucinate. She saw her father, towering above her, as children see adults, inviting her to join him in death. She cried out: "No, no . . ." and woke bathed in sweat, threw off the sheet, shivered, and slept again. Then she saw her mother, tiny on the horizon, surrounded by people with whom she was laughing. She cried out, "Mother, help!" No one heard her, and the group disappeared behind a mountain. Then Pierre appeared, thundering curses from a pulpit. He pointed her out to all the congregation with an accusing finger: "She is the sinner who must be stoned, the symbol of the decadent bourgeoisie which must be struck down; she must be expelled from the Church at once!" and a crowd of fanatics pushed her outside, spitting in her face.

Madame Hilda's husband, Joseph Petit, a foreman at Renault, didn't work on Saturday. So he turned back to the wall, groaning, when his wife got up at her usual hour for going to work. Last night she had not come back until about ten. Overtime was good on payday, but tough while you were doing it. He was a good fellow, somewhat silent, but very dependable, respected by both his bosses and the men who worked under him. He took discipline very seriously, and their fifteen-year-old daughter was first in her class and never gave them the least trouble. Madame Hilda was very much afraid of her husband's wrath. She had gotten into the habit of never telling him the truth, and she lied masterfully. So although she had described the superb coat she said she was cutting until nine-thirty without any help from Monsieur Philippe yesterday evening, the truth was quite otherwise.

Twice a year, Madame Hilda passed patterns of jackets or coats on to a German buyer who purposely arrived several days before the collection was shown. Twice a year, she climbed on a stool and took down four or five patterns, carefully drawn by herself, put them in her big bag and covered them with a scarf. She then went to the Concorde Métro station instead of the Opéra, her usual route. She got off at George V and with no hesitation asked for Monsieur Hans Pumpernicke at the Hôtel de la Trémoïlle. Herr Pumpernicke was an old acquaintance, and more than that, her first love. Frau Pumpernicke, his mother, was one of the better couturières of Stuttgart, and it was in her establishment that Hilda had started out in 1938 at the age of fourteen.

Afterward, she loved her worthy husband, Joseph, very much but never felt for him the glowing admiration that she had dedicated once and for all to the only son of that Stuttgart house, a tank lieutenant who had been decorated three times on the Eastern Front. He could have passed for the poster of the perfect blond Aryan so dear to Goebbels' and Hitler's propaganda. Each year she sent him a Christmas card with news of herself, all of which explained why one day she almost fainted of happiness when she saw the hero of her adolescence in the Place Vendôme at the workers' entrance. When he had proposed buying patterns from her twice a year, she had not for an instant considered that she was stealing from Maison Forval. All she was doing was loyally serving her first employers, besides which, this good deed would happily increase her bank account. Joseph told whoever would listen how his wife performed miracles with their two salaries, how thanks to her marvelous organization they had been able to buy a nice used car and take four weeks of vacation at Palavas-les-Flots every year.

So, twice a year, she went to Rue de la Trémoïlle, where the doorman finally got to know her, and in two or three hours, with Pumpernicke's help, she transferred all the patterns to tracing paper. When the work was done, she went home, and said she had been busy working overtime. As for Herr Pumpernicke, twice a year he pretended to be a faithful Forval customer, and without demur paid the 4,000 francs' security to see the collection. For that sum he had a right to attend the showing and return at leisure to choose two patterns. It also permitted him to examine in detail the models whose patterns he already possessed. Besides, he traded his patterns with a buyer from Brussels who bought only evening gowns. So by spending 4,000 francs' security plus the 2,000 francs he gave Hilda, he acquired the five of Hilda's and the legal two exchanged with the seven from the Brussels buyer. All that was left for him to do was go to another house which had received the best reports to acquire two more patterns. With these and what he could copy from memory he would have a very good collection. Finally, his stay at the hotel, gourmet meals, tours of the night clubs, and one or two little ladies cost as much as all his other purchases.

The arrangement was very satisfactory to the two compatriots and by now had become practically routine. So Hilda was quite calm as she got ready to leave ten minutes earlier than usual that Saturday morning, expecting to return the patterns to their place without incident. Once a seamstress had arrived before she had time to put them back in her box and she had simply spread them out on her table as if she had wanted to check them. No one had expressed the least surprise. Now she found a seat on the Métro and took out her knitting to occupy the hour and a half that she spent there each day.

Émile Benoît was forty-seven years old. He was small, sickly, hairy, stooped, weasel-faced, and sweated abundantly. He always seemed to be floating in a sort of malodorous and viscous dampness, which, from the time of his youth, had placed a distance between him and even the most compassionate souls and the least desirable girls. Every morning he hated to wake up, to have to open his shutters on his narrow, dingy court and to prepare his solitary *café au lait*.

His sole consolation was to remove the cloth covering his canary's cage, to see it shake its pretty feathers and waken joyously. The little bird would turn its head to the right and left so as to look at him out of each of its eyes—human beings always managed to stare over his head. This morning, as usual, he got up staggering, his eyes swollen, his hair hanging in long gray locks over his ears, his pajamas falling over his bare feet, which tracked damp footprints on the kitchen tiles. With his arms stretched out in front of him, he moved like a blind man to open the shutters with a great bang (intended to waken the neighbors, whom he hated), to light the gas under the pots of milk and coffee prepared the night before, and to wake his canary. It all went in unchanging order.

When he touched the flowered curtain over the cage, a big fly buzzed out the open window, and instead of finding the bird in its usual corner, he immediately saw that it was lying on its back, its claws drawn up, its little black eyes covered forever with sad gray film. Trembling, he opened the door and took the still-warm little body into his hand. The big fly had already left a dropping on the bird's eye and it made his gorge rise. While the milk was joyously evading the pan, he was looking at the poor little creature and this last demonstration of divine injustice was finally too much for him. After hastily getting into his trousers and knotting one of his two ties around his neck, he put on his jacket, stuffed the bird into a pocket, and ran like a madman to his usual Métro station where, without a shadow of hesitation, he threw himself in front of the first train that appeared. Witnesses distinctly heard him say: "This time they will have to look at me!"

Hilda had taken the following train, which suddenly stopped

101

in the middle of the tunnel. As the minutes passed, the fear of being caught opened a pit in her stomach. If her husband found out what she had been doing all these years, he would never forgive her, for he took honesty very seriously and had no sympathy with Germans, having had to work when he was eighteen during the war under conditions more like slavery than union regulations.

After half an hour she tried to get out of the Métro and take a taxi, but the train had stopped between stations, the doors were locked, and she couldn't escape. She was beside herself when she arrived at the Opéra, for it was nine-thirty and the workers had already arrived. She still had hope that no one would need the patterns before lunch and she already pictured herself putting them back in place without anyone seeing, but that would require that Monsieur Philippe have a great many fittings.

When she opened the door, she almost fainted, for he was there, perched on a stool, looking into the very box where only three of the eight patterns that had been there the day before remained. Everyone was looking at her. Seeing her so aghast, Monsieur Philippe suddenly understood the situation, took her by the arm, and marched her out of the workroom. Outside, he opened her bag and seized the five patterns. "I demand an explanation!" he said angrily.

Long afterward she wondered why she had not said that she had taken them home to correct them, but she was too frightened and stammered: "It was my old boss from Stuttgart; he was always so good to me!"

"Come with me to the manager, I don't want you to go back to the workroom. I don't want a scene there."

It was the first time that so serious a thing had happened in the firm and Chavanaux did not quite know whether to call the police or whether it would have been better to hush the matter up. Let's wait until Madame arrives, he decided. She wouldn't be long. It would be best to keep this as quiet as possible. Otherwise all the buyers will rush to buy Pumperknicke's patterns at bargain rates. While waiting, he would get a signed statement from this woman. Otherwise, if she denied it later, there wouldn't be any proof.

"Thank you, Monsieur Philippe. Madame Hilda can wait here for Madame. Perhaps you'll bring all her things so that she won't have to go back to the workroom again."

Back in his own place, Philippe announced to the workers: "Something very serious has happened to Madame Hilda, she won't be back; no use asking me about it. Do you know where she keeps her things?"

An unaccustomed silence fell on the workroom—which did not prevent the most improbable stories from making the rounds of the firm by mid-afternoon.

Armed with her signed statement, Chavanaux left Hilda under his secretary's watchful eye and hurried to Marie-Victoire's studio, where he reported the affair as he'd heard it from Monsieur Philippe.

Marie-Victoire was on the brink of tears and kept repeating: "I can't believe she's been cheating us for twenty years! What a monster!"

She thought more of her feelings of betrayal than of the material losses suffered by the firm. Chavanaux, anything but paternalistic, brought her back to the point.

"We must get hold of Pumperknicke, show him this statement, make him give back the patterns, to be returned to him in a month providing he pays the maximum—if he doesn't want to be reported to the Chambre Syndicale. But how can we keep Hilda from letting him know what's happened? If he's warned, the patterns will have disappeared."

"Try to call his hotel if he's still there. And if so, get the patterns back."

While Chavanaux found and dialed the number of the hotel, Marie-Victoire stared blindly into space. She remembered how she had given Hilda's daughter a present for her first communion, how she had defended her against Jérôme's attacks when he objected to hiring a German as first assistant, and of how she had always been kind to her. It was depressing to have trusted someone for so long when that person was only thinking of stealing from you. And, suddenly, Hilda assumed the proportions of an international swindler in her eyes. Since she had to admit she had been victimized, the more prestigious the thief, the less humiliation. What she could not bear was to think that for twenty years Hilda had liked her first employer best.

Chavanaux frowned as he held the phone to his ear.

"Monsieur Pumperknicke's line is busy," said the hotel operator, "will you wait, please?"

"No, I'll call back. What is his room number?"

"Six fourteen."

"Thank you."

If thinking about Hilda gave Marie-Victoire pain, because she saw she had never won her affection, her feelings for the purchaser of the patterns were devoid of all sentiment and frankly hostile.

"Go," she said to Chavanaux. "That rat is still there; go to his room directly and take him by surprise."

That's a good one, Chavanaux said to himself in the taxi. Does she think he's going to let himself be taken just like that? He knew Pumperknicke and remembered that he was at least one foot taller than himself. Besides, Chavanaux was too young to hate Germans a priori and he considered Marie-Victoire's antipathy a bit silly. One of two things will happen, he said to himself. Either Pumperknicke will be frightened of not being allowed back to Place Vendôme and won't want to get a bad name with the Chambre Syndicale because every year they send out a list of undesirable clients to all the houses. Or else he'll laugh at the whole thing and I'm the one who will look like a fool. Let's hope the firm still has enough prestige to intimidate him.

He entered the hotel with a nonchalant air, not even looking at the concierge, and went directly to the elevator as if he lived there. He knocked at 614 and went in without waiting for an answer.

"Monsieur?" The surprised occupant greeted him from the desk where he had been doing some figuring.

"Chavanaux, manager at Forval. We've just caught Madame Hilda in the act, and she admitted to the transactions you and she have had twice a year. You must know that I could have asked the police to search your room and that it is in your own interest to return those patterns to me. Later we'll see what financial arrangement can be made to compensate for this theft."

The word "theft" fell disagreeably on Herr Pumperknicke's ears; he prided himself on being considered one of the most honorable citizens of Stuttgart.

"Your Hilda must be a pathological liar; I have never had a single pattern outside those I buy from you every year. As for the police, let them come! There isn't the smallest sketch or pattern in this room! You can even search for yourself."

He rose and with a violent gesture, opened the drawer of the dresser and then went on to open everything in his room. He felt quite secure since the patterns had been disposed of half an hour ago at the Rue de la Trémoïlle post office.

"Very well, I see that the patterns are no longer here. But this is not irrefutable proof that you never had them. I shall report you to the Chambre Syndicale and to the police at the same time. You'll have to pay for these patterns one way or another!"

"Don't hold your breath! I'll never set foot in your damned house again. It's out of date anyway! And now, get the hell out of here!"

"You're a vulgar fellow; don't think you've heard the last of this!"

Trembling with rage and resentment, Chavanaux found himself back in the corridor while from inside the room he heard the German shouting into the telephone: "You let anyone at all into this hotel, the management is going to hear about this. . . ."

Chavanaux, fleeing hastily, ran headlong into the concierge, who was enraged at having been bawled out by a good customer and generous tipper. He tried to take out his revenge on the intruder.

"If Monsieur is the gentleman who went up to 614 without being announced, Monsieur should know that the regulations of all good hotels expressly forbid this. Will Monsieur give his name?"

Chavanaux thought he would burst. "There's no question . . ." he shouted, and plunged into the revolving door.

The few steps he took to Avenue George V in search of a taxi were enough to calm him down and he wondered what effect his account of this interview would have on Marie-Victoire. He knew she lived in a dream world and believed that any buyer to whom she refused admission would immediately throw himself in the Seine. So much the worse. He had been too humiliated. She would have to share his mortification.

As soon as he had returned, he told her what had happened, drawing an even blacker portrait of Herr Pumperknicke, but omitting the unbearable impertinence of the concierge.

Marie-Victoire was overcome at hearing of such vulgar scorn. She had toyed with the hope that Herr Pumperknicke not only would see that he was obliged to buy the stolen patterns at a high price, but also that in order to make amends and return to the good graces of the Maison Forval, he would buy five more patterns. Which would have amounted to a pretty sum.

Needing an immediate target for her wrath, Marie-Victoire exploded. "If the Chambre Syndicale were not what it is—totally powerless—a fellow of this kind would be banished from Paris!"

Chavanaux could not repress a smile. She'll indulge herself in a fifteen-minute bout of majesty, he thought.

"Of course," went on Marie-Victoire, "if the couturiers had an agreement, it would never happen again. But you can bet that even as a known copyist, Pumperknicke will be received as usual—even welcome! Those idiots! Now, let's think what to do. We may be sure that the patterns are on their way to Stuttgart. But we needn't give him the satisfaction of showing the same suits so that he can make his fortune at our expense. What a loss! But I don't see any other solution. Ask Philippe to show me the models, and we'll see if can't modify the line or the trimming. We must be able to do over at least one design quite differently. I'll see Monsieur Adrien. Then we must get rid of Hilda. I don't even want to see her. Give her a certificate saying nothing but '. . . employed the first of October 1948; left the twenty-fifth of July 1972 . . .'" The other houses will suspect that something serious must have happened and will ask for further information about her. I have a feeling that she'd better give up haute couture and take up sewing for her neighbors. I'll tell Monsieur Lecouture the whole story. But there's no point telling him what the pig said, that would upset him before the rehearsal."

Chavanaux agreed and withdrew, wondering if he should

admire this woman's self-possession, or pity her for not understanding that such a story suggested rats leaving a sinking ship.
Back in his office, he sent Madame Hilda off with her paper,
her various indemnities, and, in farewell, he advised her to
avoid further employment in the field of haute couture. Hilda
left like a sleepwalker, dazed to find herself in the street at
such an unusual hour, and not quite understanding what had
happened to her.

Chavanaux gave a sigh of relief. What a business! Then he
thought for five minutes, called one of his friends, the manager
of one of the biggest French perfume houses, and asked for an
appointment as soon as possible. Chavanaux was young, but
he knew that foresight was an important element of success
and that there must be something better in life than reaching
retirement age as manager of a haute couture firm.

Marie-Victoire entered Adrien's studio and excused herself
to the three or four people working there:

"I'm going to borrow Monsieur Adrien for five minutes, I
have something important to show him."

In her office, with the door closed, she motioned him to sit
down. "My dear, a catastrophe!"

"What?"

"Madame Hilda, Philippe's assistant, was caught in the act
of stealing patterns. She admitted she's been selling five each
season, for years, to Pumperknicke, the Stuttgart house; we
tried to get them back, but they were already gone. Have you
the time to do over at least one model?"

"You mean we won't be showing that dear little gray suit
with white mink, nor the checked coat, nor the chestnut outfit, and what else?"

"The green coat and the red suit."

"But there's nothing left!"

"Let's not exaggerate; that's only five designs out of eighty-five, and couldn't you do another cape like the one you did yesterday?"

"Really, it's beyond belief! And who do you think is going to sew five new designs? You know very well that Philippe's whole workroom is going to that wedding this afternoon. Besides which, Ingara had disappeared."

"Ingara has disappeared?"

"When she didn't show up for her fittings, Madame Suzanne telephoned her hotel, and no one had seen her since yesterday evening."

"How can that be? She's punctuality itself. She'll surely let us know. Maybe she forgot we were working today. After all, with her coming marriage, it's natural that she should forget things. Go on back to your fittings; I'll work out some other way."

Sulk if you want to, old boy, she thought. When you turn into a hysterical old woman, you make my flesh creep. I have a feeling that your little pal, Jean-Loup, will jump at this chance.

As soon as Adrien had left she dialed the number of the workroom where Jean-Loup was fitting garments on Adelaide.

"Jean-Loup, could you come to see me right away?"

"Of course."

He was a little startled that Marie-Victoire should call him directly. This was the first time she had done so. He hurried to her studio.

"Sit down, Jean-Loup, I have something to ask you."

He raised his eyebrows without answering. He felt flattered and at the same time furious at feeling so.

She explained the theft to him and added: "I asked Adrien to do another design to make up for the five we won't be showing—either to the press or to the buyers, at least not in their

109

present state. But it seems he is very tired and a bit upset by what's happened. Have you any ideas I could see?"

"Ideas! I have a hundred!"

"Unfortunately, only Sunday and Monday are left," she said, smiling.

"Adrien let me do my own three designs. They're finished. I'll have time to make another. I've seen the perfect fabric in the studio."

"May I see the first three?"

"May I use your telephone to have Adelaide come up with them?"

"Of course."

Marie-Victoire, who was expecting either to see Adelaide naked under black mousseline, or an Indian maid in a suede poncho lined in goat fur, or at best an ordinary accordion-pleated shirt dress in wine and old rose, those hideous colors that were so stylish and which always reminded her of what a seasick Italian might throw up between Naples and Capri, was very much surprised to see a black dress of very soft bias-cut angora jersey, a tunic-and-pants ensemble in raspberry red tweed worn with a heavy bottle-green sweater, and, finally, a silver lamé gown with batwing sleeves, all fluid and clinging, like the styles of 1932.

"But that's wonderful! I wasn't expecting this at all, I admit to you. Hurry and make up as many more as you can. Take all the available workwomen, we'll do the finishing next week, all we need now is to have things presentable. Thank you!"

Jean-Loup stupidly moved and for the first time in his life he bent over Marie-Victoire's hand and kissed it with the ease of a Charles Boyer. For one second he reminded her of an adorable little boy who is ushered into the drawing room before going to bed. At once he blushed as if caught in some ridiculous act, and snatching up the two outfits which Adelaide had left on a chair, withdrew very quickly.

After consulting Monsieur Philippe about changes to be made in four designs, and deciding the checked coat could not be changed, Marie-Victoire saw it was time to go to the wedding.

"I'll drive you there if you like," she said to Philippe.

"Thank you, madame, I have my own car, and it will be easier for me to get home in it. I'm going straight off to visit a friend near Milly. It will do me good to breathe fresh forest air again."

"I'll see you later, then. Do you know where the church is?"

"Yes, take the Avenue de St.-Ouen as if you were going to the Flea Market."

It's a pity he didn't come with me. He's nice, Philippe. His friend in Milly must be his rich boy friend. She watched him leave his studio, arms full of garments. He isn't bad at all and he has ideas too; one of these days he'll have his own shop on Avenue George V. Actually, I hardly know all these people I employ. We ought to talk more often, but even these days there is a wall between bosses and workers, or rather a kind of glass partition isolating one from the other as a fish swimming in his aquarium is separated from the species who live outside in the air.

"Come, Popoff, you can wait for me in the car."

She studied the road map and arrived at her destination without difficulty. The church must have been built in the twenties by an architect who lacked all sense of the sacred, and it would have been hard to imagine a sadder or uglier edifice. Several buses with rear windows decorated with white flowers were parked in front of the church and lent an air of celebration. Seeing the twenty-five Saturday brides, Marie-Victoire

111

had a panicky moment wondering how she would recognize her own, whom she had only met once or twice. At least she would remember that bride's gown. . . .

A rather pretty girl in pants and a tunic of white crepe bordered in swansdown attracted gibes from the other bridal couples: "Poor soul, at least he knows how it's going to be from the start; his wife will wear the pants. . . ."

Marie-Victoire entered the church and saw twenty-odd people grouped on one side. She recognized a beautiful evening coat in white faille, as little appropriate to this place as an orchid in a beet field. The girl saw her employer and nudged her father. This morning, in his desire to shave himself close, he had cut his chin and had to cover it with a Band-Aid; self-consciousness about it blemished the pride he felt at accompanying his daughter to the altar.

The bride's lips formed: "It's Madame!" and the party nearly clicked their heels just as if an officer had barked "Attention."

Marie-Victoire approached and said: "How lovely you look; a real princess!" And turning toward the young man, dressed in a suit of a too-light blue and pulling a pair of new gloves nervously through his hands: "My congratulations, monsieur, you have caught a rare prize."

The mother, obviously supplied by her daughter with a lace dress cut from a last year's design, was almost elegant if one didn't look too closely at her white plastic bag and shoes. The women in the family of the bridegroom seemed to have fallen into turquoise and orange paint pots, except for a fine old grandmother with a clear sharp profile, dressed in black and straight from the country. What nobility there still is in our peasants, Marie-Victoire thought. They have a great deal more style than their grandchildren in the city.

A beadle made a sign to the group that it was going to be

their turn. Immediately they all assumed important and serious looks. Four or five women picked up baskets of white flowers and placed them in front of the altar after the previous wedding party had removed theirs. Except for the grandmother, who seemed at home in the church, it was plain that this little group must not have set foot inside one since their first communions; a sort of embarrassment kept them from making the sign of the cross or genuflecting as they had been taught. Moreover, the prayers they had learned in catechism class had changed since their childhood; now the Lord was addressed familiarly and the priest had lost all his sacred mystery by speaking French like everybody else.

He got through the ceremony as quickly as possible and summed it all up in a few words: "The purpose of a Christian marriage is to have a large family." This made the young people laugh and give each other nudges and knowing looks. Twenty minutes later, the registry duly signed, flowers in hand, after having been photographed in the churchyard by Uncle Alfred, a first-rate shutter-bug, the wedding party climbed into the big sky-blue bus which would take it to dine in some large hall that specialized in weddings and banquets.

Nine times out of ten, the menu went like this: "Chef's Entrees: Queen of the Cascade with almonds, Chicken in Bridal Gown. The Embarcation for Cythera, Coffee, Liqueurs." Which in everyday language could be translated: "Salad with sausage and sardines, trout, fricasseed fowl with rice, strawberry-vanilla ice cream."

Marie-Victoire offered her congratulations and escaped as quickly as possible, happy to return again to her little beige and black Austin and her sophisticated world. This kind of ceremony always made her sad, and her reflections on the state of matrimony were rarely optimistic.

She remembered her own unquenched thirst for happiness

and understanding. Never having known the sweetness of growing old together, by far the best part of any marriage, she had a tendency to find the whole institution pointless. Obviously, she told herself, there are the Browns from Kansas City who are so perfect that they should be shown at county fairs to encourage couples the world over, and a few more like Paul and his wife. But, on the whole, there are more couples living together like strangers than there are couples really living together. If only Clothilde could find great happiness like that I would do anything to get it for her, even if she went off to the Indies. But with the kind of bearded youths that I've seen at the house, she's more likely to wind up the wife of a small-town philosophy professor.

At least she inherited her father's money, and one day she will inherit Baussigue, which is a marvelous retreat. I wish I could go there next week when all the buyers have left. Oliver could come and join me. Where would I like to go with him? Sardinia? That doesn't seem too crowded. I'd love to lie in the sun; this rain is really depressing. Some invalids go to Lourdes to be cured; others who are less religious but richer, to clinics in Switzerland; for Marie-Victoire, the Mediterranean was the only cure she wanted when there was anything wrong with her health, or when it rained too much in Paris, or when she had the blues.

She consulted her watch: quarter of six. Was that all? The prospect of a solitary evening followed by a solitary Sunday seemed insurmountable and she almost regretted not having been invited to the wedding party.

Popoff looked at her, wagging his tail. It was as if she could hear him say: "You could take me for a walk anyway!" So she answered:

"If you like we'll take a little walk around the Flea Market.

114

It's not as nice for you as the Bois de Boulogne, but tomorrow morning I promise you a long walk on the *quais*."

The Flea Market, even when one wasn't looking for anything to buy, was always fun. She stopped at a stand where an American was buying a porcelain vase decorated with a bas-relief of a large mauve lady dreaming near a green waterfall—all for a fabulous price. The American was trying to argue. *Too much, too much,* were the only two words he seemed to know, while the shopkeeper gesticulated, turned the vase around, showed a vague signature saying: "Very rare, very rare!" When people don't understand each other they repeat the same words as if repetition could strike a spark of comprehension. That American had a nice face, he was very young, the picture of innocence, vanilla ice cream, Ivory Soap, and the university. The argumentative bearded youths would consider him square.

Marie-Victoire smiled and in her English (which was perfectly grammatical but heavily accented), said to him: "Don't buy it, it's much too expensive, it's a shooting gallery vase. If you like turn-of-the-century, there's a stand that specializes in it further on. It ought to be at least a Gallé to be worth such a price."

The merchant saw them moving away: "What's she mixing in for, that tart," he shouted. "Cruising the sidewalks dressed like that!"

"I don't know anything about it," the boy admitted to Marie-Victoire, "but I thought my mother might like it."

Delighted to have found a striking example of Early America, who honored his parents instead of spitting on them, Marie-Victoire said to him: "Your mother must be about my age. I have a daughter of twenty. Tell me what she likes and we'll try to find her the right present."

115

"How nice of you, madame, French people usually aren't this nice to me."

"I adore America and I adore my own country too, it's natural to want them to be good friends and understand each other better."

"My name is Samuel King, Junior," he said, and he gave her his card.

"I haven't a card with me, but I am Marie-Victoire Forval. Perhaps you've heard of my couture house?"

"Don't you make a perfume called 'Oh' or something like that? I bought a little bottle last year for my girl."

"It's AH!"

"And you're Marie-Victoire Forval?"

He looked at her with as much delighted surprise as if the Gioconda had come down from her frame to tap him on the shoulder and say, "Hi, boy, I'm Mona Lisa."

She laughed. "No doubt about it, that's who I am."

"My girl will be so excited, that's her favorite perfume, so expensive . . . terrific!"

"If it weren't so expensive she wouldn't want it!"

He looked at her. Obviously he had never thought of that, and it was as if he had suddenly discovered a whole new philosophy. He grew pensive.

Marie-Victoire suddenly saw Hubert Mezac, Adrien's friend, his arms around a pretty wooden statue.

"My dear Hubert, what a charming statue! Heaven must have sent you. I've just met this young man," and she waved her hand as an introduction, "Samuel King, Junior, Monsieur Mezac, a famous decorator. This poor young man was about to have a perfectly dreadful vase fobbed off on him for two hundred francs. He's looking for a nice present for his mother. Have you any ideas? No merchant would dare sell you a piece of junk. All you have to do is show yourself with us."

116

Hubert smiled a bit pallidly. He was in a hurry and wanted very much to be home when Adrien got back from work. He was very touchy these evenings, was Adrien. But he still seemed to appreciate whiskey fixed the way he liked it, a warm perfumed bath, and the Japanese kimono offered him by a Hubert who was all sweetness, appeasement, and comprehension, like a very expensive nurse.

Hubert told himself that he could get rid of Marie-Victoire and her American (she really had a weakness for Americans) in a few minutes by passing them along to an old pal to whom he would make quite clear that he wanted no commission. In the language of dealers, this meant 10 per cent instead of 20 per cent—after all decorators have to earn a living too and the addresses of their dealers are like engineering diplomas!

"Now that you are in good hands," he said to Marie-Victoire, having introduced them to his friendly dealer, "I'll leave you. This statue is quite heavy and I'm exhausted from carrying it. Delighted to have seen you. Until Tuesday, then!"

He came to all Adrien's first showings and brought the "claque." Marie-Victoire was a little disappointed to see him leave so quickly, but she was much too sensitive not to know that all he wanted was to get away as quickly as possible.

"Sorry to have taken up your time and a thousand thanks for the suggestion. I'm sure we'll discover a treasure by ourselves; it won't be as easy as it would have been with you, but much more exciting."

All right, Hubert said to himself, I must have annoyed her. Ah, women, they are never happy unless they have some courtship afoot.

While they looked around the stall, Marie-Victoire asked the boy questions. Did his parents have antiques? A large house? Where? And little by little he drew a portrait of a typical American family living near Detroit. Three children, of which he was

117

the eldest, a sister fifteen, very flirtatious, and a wild little brother, who loved guinea pigs, turtles, and sea horses. Father, executive at Ford. The mother, president of a woman's club. Their living room was gold, the furniture was rustic Louis XVI from Sloane (better than gilded Louis XV!). There were low tables with large lamps at each end of an avocado-colored sofa, and his parents' bedroom was sky blue.

"Perhaps a piece of milk glass?"

Marie-Victoire saw at once from the boy's face that he didn't know the difference between a Charles X piece of milk glass and a bottle of bath salts from Hudson's, the big Detroit department store.

"Hm, she would love that," and he pointed to a Lalique glass bird. "She knows all about birds, and that one is cute."

Marie-Victoire exchanged a heartbroken glance with the dealer. After all, why not?

"Not too expensive, very nice, not too heavy to carry in your bag, either, and not too fragile. Perfect!"

With his bird nested in newspaper in the bottom of an old soap box, the boy didn't know what to say except "Merci beaucoup," as he stood on one foot and then the other.

Marie-Victoire would have been very happy to go on playing guide; she was already visualizing a Sunday full of Sainte Chapelle, the Louvre, and maybe even Versailles. But suddenly the disappointed dealer's words filled her ears: "Imagine streetwalking dressed up like that!" She returned to her *grande dame* manner, extended her hand to the American, and wished him a happy ending to his holiday, suggesting he take the boat trip on the Seine.

She saw a couple of famous antiquarians who were known by the grotesque nicknames of Sodome and Commode. She answered their greeting abruptly, and moved toward the exit

118

barely glancing at the stalls, Popoff pulling at his leash, tongue hanging.

The Flea Market had lost its charm. First her daughter, then her lover, now even strangers were letting her down; all that was left was chocolate and the movies!

Madame Hilda had spent part of the day trailing around the Galeries Lafayette and Printemps, where she had looked at everything and bought nothing, as she rehearsed the lie she must tell her husband. In the drug department, attractive metal boxes decorated with a red cross, FIRST-AID ESSENTIALS FOR CAMPERS AND TOURISTS, gave her the idea of feigning some illness which would remove her from the workrooms of Place Vendôme forever. But however unhealthy the occupation of couturière might be, it had no specific health hazards, and anyway, she had no desire to spend the rest of her life wrapped in a shawl on a chaise longue. "The lady with the camellias" in *La Traviata* wasn't her style.

What then? No idea came to her usually fertile mind. She thought for a moment about saying nothing until she found another job, but the certificate saying "employed on . . . , left on . . ." weighed a ton in her handbag. It was useless to try to get a position in another house.

Her wandering had brought her into the stationery department. Big ledgers with empty columns waiting to digest figures. They spread their red and green lines with the false innocence of carnivorous flowers waiting for a foolish fly.

There was a brilliant idea! The house was bankrupt. In a flash, from one day to the next, boom! the crash of the year. The word delighted her, real music! Obviously, it would be strange that it hadn't been mentioned in the papers. Bah! that would give her a good opportunity for saying how the rich were like the Mafia, they got rid of the workwomen and gave money to the papers to keep them quiet. What an idea! It developed in her head agreeably, like a symphony with an overture with cymbals and bass drum: "Well, my dear Joseph, I have news for you, you'll never guess. . . ."

She looked at her watch: four-thirty. Goodness, she ought to be at the Church of St.-Ouen. Little Marinette's wedding, she hadn't even thought of it. Suddenly she felt like an outcast from society, even more than she had when she had gone through the doors of Marie-Victoire Forval for the last time just now. Still two good hours before time to go home. She wouldn't admit not having gone to the wedding; on the contrary, she would describe it pathetically: that poor child, losing her job on her wedding day, if that isn't rotten luck!

What to do? Suddenly she felt stifled by the air conditioning of the big stores and her limbs felt heavy. She was not used to walking so long. She went out into the Boulevard Haussmann; it was raining. She had dressed in her nice navy blue suit to go to the wedding. Now she took out the folding umbrella from her big bag in which she carried her scissors, comb, big mirror, glass, and napkin, things which ordinarily remained in her drawer at Place Vendôme. Seeing them in her bag gave her a new shock. Where to go for two hours? Mechanically, she had turned toward the Opéra station of the Métro, like a horse going back to its stable. She looked right and left: the Paramount, there was a port in a storm. The movies are the last resort for women in distress.

The next day, Sunday, the weather was superb and this made Marie-Victoire feel even more furious at being alone in Paris. During the week, having so much to do, she had thought: I'll

120

have the time to make plans on Sunday and arrive at a final decision about my business. But Sunday was here and she could not even think seriously about her future. She was like someone about to jump from the top of the Empire State Building, who frets about the light burning in her bathroom. Instead of being frantic before that show which would seal her fate, she was imagining her daughter arguing great philosophical problems with intellectual young people around a delicious breakfast served on rustic pottery. She could almost have described the taste of the homemade jam and the odor of the big lime tree under which she imagined their table. Next, in a splendid fade-in like a movie, she saw Oliver, dressed in his blue blazer, talking about the Stock Market with another American, also in a blue blazer, as they strolled on the boardwalk in front of the Bar du Soleil at Deauville. And feeling vaguely jealous, she noticed the interested stares of the little ladies nonchalantly stretched on their deck chairs, ready to leap up at the slightest sign, like sleeping dogs who come running at the faintest whistle.

What if she telephoned Alan? One never knew, he might have lunch with her.

"Hello, Alan, what are you doing for lunch?"

"I promised a girl who works at Du Pont de Nemours to take her to Malmaison. She adores Napoleon, and Josephine's story makes her cry; she thinks that in America she would have gotten better alimony. You know my countrywomen are much more sentimental than they seem."

"It's true, I've noticed it, but tender blossoms have trouble surviving in the air of Seventh Avenue."

"Right, but this girl has nothing to do with the rag business. I know her, she was in college with my sister and she took this job so she could travel. She's very nice, so for once this won't be a drag."

121

He said this with so much enthusiasm that Marie-Victoire felt a little chill in her heart. How, after such a confidence, could she suggest joining them? Better to be alone than *de trop,* but she too would have liked to go to Malmaison where she hadn't been since her childhood.

"Good, have a nice time, see you Monday. Anyway, I should go to Place Vendôme in the afternoon, Chavanaux said that he would be stopping by and Jean-Loup has to work, too. I only wanted to see if you could lunch."

"Oh, I'm very sorry, you know I love to lunch with you. Is Clothilde there?"

"No, don't worry, you're not missing her. Bye-bye!"

And she hung up with a little laugh which was intended to be light but which really carried a weight of sobs withheld by the dam of good manners.

She looked at her telephone. That instrument, thanks to which she could speak to millions of people in Tokyo, in Sydney, or on the floor below, suddenly seemed unfriendly, as if the millions had all taken their phones off the hook so as not to have to answer when she called. Baussigue came to her mind. Papa, there was someone who would surely be happy to hear from her! Quick, the number! It couldn't be dialed directly yet, one had to be connected through Draguignan, it took a long time, it was busy. . . . Finally, a melodious voice asked what she wanted. Line One to Baussigue.

She imagined the telephone ringing in the hall. She saw her father come down the stairs, a little more slowly each year. She saw the gnats dancing in the two columns of sunshine which shone through the bull's-eye windows on each side of the big door. The phone went on ringing. Finally, the shouting voice of Mathurine, to whom the telephone would always be an object of mystery, could be heard:

"Hello, hello!" she cried, without waiting for an answer, as if she were deaf.

"Mathurine, it's Madame Marie-Victoire. Is Monsieur le Comte in?"

"Oh no, madame, he's gone to mass."

"I see, never mind then, it doesn't matter, I'll call later. Is he having lunch at home?"

"Yes, yes, Monsieur le Curé is coming too."

"Is it a nice day?"

"It's dry, very dry. There hasn't been a drop of rain since June. There are storms all around us but never on us! Madame is coming down soon with Mademoiselle Clothilde?"

"I don't know yet. Tell Monsieur le Comte that I'll try to call back at about two o'clock, but it's hard to get a connection."

"Very well, madame."

Marie-Victoire hung up. Of course, ten forty-five; she should have known her father would be at mass, but just the same she felt as if he too had abandoned her.

"Well, then, my Popoff, I promised to take you for a walk on the quais. We'll stop and buy some lunch on the way back. Thérèse hasn't left anything very interesting in the refrigerator."

The quais were covered with hippies, stretched out on the ground as if they were in India or Mexico. Popoff barked at them scornfully and Marie-Victoire hurried to climb back up the embankment for fear that she would hear things said in Dutch or Swedish, nasty things she couldn't even see the humor of.

"This is certainly a day when nobody wants us, doggy. It would be better to go home. We can take a sun bath on the terrace and while we do I can begin that fat American novel I got last week. After all, we don't need anybody else, and I can't do a thing more at Place Vendôme today.

123

In a store that sold a little bit of everything, she bought a small can of *foie gras* and a basket of raspberries for her lunch and a rubber toy for Popoff. Dogs are like children, or even grownups, they only appreciate the newest toy, and Popoff was already bouncing like a dolphin as his disappeared into its paper bag.

Chapter V

Joseph Petit almost strangled with rage when he heard his wife's account of the firm's closing. His fury reached its height when he read the certificate which he himself fished out of the bottom of her bag. He decided to take his car Monday morning and go first to Renault to ask for two hours off from work so he could threaten Marie-Victoire Forval with retribution from the union. Hilda could have kicked herself for forgetting that these days, thanks to unions, a business shutdown without notice is impossible. She had passed the day Sunday trying to calm down her Joseph, but he wouldn't listen. He was in the state of mind of a Joan of Arc ready to kick the English out of France. Nothing could stop him.

At about eleven o'clock he arrived at Place Vendôme, hesitated over parking at a meter, then did so out of fear of getting a ticket. He had put on his Sunday suit, but Maurice asked him haughtily what it was that he wanted. Instead of answering him: "Up yours, you dirty flunky," as he would dearly have loved to do, he managed to say in a confident tone:

"I have an appointment with Madame Forval. Please tell me how to get to her office."

Maurice explained how to get there and showed him the tradesmen's entrance. Once inside, there was no need to pass the Princess' desk from this entry, and Joseph went straight to Marie-Victoire's studio. Surprised, she rose.

"Who are you?"

"Petit, Joseph. Doesn't that mean anything to you?"

"I confess . . ."

"Hilda's husband . . ."

"I see."

"So you think you can get rid of all your workers without notice by pretending you're broke?"

"I'm sorry, I don't know what you're talking about. If Hilda was dismissed, she is the only one, and that's because she's the only one who stole from us. You really should be thanking us for not turning the affair over to the police."

"What are you saying? You're lying. My Hilda, a thief? Is that the only excuse you can find? Well, you won't get away with this so easily! I'm telling you, justice courts are not made for dogs! You're closing your firm, yes, that's the truth of the matter, and you're trying to get rid of your employees without paying them."

Marie-Victoire picked up the telephone: "Chavanaux, come in at once with Hilda's statement. Her husband is here trying to make a scene."

And turning back to the husband: "I think that your wife's signed statement will open your eyes. She must have told you some tale to explain her dismissal, but I assure you that no one else was dismissed. Really, Monsieur Petit, you aren't so innocent as to believe that I don't know the law as well as you. And anyway, didn't it seem unlikely that a house would get its

126

collection ready and then announce its closing two days before showing it?"

Chavanaux arrived, ready to save his boss from the hands of a dangerous maniac, but Petit was beginning to understand that he had been deceived and made a fool of by his wife. However, the poor man didn't want to seem to give in so quickly, and anyway, a man doesn't see his life falling down around his ears without trying to preserve some fragments of it. He took the paper and without even looking at it sat down on the nearest chair, trembling.

"Oh my . . . oh my!"

"Yes, poor Monsieur Petit, believe us, we felt as badly as you do. We would have never suspected your wife; we considered her a model employee. You see, happy as one may be in an adopted country, there is always some nostalgia for the place where one was born. We don't think your wife would have sold the patterns to Englishmen or Italians, and also she admitted that this German was the son of her first employer."

Chavanaux looked at her in astonishment: she was really amazing. The way she talked made you wonder if the German government wouldn't decorate its faithful expatriate. And that royal *we* . . . she isn't talking about herself and me, but just about herself in the plural. The fellow was flabbergasted, but he felt himself beginning to recover. He had come to fight with a boss and here she was, transformed into a victim of industrial espionage. Which was obviously better for him than being the husband of a common thief.

"You think she did it out of patriotism? It's not possible. She never has wanted to go back home. No, Mother was right, once a Boche always a Boche!"

"Your mother wasn't altogether wrong, poor Monsieur Petit. Anyway, you can tell Hilda that her dear ex-boss can't boast about getting our designs in advance, because we've simply removed the ones that he took from the collection. But she can boast about having cost us dearly!"

This last shot, designed to drive the criminal's husband to a shameful retreat, reached its target, and the miserable Petit got out as fast as he could, mumbling excuses.

Marie-Victoire turned to Chavanaux. She had the elated look of a trapeze artist just stepping down from her ladder and saying to the audience, "Et voilà!"

"He seemed honest, poor fellow! That will teach him that he should have married a nice girl from Aubervilliers. I think our Hilda will be having a bad time with him. And I'm not sorry to think so!"

"Just the same it's a nasty story, and we lost a good customer, too. We're lucky to get Germans, because in the long run they buy twice as much as your Americans."

"My dear, you're a pessimist. It's a state of mind which makes others besides yourself uncomfortable. The sole satisfaction in it is rejoicing at having been right when predicted misfortunes come to pass; it borders on masochism."

"I assure you, madame, I don't rejoice at all at having to scrape up money to pay for the chairs where hypothetical buyers will sit tomorrow afternoon."

"That reminds me, my dear, I'd forgotten. My friend the Baroness Swaft just sent me a check with flowers and apologies for being six months late. That will pay for the chairs and a few other things too."

Marie-Victoire was even more the trapeze artist now, as with a triumphant smile, she once more sighed with relief at arriving safe and sound on the ground.

"Heaven is on your side, madame, there's no doubt about that."

She touched wood with both hands. "Don't say things like that, it scares me."

Chavanaux only smiled like a cat with a mouse. He bowed and went out. Maybe she wasn't pessimistic, but supersititious she was, the darling, and that's as bad!

The door had scarcely closed on Chavanaux when the telephone rang and the operator asked Marie-Victoire if she would speak to Miss Fanny Wright.

"Yes, put her on. Good morning, my dear, how are you?"

"Can you see me in ten minutes? I'm nearby and I have something important to tell you."

"Of course, I'll be waiting for you."

Marie-Victoire was intrigued by the urgency of the request. *Thread Needle News,* the American magazine of which Fanny Wright was the permanent Paris correspondent, had tried, although a weekly, to beat *Women's Wear Daily* without ever managing to do so, and the rivalry between the two periodicals was legendary. I'll bet she wants permission to photograph one design more than Fairchild or something like that. It was not easy to remain on good terms with the Chambre Syndicale, which forbids the publication of designs for a month after they are shown to protect the buyers and the big specialty stores, and at the same time stay friendly with the papers which wanted to publish the whole collection immediately.

Fanny Wright arrived a few minutes later. She was a pretty woman, very tiny, with auburn hair and a light step. She had been correspondent for *Thread Needle News* in Paris for a dozen years, and was completely Parisian. Marie-Victoire got up to welcome her with a warm smile.

"Well, Fanny, what's going on? Why aren't you at Chanel? It's obvious Coco's dead. Is your paper boycotting the designer?"

"It's much more serious than that."

Marie-Victoire saw that Fanny looked exhausted and for the first time, showed her age, which no one would have guessed before.

"Sit down and tell me all about it."

"Well, here it is. My boss called me from New York on Friday. Because of you, my dear. He told me three times: 'You're fired, fired, fired!' " It was obvious that the phrase was haunting her.

"Good Lord, explain!"

"You certainly know that Big Mills of Indiana wants to buy your firm. The name would give prestige. Their other products are popular but not especially elegant."

"Yes, of course, but I haven't given them an answer."

"To make you give in, the big boss couldn't think of anything except to make you sick of the whole business by starting a smear campaign in our paper. You know that with the amount of advertising he buys every week my boss can't refuse him anything. They want me to write a bad report of the collection before I've even seen it, saying it's old-fashioned. They can't wait because the article has to appear in the Wednesday issue so that the buyers won't come to the showing. Next season, they'll make you hire a designer of their choice and then they'll proclaim a miracle. One of their executives phoned me about it Saturday and was very much surprised when I refused. I'm no saint, but I don't think a journalist worthy of the name writes smears, on things he has not seen even to please management, which surprised him a lot. I said I wanted a confirmation from New York, and then I refused again as I did the first time. So that's when the boss fired me and told me that since I was so strong for France I could ask Pompidou for the Legion of Honor. If I hadn't been so well paid, I would have quit long ago because it's impossible to write what you think; you're bombarded with memos: never mention so-and-so again, or use the 'in' word of the season every three lines. You really have to have the soul of a flunky to work there. My only consolation is that it will cost them plenty. In France, thank God, you can't fire

130

people without paying them fat indemnities. They must have had the article written by Anita Oldugle. I'm afraid it will be awful; she's not one to choke on her scruples!"

As Fanny was telling her story, Marie-Victoire gripped her desk so hard that her fingers were white and she seemed unable to speak.

"I wanted to let you know," Fanny went on, "so that when the article comes out day after tomorrow you won't think that I was the one who wrote it. I'd like very much to see the collection, but as far away from that bunch as possible!"

"Those bastards! This is really horrible!" Marie-Victoire muttered. Then, pulling herself together, she managed a weak smile and said to Fanny: "I know you'll surely find a marvelous new job and I'll do everything I can for you. Thank you for warning me, though there's nothing I can do to cushion the blow. Excuse me, in spite of this I have a thousand things to do," and she kissed her on both cheeks. "Come at ten o'clock tomorrow as usual. Alan will give you one of the best seats."

When the door closed, Marie-Victoire leaned on it for a moment, biting her lips, and thought: I don't want to cry, I don't want to cry, but just the same it's a hard blow. Her first impulse was to say nothing to anyone, but after ten minutes of thought, a brilliant idea came to her. The paper would not appear until day after tomorrow; all she had to do was telephone John Fairchild, the publisher of *Women's Wear Daily,* and tell him the story without mentioning Big Mills of Indiana, which was one of their big advertisers too. He would be delighted to be able to say that his competitor was not admitted to Forval but in spite of that had published an article on the collection there. She called Alan and told him: "Don't admit *Thread Needle News,* you must tell everyone," and explained to him why.

Alan was delighted with this theatrical stroke which would

send shock waves through the little world of couture, for he maintained that the great thing for any house was to be talked about. He immediately called *France-Soir, Figaro,* and Eugenia Sheppard, leaving urgent messages so that everyone would call back. In any case, he would see them tomorrow morning, but it would be better if the news appeared in this evening's papers. All Paris would talk of nothing else, and the criticism from *Thread Needle News* would lose all its force.

As for the reporters from the American publication, Marie-Victoire and Alan decided, if they came, they would be turned away at the door with the maximum fuss.

No sooner was this question settled than Madame Suzanne called Marie-Victoire on the telephone:

"Madame, I don't know what else to do. It's afternoon and Ingara still isn't here. I've telephoned her hotel and they say her key isn't on the board; they've knocked on her door and she doesn't answer."

"I still can't believe she would have gone off with her fiancé just before the showing, that's not like her; besides, his job depends on couture too, since he's a fashion photographer. Doesn't anyone know where to find him? That shouldn't be hard."

"I think he goes to the Ritz bar at seven o'clock every day. We can manage without Ingara in the meantime. I've never had such a thing happen to me. None of my girls has ever done such a thing. I wonder if we oughtn't send someone to the hotel. I have a bad feeling. I scarcely dare ask you, madame, but you're the one who should go; you will impress the people at the hotel, and then if she's sick you could see if it's serious. And we should settle this: she may have left some word there."

"I think you're right: we have to know where we are. I'm

not hungry today, so I'll go now instead of having lunch. Give me her address."

Marie-Victoire stood thinking for a moment. If Ingara had really disappeared, they would have to divide the collection among the other mannequins. It would be out of the question to find another suitable girl so late. With one less mannequin, there were bound to be "holes," and the press would notice. She really must be found.

The hotel was a few doors from the Folies-Bergère, and Marie-Victoire had a hard time finding a parking place even for her little Austin. What a curious place to live! she thought, walking down the street. In a tiny lobby she was greeted by a fat, badly shaven man in purple suspenders, who was carefully rolling a cigarette as he stood beside a bright green plastic plant. At Marie-Victoire's question, he deigned to stop this important operation and say:

"You can see her key isn't there; she must be sleeping."

"Do you think it's normal to be asleep at one o'clock in the afternoon when we expected her at nine for a rehearsal?"

"Oh, those girls are all crazy. They go to bed at dawn, so of course they sleep late."

"This isn't a Folies-Bergère dancer, she's a haute couture mannequin. She has worked for me for three years and she's never been late once. You must have a pass key; I want to see if she's in her room."

The fat man opened a drawer: "Here's the pass key. Take it."

"I want you to come up with me."

"Aren't you the one! If they were all like you, life would be impossible!"

After he had worked the key in the lock for some time, while girls in peignoirs came to their doors saying that they hadn't heard anything since yesterday, and they were sure Ingara wasn't there, the door finally opened, showing a spectacle which drew cries of horror from everyone, even the sleepy fat man.

Ingara, in her dressing gown, was seated before her little washbasin, her face propped on its edge, her wrists marked with two deep red lines out of which her life had flowed tidily down the open drain. Her hands were covered with dried blood and she was already stiff. Three letters were in plain view on the table: one turned out to be for Madame Forval; another for Monsieur Bill Fonk; and the third for Monsieur and Madame Nigelsen in Hillinsoe, Sweden.

"Oh my God, the poor child, what a terrible thing. She was so beautiful! This letter . . ."

"Now, now, now, wait until the police say you can have it!"

"I can't bear to look at this. Close the door and call a policeman right away."

Ten minutes later, two policemen in uniform and an inspector in civilian clothes climbed the stairs. Marie-Victoire followed them back up.

"Somebody should have checked on her yesterday. We must call a doctor, but there's no doubt it was suicide," the specialists decided.

"Can I have that letter, monsieur l'inspecteur? I am Madame Forval, here are my papers. This young woman has worked for me for three years."

The inspector looked at Marie-Victoire, then at her papers and the address on the envelope.

"Take it, but I want to read it too."

Trembling a little, Marie-Victoire tore the cheap envelope: "Madame, excuse me for not being there for the collection. When my fiancé saw my age on my papers (I was forty last month), he said he thought I was ten years younger and that I should have told him. It's true, but I never had the courage. Now he knows, and it's all over. I'm too old. I'd rather die. I ask

134

your forgiveness, and Madame Suzanne's—she was so good to me. Adelaide can wear almost all my dresses. Ingara."

Marie-Victoire, with tears running down her cheeks, held the letter out to the inspector while she searched in her bag for a handkerchief.

"Terrible!" said the inspector. "Who is the fiancé? He must be told."

"It must be the Bill Fonk this other letter is addressed to; the third is to her parents. I don't know where he lives, but I'm told he goes to the Ritz bar every evening at seven. He's a fashion photographer. I'll go there myself to tell him the bad news before he hears it from someone else."

"Anyway we'll be able to find him easily."

"May I leave?" With a weak smile: "My collection is being shown tomorrow morning and I must replace this poor child. She was a marvelous mannequin. Everyone liked her. Where are you going to take her?"

"To the morgue."

Marie-Victoire shivered. She had only seen the place in films, but having one's body laid out there was like ending up on a butcher's block.

"Can you let us know when the body may be claimed? We'll see that she has a proper funeral, at least. Here is my telephone number."

"Thank you, madame, you can get her on Thursday."

As Marie-Victoire went back to her little Austin, she thought: now the order of the mannequins must all be changed around. But she could not concentrate on the task, could not stop thinking of the strange life that mannequins led, going from fantastic luxury to shoddy hotels, wearing better than anyone else could dresses finally sold to fat rich women. Their demands and whims must be forgiven them, she told herself; it's natural

135

that they should try to seize a few days of comfort when they're on trips. There are some who overdo it, of course; that English girl in Munich (was it Munich or Bayreuth?) who had champagne and caviar sent to her room. What nerve! but she was really a very vulgar girl. Since then, we've warned the hotels in advance that we won't authorize extras on the bill beyond cups of tea and bottles of mineral water. And that Austrian, the compulsive gambler, whom you couldn't let near a casino! And Simone, whom nobody wanted to share a sleeping car compartment with because she never washed below the neck. And that lesbian couple, both absolutely beautiful, but you had to hire them together if you wanted one of them. And the penniless Hungarian who was on intimate terms with all the crowned heads of Central Europe. How many of all of them who had shown clothcs for the house made some kind of life for themselves? Perhaps a dozen, not many more. In their strange occupation, they needed a much more level head than most women and above all, must know the moment to quit. Poor Ingara, so conscientious! For a mannequin, turning forty is as fearful as opening a door over a black precipice. A clumsy word from her fiancé was enough to make her decide to open it a little sooner. If he really loved her, I wouldn't care to be in his shoes. It's true that suicide is more common in Sweden. But what could he have said to her? Men are so clumsy! Will he feel desperate over it? Good, here's Maurice, everyone will have to hear about it. . . . There are days when a desert island would be paradise!

"Sad news, Maurice. Ingara has committed suicide."

"My God, that's terrible! Such a beautiful girl, and so serious. *She* never asked me to get a rich man or woman for her!"

Marie-Victoire started: "Do the others ask you to do that?"

"Well, not all of them. You remember the two lesbians? They

were the ones who did it the most, they needed money and would do anything."

"I can't imagine you canvassing the customers to see if they would be interested in a lesbian orgy!"

"People ask me more things than you might think."

"You're right, my imagination is limited in that area."

Maurice looked as if he thought his boss would do better to be less chic and more sexy. This was the natural reaction of a real womanizer, and he barely restrained a shrug as he opened the door for her. He watched her disappear and put his cap back on, thinking with a deep sigh, "What a pity, such a pretty woman."

Marie-Victoire went directly to the dressing rooms where she beckoned Madame Suzanne out. "My poor Suzanne, you were right; she committed suicide."

"Poor little thing! She should never have been left alone on a Sunday. I felt something awful had happened: I'm sure her fiancé let her down!"

"Here, read her letter. She was so fond of you; she asked us to forgive her for all the trouble her death would cause us. She even thought to tell us that her models would look well on Adelaide. The poor baby, she was so conscientious—thinking of her gowns before slashing her wrists!"

Madame Suzanne wiped her eyes as she read the letter. "What a terrible thing! How can we tell the other girls? It's awful!"

"Yes, and in spite of our feelings we must reorganize the whole showing. Try to divide her gowns up among the others. I'm going to ask Monsieur Alan if perhaps he doesn't know some girl who might be still free, but I doubt it. The rehearsal will still be at four o'clock. And I'll have to see Monsieur Adrien: he designed that last cape for her. What a blow to everybody! And her poor parents! I can't even write them, they probably don't know a word of French or English. But I'll ask the Swedish ambassador what can be done. Do you know if she had brothers or sisters?"

"No, she was an only child."

"Poor souls! Could anything worse happen to them? I certainly couldn't survive a tragedy like that!"

Her thoughts went to Clothilde. How I would like to have her near at this moment! She felt a physical need to touch her child the way she touched wood. This terrible tragedy which had befallen a distant Swedish family gave her the feeling that a storm gives a mother hen; she spreads her wings to protect her nest.

Adrien was in the midst of checking an evening gown on Daphne and seemed to be in a very bad temper.

"Don't just stand there staring at me as if I were an icon; turn around! Madame Alphonsine, didn't you notice that this gown breaks in the back, or were you too lazy to fix it? You'll have to take up the whole thing for me!"

Madame Alphonsine and Daphne looked sour, furious at being criticized in front of their employer.

"I'm sorry to bother you, but I have some very bad news: Ingara has committed suicide."

"What an idiot!" said Adrien.

"Oh, the poor girl!" said Alphonsine and Daphne together, immediately bursting into tears.

Adrien went on: "What got into her—the day before the showing? She could have waited forty-eight hours!"

He looked as if he were really having one of his bad days. Marie-Victoire thought, I've never seen just how nasty he can look, and to say a thing like that, it's almost indecent. Then she said: "Before the rehearsal, Madame Suzanne and I are going to try all the models she was to wear on other girls, unless Alan can find a new girl for us. Don't worry about that, Adrien, you'll have enough to do."

Daphne dried her tears with the back of her hand: "Do you want me to wear the cape?"

"The cape!" Adrien exclaimed. "You're crazy, it isn't your character at all, but you might try the red dress."

Goodness, now he's going theatrical and mannequins must be type-cast for his clothes; he's getting delusions of grandeur, thought Marie-Victoire. And Daphne was hardly thrown off stride, either. They haven't even bothered to ask why Ingara committed suicide—they're much too busy dividing the spoils. To think I cried for a week when I lost Popoff's predecessor: I must be mad, too! A little sickened, she left, saying: "I have to see Alan."

Alan was either more intelligent or more sensitive than Adrien because he liked women, and he reacted to the news appropriately. He also saw that Marie-Victoire was upset and that he must console her. He asked to see the letter, spoke of how touching it was, asked to keep it until that evening, sighed as he looked up a telephone number to call a mannequin he knew that wore the same size. He was sure she would come the day of the press showing and for the first buyers' showing, as a favor to him. And accompanying Marie-Victoire to the door, he advised her to go rest a little, he would take care of everything and keep her informed of just what was happening. Yes, he would go to the Ritz this evening to meet Bill Fonk.

Marie-Victoire had hardly left when he picked up the telephone. First the mannequin. He had been in her bed the previous evening and he knew that at this hour she must be at Venet. He had trouble reaching her; the showing was just

139

starting. It was terribly important, he insisted; finally he got her on the telephone.

"Come to Forval as soon as you're finished."

"But I'm showing at Ricci at five-thirty."

"That leaves you an hour and a half between. Ricci is only two steps away: you're going to replace one of our girls tomorrow. I'll explain it later. Come on, I'm counting on you."

"All right, I'll be there at four-thirty."

One down, he triumphed, and called Marie-Victoire: "I have a mannequin; she'll be here at four-thirty and I'm sure that Ingara's dresses will fit her perfectly. Madame Suzanne must get everything ready; she'll have barely half an hour to try them on and she can't stay for the rehearsal."

"Thank you, Alan, you're a magician!"

"*France-Soir* . . . give me Monsieur X, please. Hello, Alan Harside from Forval here. I thought you would like to be the first to know that one of our mannequins committed suicide because she'd just turned forty. She left a terribly touching note which will make women everywhere weep. If you send someone right away and promise to print it on the first page of your last edition, I'll give you the letter and all the pictures you want of the girl."

"We'll be there! Meantime, I'll get to make-up and change the first page. Five minutes later and I couldn't have done it, my friend!"

Alan got everything ready in an envelope, plus a little story with the name Forval in every line. Then he called press agents, morning papers, *Women's Wear,* weeklies, in fact all of the press, radio, and television. He rubbed his hands, it was a terrific piece of publicity. You couldn't buy anything like it, not for tens of thousands! He had a grateful thought for Ingara: what a treasure, committing suicide just before the collection! She was really a fantastic girl! In fact he must organize her funeral: lots of flowers and every mannequin in Paris on hand. He must be sure not to have it conflict with the Saint Laurent showing. He sighed; obviously it wouldn't be as big as Dior's funeral, where you had to have an invitation to get into Saint-Honoré-D'Eylau, but it would still be something! If that didn't raise perfume sales at least ten per cent, he'd be hung!

The news spread through the house like a forest fire. People stopped in the corridors, whispering, sniffling. When she was so beautiful, how could she have been so unhappy? The little seamstresses had red eyes. The saleswomen took it as an opportunity to tell about all the suicides they had known over their long careers and sighed: "Imagine killing yourself at forty! That's childhood!" If only they could be that age again!

Chavanaux made a note to ask where he should send Ingara's salary and how the firm could get back the clothing that had been loaned her for the season. He remembered an actress who was buried in a superb pink crepe dress bordered in mink only lent her for a party, and how the widower had never wanted to pay for it. He thought that if Ingara had not worked in such an artificial world, where chic took the place of virtue and the first wrinkle killed, she would never have thought of committing suicide. And he imagined her quietly happy in her little Swedish village with an engineer husband and three beautiful blond children. The more he knew of it, the less he could stomach this world of false values. To succeed in it, he mumbled, you have to have a three-way mirror instead of a heart.

The rehearsal began at four-thirty. Everyone gathered in the salon: the saleswomen; the employees from the accounting department, who must be familiar with the models; the

141

chief supplier in case a fabric had to be changed later. Each time a customer wanted a garment in a fabric different from the original, even if it cost less than the original fabric, she must be sure to see that the final price was higher: there was always a charge for any change made.

Adrien and Marie-Victoire arrived last: they came from the dressing room where they had met the new mannequin. Alan was right, she could wear all Ingara's models perfectly. However, they looked quite different on her: she was less stately and more intimate, like Bach's music arranged by Mozart. Adrien, naturally immune to all feminine sex appeal, found her "vulgar," but Marie-Victoire praised her enthusiastically and thanked her for having come so promptly. Unfortunately she would not be able to stay for the rehearsal, but now that they knew she could wear Ingara's models, they could arrange things . . . as long as she could come at ten tomorrow morning.

All the women had brought notebooks to list the names and numbers of the models, with descriptions, for after tomorrow afternoon they must be able to find each garment requested by the impatient buyers as quickly as possible. The hairdressers were there, too, ready to decide on any changes to be made.

Marie-Victoire spoke to Chavanaux: "Chavanaux, my dear, it's going to be harder to keep track of the order of appearance than usual, since the girl who is replacing Ingara had to leave to go to Ricci, but never mind. Madame Suzanne will show Ingara's models by hand when they're supposed to appear so that we'll know what order they're in."

A thick silence greeted this statement, and Madame Suzanne held up Ingara's gowns with solemnity appropriate to those cushions covered with medals at state funerals. Everyone shivered and held her breath to see each of the twelve models deprived of life like shrouds for cold flesh. The audience only breathed again at the appearance of the other mannequins, quite alive, and the saleswomen once more made their usual bittersweet comments to make it plain that they weren't to be intimidated by a ghost. Madame Annie, the new one, who had never seen Ingara, was undisturbed and very enthusiastic over several garments. The old guard exchanged scornful looks as if to say: She's showing off, but it takes more than that to impress us.

Jean-Loup's first model passed unnoticed. It would have been necessary to show an ankle-length skirt when the fashion was at mid-thigh to make these so-called connoisseurs notice anything new. If the change was subtle, cloth more clinging, or a line followed the body more closely, they dismissed it by saying it looked like Vionnet or Poiret: they'd already seen that in the 1930s.

Jean-Loup came out of the dressing room to say to Marie-Victoire: "My last model is still on the cutting table. It would have held things up too much to put it together to show now. It's a Phileas Fogg coat which can take the place of that checked one you took out of the line: it has a faint geometric print in chestnut, black and white. Thank God we could find some trimmings at Printemps in the same shade of chestnut."

"Good. Have you given it a name?"

"It's number ninety-nine and I'd like to call it Vasarely."

"Perfect. One more, mesdames, and that will be all."

Marie-Victoire always enjoyed giving names to her dresses, and she was almost the only one who still did it; most of the other houses had adopted the little numbered card held up by each mannequin. But a name was easier to remember than a number. On the other hand, if the name was not well chosen or well pronounced, it could make for dubious jokes. But the best argument Marie-Victoire found for keeping this slightly old-fashioned tradition was that when there were sales, one could immediately spot the season when the dress was made, because they went from flowers to musicians, with cities and quarters of Paris in between, or, as today, painters.

Adrien sent another model forward.

"My dear Adrien, I think it's useless to show this gown to the press. Besides, I see there is only one pair of red shoes and we need them for the next one."

"It's a good customer dress," said Madame Nicole.

"I think so, too, and that's why it won't interest the press people. No use boring them. They would not care less about women being well dressed by a couturier. All they want is something sensational, and if they don't find it, they'll immediately put you in the 'little old lady' category!"

The mannequin stood quietly in the middle of the salon, waiting for a decision.

"If it's only a question of shoes, we can put it in later."

"No, really, believe me," Marie-Victoire persisted. "I'd love to wear it myself, but it is of no interest for tomorrow. And it's almost exactly like the one with the camel's hair coat."

"All right, all right," said Adrien, turning pointedly to the next mannequin. "Oh my, my little gray suit! Its white mink collar is all changed!"

"I see you've forgotten the Pumpernicke incident," Marie-Victoire snapped.

"I see, this is the first victim."

The saleswomen looked at each other and the one who used to wait on Pumpernicke stiffened: "May I ask what my customer has to do with this suit?"

"I'll explain it to you later, remind me to see you."

Another disagreeable aspect of this affair which Marie-Victoire had not thought of: the saleswoman would be furious at losing her commission on this regular customer.

The rest of the rehearsal went well enough. A few accessories were changed. Marie-Victoire insisted on getting rid of all dark-colored stockings worn with models in deep colors.

"I don't like them any more. Also, I want gloves with the coats. Not with the dresses, but you can't make me believe that an elegant woman goes out without gloves, especially in winter."

Jean-Loup spoke up. "An elegant woman has her heated car at the door. Gloves are 'little old lady.' "

"In that case, long live 'little old ladies.' At least little old ladies from Forval won't have chapped hands."

There was laughter. It was true, a woman without gloves in the city looked terrible, the saleswomen agreed. These days people dress all week long the way they do for a weekend in the country. Not so long ago no one would have dreamed of wearing the same outfit in Vichy and in Deauville. Today, in New York and Saint-Tropez both, women go without stockings when it's warm and wear winter sports outfits when it's cold. We'll all end up in quilted blue uniforms like China and the next thing we'll be breaking rocks in the roads too! Haute couture saleswomen are incorrigible capitalists.

After his embroidered gown with its tulle cape, Adrien announced: "We won't be showing the wedding gown. It will be finished in time for tomorrow, but only if nobody puts down her needle until eleven o'clock tonight."

"Well, it's certainly expensive enough, so let's hope it will be fabulous!" murmured Chavanaux.

Madame Sylvette, who had been called to the telephone, came back to the salon with her eyes popping like a madwoman's. She looked like a living statue of a "The Bearer of Bad Tidings" in the 1908 Salon of French Artists.

"Madame, madame, a terrible tragedy! Princess Herminie was badly injured this morning in an automobile accident! That

145

was her lady-in-waiting who just called. The whole order is canceled!"

There was a long silence, then Marie-Victoire said: "For once, Madame Sylvette, you're right. That is a real tragedy. The poor princess was really lovely, let's hope she won't be disfigured. God must be blind to allow such misfortunes! It's horrible to speak of money now, but it's a tragedy for the firm too . . . nearly 300,000 francs, not to mention the publicity!"

The other saleswomen gathered around Madame Sylvette with pitying looks, murmuring their condolences. Madame Nicole (who always put her foot in it), her head shaking, her jowls trembling, blotchy, mauve with too much white powder, like a strawberry gelatin on which someone had spilled flour, sniffled: "Never two without three! Oh my, what will happen next?"

Marie-Victoire, furious at the importance she attached to this kind of superstition, looked at Madame Nicole so fiercely that the poor old woman burst out sobbing. All these ladies, ready to commit the worst backstabbing among themselves and to carpet the corridors with banana skins under each others' feet, were immediately united in a spirit of solidarity when one of their number was attacked. Madame Nicole was immediately surrounded.

"Come, my poor Nicole, emotions like that are bad for your heart, come now, take your drops."

The youngest shook their heads. What a misfortune to work at such an age! Each one summoned her own reassuring mental images of bank books, treasury bonds, or retired husbands, feeble fortifications against impoverished old age.

Chavanaux approached Marie-Victoire: "Were any of the outfits already cut?"

"Unfortunately not. If they were, we would still be paid for them. The Princess was to come tomorrow evening after

146

the buyers' showing to see if she didn't like some of the new models better than the designs made specially for her. I had already told Madame Sylvette to ask her lady-in-waiting discreetly to make a deposit so that we would have some cash in hand. It's bad enough and that makes it even worse."

"It couldn't be worse than being paralyzed or God knows what at twenty-two!"

"Don't think me heartless, my dear, but I can't help feeling personally attacked by this last blow of fate, after the series of misfortunes which has fallen on our heads in the last four days. The disappointment of losing such a large order and such publicity overwhelms the sorrow I would normally feel for such an accident. I haven't read my horoscope lately, but it can't be very good!"

Alan came over to her: "Are you ready to go to the Ritz? It's seven o'clock."

"Oh yes, there's still that! Give me a few minutes to comb my hair and get my bag."

"I've learned something else that you ought to know. Can I come up with you?"

"Another piece of bad news?"

"I'm afraid so."

"Really, I've had my share for the day. Can't it wait until tomorrow?"

"I think you'd regret it if I didn't tell you."

"All right, let's go."

With resignation she looked at herself in the mirror as she powdered her nose.

"The person who is probably behind that idea of Fanny Wright's article for Big Mills of Indiana is none other than Oliver Mayer."

"What?" she dropped her powder puff and looked down at a cloud of pink powder on the white carpet in stupefaction.

147

"Oliver Mayer became a vice-president of Big Mills last month."

"But I've never spoken of him to you! How do you know that I know him?"

"It's my business to keep up with things. I'm sorry, but I didn't think it was a secret. People saw you together last year in the Balearics and one of my friends told me that you were having dinner together Friday evening at Maxim's. But I suspected you didn't know of his connection with Big Mills."

As she didn't answer, seeming to be busy cleaning up the powder, Alan went on: "But you're going to have to work out a solution for the firm anyway. Haute couture is no longer profitable as a primary operation: you are too much at the mercy of some accident like the Princess Herminie. Americans have skimmed the profits off French innovators for too long. If they had to hire great designers of their own, they would pay four times as much as they do for taking our ideas. Then they'd only have one line apiece instead of borrowing ideas from all the best in the world. We're a bunch of suckers. The only solution is to exploit your own ideas, like Cardin. Don't sell out to Big Mills. They've used really dirty methods. I'd like to invest in the kind of business you've been dreaming of: a luxury boutique where you could sell your own ready-to-wear to the whole world. I've told my father about the idea and he's ready to advance the money. Of course, if Clothilde would marry me it would make things easier."

This is blackmail! Marie-Victoire thought, and for a moment she forgot her rage at Oliver's treachery. At last, she said: "My dear, I love my firm, but not to the point of selling my daughter to save it. Besides, I have no control over her feelings, and while she likes you very much, I don't have any impression that she's in love with you. You have to be a little older than she is to appreciate the value of a marriage of

148

reason. Anyway, with her modern ideas, I can't quite see her living in Akron, Ohio. Even at my age I doubt if I could live . . ." she was about to say, in Dallas, she caught herself, "in America."

"Just the same, if I could have your blessing, I'd feel encouraged."

"My dear Alan, of course you have my blessing. I certainly prefer you to some bearded revolutionary, but don't depend on my influence on my daughter. Just between ourselves, it would probably be enough to finish her interest in you if she thought you were my official candidate. But I want you to understand clearly that my business and my daughter are two completely distinct matters, and if the first interests you, the second does not go with it. . . . Now, let's talk about this some other day, because I'm really very tired this evening. Let's go see this photographer at the Ritz and soften the blow for him a bit. I hope the police haven't already told him."

"All he had to do is read *France-Soir*."

"How would the reporters know? Have you the papers?"

"Here it is. Too bad Princess Herminie's accident cut Ingara's photograph by half, but you could say that our firm is the star of *France-Soir*. They mentioned that she ordered her whole trousseau from us."

Marie-Victoire sat down again. Ingara's photograph was there in the lower right on the first page: *"Haute Couture* Mannequin Commits Suicide. See page 8." She turned quickly to page 8, where a reproduction of the pathetic letter was spread. Marie-Victoire turned pale. "How dare you give them that letter?"

"But look, it's a marvelous article, pure gold as publicity! You'll see, all the papers will pick up the story tomorrow."

"Have you neither heart nor decency?"

"Oh now, look, decency and publicity . . ."

149

"So you're satisfied with yourself? That letter was addressed to me, you had no right to use it without my permission, it was an abuse of confidence! What will people think? To make use of such a tragedy for publicity, it's perfectly abominable! It is monstrous vulgarity! I won't dare show my face."

Alan was startled by her violent reaction. He had suspected that she would not approve of his use of the letter, but he thought that he would soon make her understand his reasons for doing so when she saw how much coverage it got.

Marie-Victoire went on: "If I were in that photographer's place I would bring you into court. At one time, duels were fought for less than that. You must have no sense of honor whatsoever and not only will we get bad publicity from it, but you have lowered the firm in general and me in particular to the level of scandal mongers. You should be doing publicity for a Pigalle night club, not for a haute couture house! It is absolutely essential that everyone be informed that I knew nothing of this story. You can cope with your journalistic friends and for a beginning, you can go to the Ritz alone. If that photographer is a man, I hope with all my heart he'll break your jaw . . . that would be excellent publicity! You can sell film clips to Paramount or Fox! I hope you realize that I have nothing but contempt for you."

She declaimed this like a speech from a Rostand play, Alan thought, but underneath he knew she was partly right.

"I'm really sorry, I shouldn't have used that letter, but I didn't think I'd get the photograph on the first page without it."

"So having the photograph on the front page of *France-Soir* is the height of success to you!"

"It's not so easy."

"If you like, I can tell you a dozen infallible ways. For one, Alan Harside, press agent for Marie-Victoire Forval, and tire

150

heir from Akron, was seen walking naked in the Place Vendôme."

"You're very witty!"

"I'm not witty, I'm sick at my stomach, and I wonder if I shouldn't call a photographer to immortalize the picture of Marie-Victoire Forval firing her press agent for vulgarity."

"You aren't serious?"

"Vulgarity is the one thing I've never forgiven anyone. As for Clothilde, if her criteria aren't quite the same as mine, don't deceive yourself about this, she can't stand it either. At this moment, the only way I can see of clearing myself in the eyes of the world is to get rid of you. If you can find a better way by tomorrow, we'll see. I cannot permit the world to believe that I gave that letter to the newspapers so that I could profit by the publicity. I am going home and try to sleep. It's quarter of eight. Maurice must have left. I haven't even the strength to get the car out of the parking lot. I'll take a taxi."

"I'll go get your car. I feel terrible that you're so upset by this story."

"You're not an entirely bad boy, but there are some things you simply don't understand."

She drove her car like a somnambulist. She was so tired she thought of almost nothing but her bathtub. She imagined herself floating, her ears closed to the outside world and full of watery noises, her hair drifting softly around her shoulders: her whole being encased like a foetus! If only I hadn't told Thérèse that I wouldn't be dining at home this evening, she would have brought me a tray in bed. Why did I tell her that? Oh yes, Oliver was to dine with me. I don't want to see him. Oliver conniving with *Thread Needle News,* it's too awful! He can't want to make a fool of me that way!"

In the elevator, she leaned against the paneling and closed her eyes. She had the key to the apartment in her hand when

151

she got to her floor and saw a man standing there. She was about to scream with fright when she recognized Oliver.

"You're very late. Did you forget that I was to come for you at seven-thirty?"

Without further ado he took the key from her hand and pushed her into the foyer, closing the door with his foot and plunging them both in darkness.

Fear, then anger and rage at his presumption made Marie-Victoire lose all control. Before she knew what she was going to do, she slapped Oliver hard, on one cheek and then the other.

He quickly caught her arm in an iron grip and, letting her feel his strength, twisted it a bit.

The moment of blankness over, Marie-Victoire took a deep breath and tried to steady herself. Above all, no hysterics in front of this cad: never! Forcing her voice down two octaves, and making herself speak slowly: "I'll thank you to let go my arm. I'd like to turn on the lights."

Oliver, without a word, let her arm drop and Marie-Victoire switched on the lights. She blinked when she saw Oliver two paces away, with whitened cheeks and a lump beginning to swell and bleed slightly where her big ring had hit him.

This man is utterly maddening, she thought, but continuing in her role of woman-who-keeps-a-cool-head-under-all-circumstances, she rose to the attack: "Don't expect me to apologize. You deserve a dozen more. I'd prefer to have heard from you about your connection with Big Mills instead of from my press agent." And moving toward the door to the corridor, she opened it wide: "Now, please be good enough to leave at once."

Oliver, quicker than she, closed the door again and leaned against it: "I will not. Don't think that I waited a half hour sitting in the dark on your staircase to be slapped for the first

152

time in my life and then just disappear—even my mother never hit me! And at least in America the halls are lighted! This French system of three minutes of light when the button is pushed is the kind of penny-pinching you'd expect from an underdeveloped nation! I came to talk to you and you're going to listen."

"I am not. There's nothing you can tell me that I don't already know. So if you're going to be difficult . . ." and she moved toward the telephone.

"You're not going to make such a fool of yourself as to call the police to get rid of a man who spent Friday night here! Come now, be reasonable!"

Marie-Victoire thought she would explode at the sound of the word reasonable, but she had a strongly developed sense of the ridiculous and had never had anything to do with the police, except on this very morning.

"Very well, allow me to go to my room, then, I've had a very tiring day. When you're tired of waiting, you know where the door is."

Oliver was not the man to be overwhelmed by the grand manner. "Please stop acting the outraged princess and listen to me. I am under no obligation to justify myself; business is business. But, I'm not scheming to take over your firm for nothing. I've been on the board of directors of Big Mills for a month. Your business is a very small matter to them, but it's natural that they want to buy it at the lowest possible price. Will you believe me when I tell you that I hadn't heard of the tactics they were using until this afternoon from Lefebvre? I can understand your anger, and in a way I even find it flattering—it proves that you care a bit about me. And I saw the announcement of Princess Herminie's accident and the news about your mannequin. I was rather surprised to see that pathetic letter in print, though. That isn't like you."

153

"It's so little like me that I am going to fire my press agent, Alan Harside, your brilliant compatriot, who betrayed my confidence. He said 'What a touching letter! Let me have it until this evening.' And I, like an idiot, didn't question him. Meantime, he sent it to *France-Soir*. It's absolutely abominable. You yourself were shocked! Really, today has been too much!"

"If you want me to I'll go away and let you rest."

He was already at the door when, in a small voice, Marie-Victoire asked if he didn't need a compress for his cheek. She added that she had some ointment, an old herbal recipe of her grandmother's, which would heal the inflammation in a few hours. Oliver turned, and with a smile he tried to make as little triumphant as possible, accepted.

In the bathroom, she made him sit on the little stool in front of her dressing table. She began by washing her hands and removing her rings.

"That's quite a weapon you've got there. . . ."

She smiled and busied herself with taking a bandage and alcohol out of her medicine cabinet.

"Grandmother's ointment will make it feel better right away. She used it to heal all my bumps and scratches when I was little."

With both hands, she rubbed his cheeks so gently that it was more a caress than massage, but she stopped as soon as she saw his eyes fixed on her face. And he saw through her; putting his arms around her waist, he pulled her to him.

Marie-Victoire, her hands covered with cream, could not put them on his shoulders to push herself away. Leaning back, she withdrew the upper part of her body. Oliver gently increased the pressure.

"Come on, tigress . . ." and getting up without loosening his grip, he took Marie-Victoire in his arms.

Still holding her hands up, she had such a comic air of

supplication that he burst out laughing and kissed her on the nose. Then, keeping her pressed close to him, he made her turn around so that she could reach the box of Kleenex on her dressing table. Marie-Victoire wiped her hands, while Oliver, his body close to hers, covered the nape of her neck with long kisses.

Then he licked her ear and bit the lobe; he knew what effect this would produce. Marie-Victoire closed her eyes, not wanting to look in the dressing table mirror at the reflection of what her mind called a defeat, while her whole body told her secretly that it was a victory.

Oliver took advantage of this short moment of weakness to lift her up and carry her to the bed. He didn't trust her reactions and still held her with one hand while he undressed her and took the telephone off the hook.

What a man, sighed Marie-Victoire, he knows exactly how to unzip my dress! Is he copying them on top of everything else?

She gave in completely, though trying not to respond too quickly and too fully to Oliver's fingers and mouth as they moved over her whole body. But she could not keep her skin from shivering and her breasts from offering themselves to the big hands that knew so well how to hold them.

Because she had not opened her eyes, she gave a cry of surprise when Oliver's body came down on hers and his soft warm skin met her own with a tremendous shock which went through her like electricity. She completely abandoned herself, moving with him, greeting his desire, answering this hunger that seemed to possess him. The joy he gave her was long, intense, full to overflowing.

She held back nothing, letting herself go completely, discovering in herself groans she had never heard and desires of which she had never been conscious. She surprised herself by asking, demanding, even begging. Oliver, intent on triggering Marie-Victoire's most intimate responses, forgot his own pleasure for the moment so as to devote himself fully to her joy.

He had no trouble surmounting those barriers that Marie-Victoire had unconsciously built in her years of solitude, damming a sensuality that she had glimpsed only briefly when she was very young, and that had just begun to surge again since she had known Oliver.

In a moment when Oliver was making love very, very slowly, as if he wanted to waken every fiber of her womb, Marie-Victoire felt a kind of chrysalis bursting within herself as if she were witnessing her own birth.

Drifting slowly upward from her ecstasy, she opened her eyes on a grave and tender face where a slightly troubled look was filtering through the passion. Oliver, reassured by Marie-Victoire's innocently wondering look, measured the extent of his triumph. She murmured very low, so that he almost had to read her lips: "Thank you . . ."

In as long as he could remember, never had another woman behaved with such natural simplicity in his arms, with such real abandon mixed with such great sexual need. Not leaving her body, he let himself down on his forearms to scrutinize her more closely.

Marie-Victoire seemed to be surrounded by a mist which softened the contours of her firm body. A light sweat made her skin shine softly, she seemed both near and far at the same time, lost in herself, in the transmutation that he had worked at and achieved with the patience of some insect simultaneously inseminating and removing the substance from the heart of a flower.

Neither of them wanted to stop. Both felt they had got through to the other side of the looking glass, that they were

156

living in another rhythm, the rhythm of two bodies in harmonious dialogue. They were so united that both fell asleep at the same moment. He did not leave her body until dawn and Marie-Victoire gave a long groan as if he had taken half her being from her. She confessed to him later that she had had a horrible feeling of becoming an empty shell thrown up on a dry and hostile beach. When at last she came to the surface, she felt she was dying of hunger.

"Thérèse doesn't come until eight o'clock, so we have two hours. Darling, I'm starving; I haven't eaten anything in twenty-four hours. I'm going to make some bacon and eggs."

She washed, dressed in a beautiful *broderie anglaise* negligee which made her look young, cleaned the traces of yesterday's make-up from her face, and left her hair down. In the kitchen she quickly prepared a substantial breakfast and took it to the terrace. The world seemed newborn: the one Adam and Eve enjoyed before they ate the apple. The sky was clear and pink, the air was cool and gentle, a light mist was rising from the Seine. Oliver was already dressed and watching her as he leaned on the wrought-iron railing of the terrace.

"How well you go with the apse of Notre Dame!" said Marie-Victoire.

He was surprised at this odd compliment and thought she hadn't said what she meant: "What do you mean by that?"

"During parties I've often observed men standing on this terrace, and there aren't many who fit into the view. Unless they have a civilized background they are reduced in stature by its beauty. By the way, where does your family come from?"

"Portugal."

"The nobility of the Jewish people, if I'm not mistaken."

"So they say. I still have relatives who are bankers in Lisbon. My grandfather left because after his mother died, his father married a priest-ridden Catholic. She undertook to convert the whole family, especially her stepson, whom she dreamed of making a priest. But there wasn't much of the priest in him—all he wanted was a certain rabbi's daughter and oil wells! And that's how my grandfather came to settle in Dallas."

He smiled at the French mania for only liking or trusting people after they knew "where they came from." He himself had never given any thought to his European ancestors; he was American and judged his contemporaries by their intrinsic worth, not by their family background. He believed in hard work and native shrewdness, and was proud that he had increased his own inheritance at least tenfold. He would not have cared if his father had been only a poor furrier from a ghetto. But if that were the case, he thought my profile wouldn't look so well against that damned cathedral! The French are really decadent!

Like an old married couple they breakfasted almost in silence, for both of them were hungry. There are certain blessed moments in life when everything reaches a perfection one does not risk spoiling by a word.

"There's nothing better than bacon and eggs when you're hungry."

"I've never eaten jam like this."

"It's made of figs and lemons; I made it in Baussigue."

"Baussigue?"

"It's our family property; it's completely remote from modern life."

"Come now, modern life isn't as bad as that."

"I find it worse and worse. If the hippies weren't so dirty, I'd agree with them."

"You? Fighter that you are? Come on!"

158

"You're right; when I was in boarding school in England, my friends called me 'the fighting frog!'"

He laughed. "That fits you very well, my darling fighting frog! Look at my cheek!" And he took her in his arms. "I'll leave now so I won't meet your maid, who looks like a dragon! I'll come to Place Vendôme at about noon to see how things went with the press. If you have time, we'll have lunch at the Ritz."

Dreamily, Marie-Victoire went back to bed, and before falling asleep she decided: I'll tell Thérèse that I had dinner last evening with a friend. I'm really too tired to wash the dishes and put them away."

That morning, Clothilde was even worse than on the two preceding days. Her abdomen was hard and swollen and she was almost unconscious. Sometimes she felt as if she were roasting and threw off all her covers, sometimes she shivered, and the sweat that had soaked her two minutes before felt like ice water. After a long time, she realized that the sound she heard was not just her teeth chattering but someone knocking on the door. She got up, and leaning against the wall, managed to go to it and open it. Simultaneously, a flux of blood burst from her and spread in a pool at her feet. Agnès had to drag her back to her bed, for she had fainted. Terrified by the size of the hemorrhage, its dreadful odor, and the hardness of Clothilde's abdomen, Agnès decided Clothilde must go to the hospital but did not know how she would manage to get her there alone. She was hurrying downstairs to telephone the police station for an ambulance when she heard someone coming up the stairs. It was Pierre, coming back to get his laundry.

He entered the apartment, saw the frightful spectacle, and muttered like a madman: "Poor little thing, if she had only listened to me."

Agnès called the police and rushed back upstairs. She tried to clean her friend a bit, but soon used up all the cotton. Almost fainting herself, she opened the window. Fortunately the ambulance came in record time, the attendants rushed in, put Clothilde, wrapped in a blanket, on a stretcher, asked Agnès to put Clothilde's bag beside her, and drove post haste to the Hôtel-Dieu, the nearest hospital.

Agnès was left with Pierre in the little apartment, and neither of them dared speak. From the window, they watched the men in white shove Clothilde into the ambulance like bakers putting a loaf of bread into an oven. "If only they can save her!" they both said at the same moment. They smiled at each other sadly, and Agnès added: "I'd better let her mother know. I don't know if they'll call her from the hospital."

"Yes, you'd better; I'd rather you did it than I."

Agnès looked at him without saying anything. Men have enough courage to kill other men when they know they'll get marksmen's medals; when it's a matter of taking real responsibility, there's no one around.

"Ciao, you lousy revolutionary. I hope you aren't very proud of your ideas on abortion. If she'd done it in a hospital she wouldn't be between life and death today."

With that, she left him to go and telephone from the bistro where Clothilde always made calls. She tried a dozen times but the number was always busy, so at last she gave up.

Thérèse noticed that the telephone was off the hook at the same moment when Agnès gave up trying to call.

"That's funny, madame, that's twice the telephone has been off the hook. Did madame take it off?"

"No, Thérèse, I don't understand what could have happened, no one called me yesterday evening."

Thérèse tightened her lips. Mysterious things were happening in this house. Someone had eaten breakfast with her in the evening, so Madame said. Popoff was sulking, Mademoiselle didn't come home, Madame was dead tired, and the bed was all messed up. I wouldn't be surprised if that American were at the bottom of it. And before her eyes there arose the horrible vision of men's shirts to wash and iron! Waiting on two single women was ideal, but a man in the house complicated everything. They'd eat meals together, he'd dirty lots of linen, he'd never be satisfied. She shivered. And if her mistress should go to America? Going back to Baussigue was all right for vacations, but Thérèse had a passion for the movies—she spent almost all her extra money on them—and there were no movies in Baussigue. To get another job in Paris with "strangers" like Mitzie or Lydia, how awful! She crossed herself quickly to ward off bad luck. Madame really wasn't so bad! She almost felt affection for Marie-Victoire, who was still in the bathroom.

"I hope madame's collection is going to go well. What dress shall I lay out?"

"Good heavens, I don't know."

"Madame doesn't know?"

Thérèse couldn't get over it; usually the outfit for the day of the press showing was planned at least three months in advance.

"Oh yes, of course, what am I thinking of? Adrien decided that I should wear the green linen dress with the coral brooch and the shoes I had dyed in the same color."

"I'm afraid it's going to rain."

"How can that be? It was a beautiful day at six o'clock."

"Madame got up at six?"

"Oh . . . no . . . that is, I woke up and went back to sleep again."

This time there was no doubt of it, Thérèse grumbled to herself, the American must have spent the night here.

Chapter VI

With the dress for her press showing selected, Marie-Victoire also had to compose her face to erase the traces of the trials of the past two days. With her favorite cosmetics, she made up her mask of successful couturière. Unfortunately, she thought, the mask is all there is; my heart is not as hard as my face. Women who can stay soft and permissive all their lives are lucky, but the ones who have no protector are forced to wear armor. Strange how the whole world applauds women who take on masculine responsibilities, astronauts and the rest. But the ones who deserve the most admiration for their courage may be the ones who don't try to compete with men, leave the management in their hands so as not to damage their fragile self-confidence . . . though they're quite as capable. I don't think you'd find many successful women who are satisfied with their romantic lives. Perhaps men will accept true equality some day, but for the moment they still prefer pretty admirers. There's a lesson to be learned from Japan, where geishas are paid an enormous hourly rate just to tell a customer that his gold teeth are as fascinating as his tie.

. . . Come, come, my girl, enough philosophy! Your job is to dress those fragile little things so that they can better win the man of their dreams or make their dear girl friends jealous. The ones who dress to please themselves are in the minority, but they are the only ones who have the right to be called elegant women.

After a last critical glance, she decided on a pair of beige gloves after trying on some white ones. She looked for the key to the Austin in her bag.

"Where did I put that miserable car last night? I remember finding a parking place and not taking it to the garage. I was so tired that it can't be far away."

In fact, the little black and beige Austin stood quietly at the sidewalk just opposite the house, like a domestic animal, and purred like a friendly cat before it leaped forward.

Place Vendôme; she must see that everything was in order.

The first thing to see to was the assistant saleswomen's dress and she asked the Princess to call them together. In some houses, like Dior, these were young women who received a fixed salary and who soon went on to become regular saleswomen in some second-rank house. But Marie-Victoire had a different system. Each year, one or two commercial schools sent her very young girls who drew a low salary and spent a two-year term in her salons. These apprentices were obviously not from the best of society, which was why some saleswomen in haute couture were unbelievably vulgar in spite of their contact with a sophisticated clientele.

To avoid major errors of taste or outfits that were too shabby, since some of these young girls came from very poor families for whom this period represented a real sacrifice, the house furnished them with navy blue uniforms. All of them envied the mannequins and tried to imitate them with make-up, or by wearing earrings or an elaborate coiffure. So it was important to check them from time to time, comb some of them out, and remove excess make-up. Even footwear was a source of contention; it was necessary to forbid boots in winter and white shoes in summer. It was quite hard to keep these girls in order. Certain saleswomen, only too happy to have slaves under them, brutalized them with errands, advice, or rebukes on the pretext of training them, and it was quite usual to see one of them sobbing in a corner like a child. But other saleswomen tried to make life easier for them, remembering their own apprenticeship. They realized what a disastrous effect the whims of vain customers could have on a fifteen-year-old mind when compared to the thankless labor of a poor family. Luxury trades in general, and haute couture in particular, may support a great many people, but they also represent a crying social injustice to the working class.

All the little group was there, waiting for inspection. Marie-Victoire, who called all of them *ma cocotte* because she could never remember their names and seldom their faces, told one to take off her first communion medal, another her earrings.

"Madame, my ears are pierced," the blushing girl said.

"My poor child, I can see that; it's dreadful."

Marie-Victoire had always fulminated against the bad taste of parents who mutilated their child this way.

"Try to cover them up with your hair."

Coming to a lovely blonde with her hair in a simple knot, her skin smooth and pink, devoid of all make-up: "You, ma cocotte, you stay with me to show the journalists to their places." Then, turning to the others: "Here is a perfect hair style; you should all imitate it."

The girl turned red, and the others were furious: they would make her pay dearly for the "boss's" sudden favor.

164

Marie-Victoire asked the Princess in an aside: "What is her name?"

"Christiane, madame, she's Madame Annie's, the new saleswoman's 'baby.'"

"She's a darling, have her mother come in, she ought to learn English, she's worth taking some trouble with."

And another she called up: "You, I'd like you to spray all the rooms with Ah! It should smell delicious here. You three, you go to the dressing room to help Madame Suzanne dress the mannequins. The others will move between the entrance and the salons to show everyone their places. The cards that have an S in the corner are for the second salon, an E for the entrance and an I for the first salon, which is the most important. Don't make any mistakes about this. The numbers go clockwise. In case of any complaint in the first salon, call me. If it's in one of the others, ask Monsieur Harside or one of his assistants. Don't forget that the mannequins are the only ones in the house who have a right not to smile. I don't know who started that idiotic style of thinking it's more elegant to walk around with a stony face than to be friendly. Don't forget that this is neither a fair nor your cousin's wedding. You must be friendly but dignified so that our guests will feel honored to have been invited. If you make the house vulgar or disorderly, you can be sure that the guests will behave badly too. But if you are quiet and efficient, they will be polite. If you remember this advice in your daily life too, you'll be glad of it."

A young girl arrived very much out of breath with a pile of press releases in English. "Will you look these over?"

"Yes, of course."

Many of the journalists, though they made great scenes to be sure of getting a seat, were satisfied to copy word for word the description the house had provided. The models were

165

generally described in flowery terms and instead of simply saying that the gowns had floating panels, the releases would say: Monsieur X . . . transforms women into dreamlike butterflies this season, whose fluttering rainbow-hued wings capture our hearts. . . ."

Marie-Victoire had always said this kind of literature turned her stomach. Nine times out of ten the designer only liked other boys, not butterflies, and the so-called message of haute couture made her laugh, for these gentlemen's ideals were no higher than the cash register. If the reporters of *Cantal Libéré* and those of the *Petit Patriote Normand* wanted to write in this old-fashioned and ridiculous way about couture, they ought to invent their own asininities. Besides, she didn't see why anyone should pay someone to write this kind of treacle, when all he had to do was literally describe the trends of the collection.

So the release was very much simplified and abbreviated to telegraphic form. It spoke of colors, fabrics, lengths, widths, and sleeve styles. Marie-Victoire had translated it into English herself, and if the reporters added flourishes, at least she didn't feel responsible for them.

Suddenly she jumped. A gross typo was printed in capitals. In place of *cut* was the word *cunt,* which was quite impossible, she explained emphatically, it was a four-letter word which could not be printed in newspapers. Let everyone get to work on it: two hundred corrections wasn't such an enormous job. It must be crossed out with a felt pen so that the word couldn't be seen underneath and the correction written above, or all of America would be laughing at them. She called back the second saleswomen and told them to distribute it as quickly as possible among the saleswomen and show them the correction.

Tension mounted like the tide at Mont-Saint-Michel. With the press release, what was called an outline of the trends

166

was distributed. It was a very stylized drawing that the dailies were permitted to publish immediately.

The Chambre Syndicale had worked out all these rules on immediate publication of designs in a series of complicated negotiations with the couture houses. The Chambre wanted to protect the interests of the specialized magazines that would only appear a month after the collections. Then, too, all that buyers would have had to do to make up a bargain collection each season would have been to copy newspaper illustrations. Unfortunately, the situation wasn't so simple, since Madame Publicity, the Great Devourer of our time, would have lost her bread and butter.

Some houses thought that by resigning from the Chambre Syndicale they could still show their models and continue to profit by the publicity given to others. Chanel began this. Since she never changed her line, she wasn't risking much. Inexplicably, houses like Balenciaga and Givenchy, which made it a point of honor not to receive journalists until a month after everybody else, in spite of this got an enormous amount of publicity in *Women's Wear Daily,* which published dozens of sketches of mysterious origin. This put those who had been faithful to the Chambre Syndicale into a cold rage, for they realized that in spite of its good intentions, the Chambre had hindered them more than it had helped them. No one wanted to be its president, a title which automatically invited the maledictions of some three hundred journalists. Now each house followed its own policy. Marie-Victoire still respected the ukases of the Chambre Syndicale, which had become more flexible this year, authorizing three photos of models chosen by the house in addition to sketches.

Marie-Victoire examined the sketches, which were to be distributed at the same time as the press releases, and made a little face. Adrien didn't draw badly, but if his sketches were perfectly legible for the workroom, they were a bit flat and "little old ladyish" for a newspaper. If only he would let me have Joe Eula or Kenneth Paul Block do them, she said to herself, they'd be much more attractive and it would be well worth the expense, but he would be so annoyed that she didn't have the courage to do it to him. She went to inspect the buffet.

When the table where the Princess usually sat was removed, the landing was large enough for the buffet to be placed at one end of it. The three maîtres d'hôtel, the same ones as usual, were busy building a variety of edible pyramids. Always interested in food, Marie-Victoire asked if this were the chicken puff pastry she'd been told about.

"Yes, madame, it's always a great success and disappears before anything else when we serve it."

"It really looks very good."

She would have liked to taste it, but she didn't dare to be greedy in front of her staff.

"I told them to be sure to have iced tea. Is it made?"

"Madame is right, though it isn't much in demand. Less so than champagne anyway, especially with foreigners."

I wonder, she said to herself, who will be the first to dare break this whole terribly expensive tradition, especially when you think that the big wheels of the profession, the Eugenia Sheppards, make it a point of honor never to eat anything, and the ones who drink up the champagne are the parasites and even the saleswomen.

Alan's assistants were placed at a little table at the head of the staircase where they could check each invitation. In case of an unknown, they would also ask to see his press card. In general, and especially on the first day, everyone had to be legitimately invited; gate crashers waited until the surveillance was a bit more relaxed. The biggest problem this time would be to keep out the journalists who had invitations for the following days. So the two assistants must first check the date entered on the cards.

Since the whole reception system was in order, Marie-Victoire decided to check the dressing room next.

If the studio of a couture house is its brain, the mannequins' dressing room is really its heart. And on the day of the collection, it was beating like a mad thing. When she entered, Marie-Victoire saw that Jean-Loup was there before her and at once she felt that something odd was going on. Respecting the hierarchy, she spoke to the wardrobe mistress, dear Madame Suzanne, who seemed tense.

Today she had an enormous amount of work to do, which was more than just a matter of massaging the neck of one of the young ladies (a specialty of hers) or giving others smelling salts. But on the days of collections, the mannequins really had to be at death's door before they complained, for it was in their own interest to be noticed and hired by reporters to model clothing for magazines.

Since morning, Madame Suzanne had been on the house telephone getting the models sent up from the workrooms. Thanks to the big chart, reworked for a final time by Marie-Victoire and placed in the middle of the dressing room, she knew exactly what she must get from the workrooms and where each garment should be hung. The mannequins always followed each other in the same order, and it was not unusual, if no one kept an eye on the line-up, to see a girl dressed from head to toe waiting behind the curtain while the preceding one who belonged in the salon was still in her girdle.

So each mannequin had her outfits arranged in the order in which she was to show them, and even the temporary mannequins who didn't speak a word of French managed very well. But it wasn't only the garments; there were acces-

sories too. In front of the place where each of the mannequins put on her make-up, Madame Suzanne had placed a
shoebox in which she had put jewels and colored pantyhose.

When the dressing room had had a dozen permanent mannequins, there had been time for many refinements, but now that
she had only five or six, everything became much more complicated. Stockings and accessories couldn't be changed without
slowing down the presentation, and a collection must go as
quickly as possible if you didn't want your audience to go to
sleep.

Madame Suzanne indicated to Marie-Victoire with a look
that Daphne was the fly in the ointment, and on the pretext
of showing her the hats that were hanging outside the dressing
room just behind the curtain which opened onto the salon,
she told her the story in a low voice.

"Monsieur Jean-Loup came in. He began giving instructions
to Adelaide and Veronica, who are wearing his models, saying
that they were the only fashionable ones in the collection,
that all the others were all 'little old ladyish.' So Daphne
made a face and hissed that obviously a whore couldn't very
well look like a little old lady without losing her clientele.
Adelaide asked if Daphne meant her. Daphne answered that
you really had to be pretty desperate to agree to wear certain
things, etc., etc. Daphne went out for a few moments and
while I wasn't looking Monsieur Jean-Loup stuck a big hatpin
with the point up in Daphne's chair cushion. When she sat down
the pin went into her flesh so far that the cushion stuck to her
buttock. Poor girl, it bled a lot, and after I washed it with
alcohol, I had to put a bandage on it. That's really wicked,
what he did, not worthy of a designer! And today, when
everyone's thinking of Ingara's death! How can you respect
him after that? Monsieur Adrien wouldn't do a thing like that!"

Marie-Victoire sighed. Impossible to make a fuss an hour before the collection. Daphne was really an idiot and Jean-Loup was a nasty little boy, but he had made a real effort for her, and this was no moment to scold him.

"Madame Suzanne, I woudn't want you to think that I would have dreamed of giving Ingara's letter to the papers. It was Monsieur Alan."

"Oh, I *am* glad! I was really surprised."

The assistants of Alexandre, the hairdresser, had arrived. They were very young men dressed in too-tight clothes. They got the hairpieces ready and began to do their last comb-outs or raise puffed hair with the tails of their combs, spraying copiously. Aurore was very nervous and sprayed her armpits with anti-perspirant one more time, for she was haunted by the fear of rings of sweat under her arms. Véronique was likely to break out in red spots at the slightest emotion and was doing breathing exercises as her doctor had recommended. Amalia had forgotten to shut the toilet door and one of the temporary Americans, in Paris for the season, recoiled in horror when she passed by: "Disgusting!" Svena, the Swede, gave unintelligible cries; she had lost a contact lens, she was nearsighted as a mole and only spoke a few words of French; finally it was understood from her gestures that she needed help in finding it; it had fallen on her powder box and Suzanne fished it out. Adelaide carefully pulled on her pantyhose and complained about their length. The fact of having to change from one color tights to another to match different outfits had complicated the timing of the showing a good deal, and because of it an extra mannequin had to be hired.

The little assistant saleswomen busied themselves arranging the models at Suzanne's command and stared greedily at the mannequins making up their faces. They painted at least four different colors on their eyelids and glued enormous curled eyelashes to their upper and lower lids. Close up, the result

171

was grotesque and very ugly; it looked like a spider's nest. But from a distance, even those who had only shoe buttons seemed to have the most beautiful eyes in the world.

Adrien arrived and said: "Hello, girls, I hope everything is going well."

They all answered together: "Yes, monsieur, very well!"

Except for Daphne, who clothed herself in wounded dignity and ostentatiously sat on one buttock as she put on her make-up.

Adrien looked at the big chart where under each manne-quin's name was the list of her models and their names, their numbers, and a little square of the fabric of which they were made. For a last time he wondered whether it was right to group all the blacks and all the reds together or if it would have been better to have held out against it. Cardin had been known to leave four or five mannequins wearing the same style dress on the stage at the same time. But, he calculated, that must have taken at least eighteen mannequins: easy to see that he was rich! He looked at Jean-Loup's coat and began to regret not having used that fabric himself.

"Your coat is really stunning!"

Jean-Loup shrugged. He hadn't missed Adrien's conde-scending tone, and he turned his back on him.

Adrien said nothing, but he was furious. He turned to Daphne, murmuring: "You'd think his five models were the only ones worth showing and the rest of the collection was of no interest. Really, he's like a child who's just made some-thing with his first Meccano set! What a bore!" He sighed. "How exhausting it is to have to fight all the time." He felt so tired that even the excitement of the opening didn't make his heart beat the way it used to. Once he would have had stage fright gnawing his stomach, but at the same time he would have felt as high as if he had drunk a bottle of champagne. It seemed

172

to him today that everything was futile, that he was walking down a Métro tunnel, he would never be able to get back to the fresh air, and nothing seemed real.

"Why," he went on, still speaking to Daphne, "spend so much energy, so much talent and money to make elegant clothes? Elegance . . . it's an old-fashioned word. People are still elegant in the provinces, but in the big cities you have to be 'far out.' Anyway, they say clothes give people neuroses, and that all we have to do to get rid of them is to go naked. We'd all better become masseurs instead of couturiers. We can't fool ourselves any more, the haute couture of the good old days have been dead ever since couturiers started showing their ready-to-wear collection three months before the haute couture line. They've made themselves old-fashioned, like those stupid insects whose name I've forgotten that eat their own legs. . . . It was really a pleasure to dress a society woman, to see one's masterpiece worn where it belonged, with proper accessories for each hour of the day. These days, manufacturers copy everything they can from couture. . . . How can we ever say that we still create fashion? If hippies start wearing Indian styles, that's enough to make so-called haute couture—it's only high in terms of prices—show fringed deerskin dresses and forehead bands next season. I don't remember which head of a couture house was frank enough to say on television that nowadays haute couture is for old women and hunchbacks who can't find their size in ready-made clothes. If it wasn't tactful, it certainly had a grain of truth in it.

"The young designers come right out and admit that special customers no longer interest them. What they want is to see their clothing worn by the maximum number of young people of both sexes around the world: so they multiply their outlets and manufacture in quantity. But even if I had a chance to do that kind of couture, I don't think I could."

173

Daphne realized that he was talking to himself, not to her, and ostentatiously turned her back. He hardly noticed and continued to vent his bitterness and his desire to go into another profession.

"Looks out of sorts, our 'Mother Adrien,'" said Jean-Loup under his breath to Adelaide. "She's losing her grip and if the boss doesn't offer me her place, I'll have to split this place fast. If the Yank I'm meeting this evening really wants me to work on Seventh Avenue and if he looks nice—zap! I'm off for the land of hamburgers and gold-plated Texans! Or even a middle-aged but gilt-edged baby doll! Although the feminine species do not have a very good reputation over there. Well, we'll see: I'm still young and beautiful!" And he preened in the big mirror that covered one wall of the dressing room. He was wearing a new outfit of plum-colored velvet with a turquoise shirt, and he was already visualizing his photograph on the first page of *Women's Wear Daily.*

A big bunch of flowers arrived for Adelaide, who put it carelessly on top of a cupboard. Suzanne murmured to Marie-Victoire: "If only she would marry the boy who sent those flowers. He's very rich, and I saw him the other evening; he's not bad at all. But she's rather flighty, and I'm afraid this one won't end any better than the affair with the Venezuelan last year."

Being a mannequin was a hard profession, and the papers were full of sob-sister stories about their ephemeral careers. Madame Suzanne had collected and hidden anything that looked like a newspaper, and she had forbidden anyone to mention Ingara's death. She'd also got rid of a woman who wanted to interview them all and tape their sobs.

Maurice had received strict orders not to let any reporters in. But how could he tell the difference between a fashion reporter and a news reporter? Like sheep, the other papers had all copied *France-Soir* and were trying to outdo each other. The mannequins' union had already taken advantage of the occasion to protest against foreigners invading the market and to demand that a higher percentage of French girls be hired in every house.

The temporary Americans laboriously explained that they did not understand how Ingara could have felt so desperate at forty. In America, they said, there were plenty of mannequins in the big stores who were neither terribly young nor terribly thin. They circulated among tables in restaurants for ladies in town for shopping to watch as they consumed calories and imagined themselves as well-dressed as women of normal weight. It was a very sensible idea, they added, for those ladies couldn't identify with a sylph of eighteen any more than they could with a ballerina doing entrechats in *Swan Lake*.

And in any case, there was a real question as to whether showing weird-looking dresses on mannequins hadn't turned certain timid women away from haute couture. The reaction of a normal woman was to skip over the photographs in fashion magazines where the mannequins wore butterflies painted on their cheeks or green wigs on their heads to jazz up uninteresting dresses. Marie-Victoire had always refused to indulge in this kind of buffoonery. It was always a serious psychological error to call attention to something other than the object for sale. While the buyer was being amused by the tattooed mannequins, she forgot to look at the dress.

Marie-Victoire consulted her watch and saw it was time to go back to welcome the reporters.

The tailors and the first hands were grouped at the top of the staircase, as conscious of not being part of the extravagant world around them as a worker from the Rolls-Royce factory meeting his well-waxed product parked in front of an embassy.

Madame Sylvette was waiting for "her" viscountess and

175

"her" duchess. Madame Estelle was waiting for Estée Lauder, Madame Callianis, and Claudia Cardinale, who, she hoped, would make appointments. The other saleswomen were vaguely jealous and jeering, except for Mademoiselle Huguette who "had" the biggest customer of all, literally and figuratively, the good Madame Durand, and who frequently remarked: "Stars are all very well, but I can count on mine for real money! And I don't have to give her any presents either! When I think that I had to put up a fight to get her an invitation for today, it's unbelievable that anyone could be such a snob!"—all this with a vengeful gesture of her chin toward Marie-Victoire.

Chavanaux, in his eternal gray suit and dreary tie, was quite nervous. By this time he knew that dresses couldn't be sold like aspirin tablets (his first job was in Rhône-Poulenc) and he learned to recognize the value of an unsalable model that "made" a page in *Paris-Match*. He also realized that the best publicity couldn't be bought and, anyway, at 5,000 francs a page in *Vogue,* your money didn't go very far. This season he hoped that the spectacular unsalable models wouldn't outnumber the reasonable ones, for, though you needed publicity, you also needed buyers! Would they achieve the ideal balance this season? Although he had already seen the collection he could not guess what the journalists were going to think, and he stared at these ogres on whom his salary depended.

The corrected press releases waited in piles beside the photographs and sketches for the arrival of the horde which would soon be arriving on foot from the Lanvin showing.

The first to come was the *Combat* reporter. He was young, amusing, and dynamic: he walked more quickly than the rest. The ladies from the Wool Bureau came next; since they weren't interested in evening models, which were rarely made from their product, they always left early. Then came *Madame Express* with Friedlander, the representative from *Madam,* the German magazine, who had been placed in the second salon and only got a wave and a smile from Marie-Victoire.

She never budged from the threshold of the first salon which she seemed to be defending like the faithful Roustan in front of Napoleon's door. She did move forward, though, to shake hands with Nathalie Ordioni from *le Monde,* an old friend, and to ask in a low voice:

"You just came from Lanvin, didn't you? How was it?"

"Stunning, youthful, and sumptuous, too, a good combination. A great success for Crahay, the Americans went mad over him."

"Ah," she sighed, "they'll be all the harder to please here!"

But here was Claudia Cardinale. All the little assistants stared at her as if an angel had appeared on the landing.

Marie-Victoire rushed to greet her: "How lovely you look! Come quickly, I've given you the seat of honor, next to the duchess."

She took her arm and rubbed it a bit, like a cat against fur; celebrity gave off a warm glow! Also Claudia had a satiny quality to her skin that Marie-Victoire had never found in anyone else except Princess Paola: it must be an Italian specialty.

A wave of newcomers moved toward the entrance and paused there. To Helen Lazareff, of *Elle,* slim and blond, Marie-Victoire cried: "My dear, how do you grow younger every year?"

And turning to Christiane: "Madame Lazareff is Number 15 and has three chairs in the second row for her assistants.

"Heavens, Grace Mirabella, Eugenia Sheppard, and June Weir. . . . All the crowned heads at once . . . this way . . . this way . . . you look marvelous!"

"Oh, Mrs. Hamilton, how are the dogs?"

"Dear Monsieur Dabadie, you look splendid. You've gotten

thinner, it's amazing! Here is your place, near *Harper's Bazaar* . . ." and to herself: let's hope they come.

Madame de Turkheim was there. . . . "My dear, I adored your last article!"

Ah, Monsieur de Gunzburg from *Vogue,* always so formal. "How nice to see you, you look marvelous. You have your usual chairs and Susan Train is waiting for you. . . . !" She gave him a big smile which she tried to make as affectionate as possible, but she wondered whether, if she had come to meet him walking on her hands if he would have even smiled!

An enormous burst of sound filled the entrance and Marie-Victoire told herself that it must be *Thread Needle News* arriving. She pushed her way through and saw a strange young woman with the editor-in-chief of the Paris office both shaking their invitations under the Princess' nose. She came toward them and said in an extremely clear voice:

"No, it's not a mistake. Since you received these invitations the house has had good reason to cancel them and I don't wish to receive your paper. But since your article is already written, it shouldn't bother you too much!"

Seeing that their position was untenable, the two Americans retreated, white with rage, among exploding flash bulbs, for the photographers were delighted by this windfall.

So triumphant over her effect that she almost forgot the harm the story would do her, Marie-Victoire shot a triumphant glance at Alan and welcomed Juliette Greco and her sister effusively:

"Juliette, how nice! Oh my God, where am I going to put you? You should have let me know you were coming. But I'm sure this nice gentleman from the Chambre Syndicale" (damn, I've forgotten his name!) "is going to give you his place and take the chair just behind"—and turning to the gentleman—"Of course you know our great Greco?"

Greco: "No, no, monsieur, you have work to do, I don't want to trouble you, my sister and I will sit behind you; we'll be perfectly all right."

"What a dear, what a love, she's marvelous!" cried Marie-Victoire.

". . . Ah, here's that nanny goat, Edwina Callianis. I really don't know what Adrien sees in her. She does look stunning, though, all in white with her emeralds and her mahout's turban. If I had been there I would not have let her order it, though it covers her red hair. How much she looks like a camel; camel, plus mahout, plus emeralds; you'd think she was a Taj Mahal's guide.

"Dear madame, you're on the other side of the duchess. . . ." My God! I hope she arrives. . . . "Christiane will show you."

Estée Lauder, at last, how good she smells! "Estée, my dear, how nice of you to come, you sit next to *Vogue*," and, in her ear: "I'm sure they must love you with all the money you spend on advertising!"

. . . Oh my! Here's Mother Durand, I shouldn't have given in to her saleswoman. When I think she spends 200,000 francs a season here and she always looks like Mâme Michu on the day of her little one's first communion! And all that jewelry she must have bought in 1943! . . . I really must tell her that you can't wear a gold and ruby clip when your tits are as big as hers. . . .

"Dear madame, you won't be comfortable in this crowd, tomorrow we could have given you a seat in the first row."

And the good lady modestly replied: "It's very nice of you to have invited me today and I'm so glad because now I can order tomorrow morning before I go on vacation."

"Come, here's a nice little place beside these ladies from television."

"The telly! Oh, how nice!"

179

. . . Good, at least it doesn't take much to make her happy.
. . . But what can have happened to the duchess? We'll have
to start in five minutes . . . and that viscountess isn't here
either. If she can do this to me she can whistle for that thou-
sand-franc rebate she expects on her order. Ah, here she is.

"Dear madame, we were only waiting for you to begin. I've
had a hard time holding a seat for you!"

And turning to the photographer, she murmured:

"You haven't forgotten Peter Ustinov beside the English
ambassador's wife—that's a real coup! It's the first time she's
been here!"

Then aloud:

"One more picture and then I'm going to have to ask you to
leave."

Chavanaux, always watchful, came forward to escort the
photographer to the exit with a firm grip. Since they had decided to respect the last directives from the Chambre Syndicale, the photographer must be sent away before the first
models appeared.

After a glance around, Marie-Victoire went to the little
stage, stuck her head through the curtains that covered the
entrance to the dressing room, and whispered:

"Are you ready? Everyone is here except the duchess: she
must not be coming."

The twelve mannequins were waiting, fully dressed. Now it
could begin.

She gave a signal to Madame Estelle, whose English accent
was perfect, to come to the side of the stage and announce
the models, which would be done in French and in English.
Estelle came with her list in her hand, while Marie-Victoire
slipped back to the entrance hall, where, sitting on the fifth step
of the staircase, she could watch the collection unfold.

180

Madame Estelle, in a clear voice which called for silence, announced: "Number one hundred thirty-three, 'Zurbarran.'"

"Zurbarran" was an outfit of chestnut and black tweed trimmed with brown astrakhan, worn with black accessories, which looked more like the first-class cabin of a Pan Am Boeing than the flea-bitten monks the artist loved to paint. It was called "Zurbarran" because of its color.

Madame Durand, having no idea of how the name was spelled and not knowing whether it was a beach in Zanzibar, a Hindu festival, or a Persian dignitary, hurried to write "133" on the note pad balanced on her enormous crocodile bag from Hermès. She was to go to New York with her husband for a convention in October, and Mademoiselle Huguette had convinced her to do honor to the French concrete merchants (even if some of them had made a fortune building Herr Hitler's Atlantic wall during the war), and to Marie-Victoire Forval as well, by changing her clothes three times a day.

June Weir gave a pitiless glance at the outfit, as if to say: Nothing new there! For five seasons Lecouture had been showing models with skirts just below the knee while other houses had hemlines anywhere from the middle of the thigh to the ankle; the square armhole did give a new importance to the bodice though—that was the only detail worth noting. She turned a little in her chair. It was plain that Adrien Lecouture had no surprises this year either and she thought his day was over.

The other reporters wrote quickly, in abbreviations: 133-coat ¾ length—skirt 4 in. below knee—tweed chestnut black —sq. armh.; looser waist—black belt—shawl col. br. astrakhan—classic shoes, no platform.

The mannequin stopped between the two salons to put her coat on again and another saleswoman who knew a little English announced the number and name once more. The mannequin began to repeat her movements in the crowded entry where another assistant saleswoman, pale with stage fright, did quite well except for pronouncing her "eights" as "hight."

Back at the door of the dressing room, the mannequin dropped her nonchalant air and ran to change as quickly as possible.

Adrien called to her as she passed: "How's the atmosphere?"

She made a face. "Can't really say yet."

He remembered his great success with the '63 collection, when the salons crackled at the appearance of the first model, "Asphodèle." That was a year of flowers in every sense of the word. But then it had still been permissible to be elegant. Poorboy fashions, which grew out of the '68 riots, hadn't yet taken over, and pretty women didn't want to get themselves up to look like Israeli sergeants.

The first mannequin had scarcely reached the second salon when Daphne made her appearance in the first in the bottle green suede suit with matching boots, a felt hat with the brim turned up on one side, and a frivolous white lace collar: "Velasquez." The outfit was stunning and looked like one of the Three Musketeers. Mother Durand, in a lucid moment, decided: I don't really think that Mademoiselle Huguette will try to palm that one off on me!

Feeling defiant, Daphne raised her chin and turned with precision, her eyes fixed over all the heads. She seemed to live in her costumes and change personality with each garment. From the wife of an English milord visiting a farmer's wife who has just borne her sixth baby, she would transform herself into a lady from a Sargent portrait in a black suit with a white satin blouse. Next she came down the steps of the Madeleine after marrying her daughter to the eldest son of the Duc de Z, wearing "Monet," a printed velvet ensemble. But as soon as she put on "Botticelli," a long sheath embroidered in blue beads, reminiscent of a mermaid rising from the waves, she assumed the condescending amiability of an ambassadress receiving guests at the top of a staircase. Finally, no sooner had she slipped into "Matisse," gathered harem pants with a tunic embroidered in brilliant colors, than she became an impatient mistress awaiting her lover's first visit.

There was no way of knowing whether she would have put so much of herself into it if she had had to work for another designer than Adrien. She wasn't such an extraordinary mannequin, yet she turned the creations of the man she loved with a frustrated passion, into triumphs. All the other mannequins thought first of their own appearance and wanted to achieve a personal success. She alone made a scent of incense rise around Adrien's gowns. She didn't present a collection, she celebrated a rite.

Adelaide followed Daphne, in her anachronistic outfit of green suede, with "Vasarely," Jean-Loup's first coat. It was a full-cut greatcoat which woke up the reporters, who were resigned to living through the adventures of D'Artagnan at the court of Louis XIII in eighty episodes. Amazed to return to the present, they burst into applause. At once the *hoi polloi* in the second salon took courage and imitated them. Marie-Victoire was not surprised: novelties never passed unnoticed. They might forget to mention them in their reports; for no reason at all they might decide to emphasize something else; but at the moment they missed nothing. . . . If they didn't invent fashion, they still created it by selecting the trends to emphasize at all the houses. Since there were always many lines to choose from, if the reporters hadn't existed there would have been no fashion. But you can go out of your mind with frustration if a trend you bring out this year goes unnoticed only to be praised next season at another house

183

which just copied it. This had happened with Crahay's long skirts at Lanvin, when Saint Laurent got the credit for them the next year. . . .

Edwina Callianis did not know that Jean-Loup had designed this coat, and soon would hurt Adrien's feelings dreadfully by telling him that she absolutely adored this garment and couldn't live without it. She usually tried on the whole collection and made Adrien help with her final choice. As a matter of course, she only paid 50 per cent of the price and was insufferably demanding about details. She claimed to give the house a great deal of publicity, in New York as well as Paris, which was true in a sense, since she was talked about a great deal— though more often than not with derision.

Marie-Victoire remembered a tea at the French consulate where practically nothing was discussed except the sudden demise of poor Edward Callianis, a charming and popular Greek, great lover of flashy women, who made the mistake of marrying this flamboyant Caucasian for his fourth or fifth wife. In Sacha Guitry's immortal words, it was she who had closed his eyes and opened his safe. Not finding it as well filled as she had hoped, she fell into a deep depression, but that had not stopped her from appearing at a cocktail party two weeks later, dressed in black mousseline, her head decked in an enormous black ostrich-feather hat which came down to her nose, in token of her mourning.

When she had asked Adrien if the house wouldn't take her on as public-relations woman in America, Marie-Victoire had let him know in what low esteem Edwina's so-called dear friends held her and he hadn't dared insist.

Chavanaux thought: "I don't understand any of this." No matter how much they applauded, he would never have let his wife be seen in a coat like that.

The saleswomen shook their heads, except for old Madame

184

Edith, who specialized in remainder sales and thought of her little actress clients, who would rather attract attention by dressing like a bear at a fair than go unnoticed.

Alfred, the tailor who had cut the coat, explained to Philippe, the other tailor, that he had to raise the front a great deal to keep the whole thing from looking like something bought from an Armenian rug merchant. Christiane thought it was funny-looking and, never having been at a winter sports resort, wondered who would dare wear such a thing.

Madame Annie noted it down, for she had a client who would buy almost anything with her eyes closed. As her sales-woman, she must hurry to get her to buy as much as possible before she closed her eyes forever. This was a very rich Englishwoman who lived in an apartment in the Ritz and had three nurses in relays around the clock keeping her alive with injections. She had always had a passionate love for clothes and had not even thought of remarrying when the millionaire lord who married her late in life went on to the next world. For ten years she had lived alone, without so much as a dog or cat, as near as possible to her dear couturiers, warmed only by the eager affection of saleswomen. Though bedridden for the past six months, she had gone on ordering dresses, which a mannequin came in to show her at home. (She was to die just after this season's collections, as if she had kept on breathing only to be present for that important event one more time. As her last act, she asked to have her whole wardrobe hung up before her so that she could choose her shroud; she decided on a gold brocade gown, embroidered from neck to hem, which weighed nearly as much as she did. Her sales-women were heartbroken because she hadn't had time to place her seasonal order.)

Madame Annie, while keeping her dying Englishwoman in mind, watched the Baroness de Stock out of the corner of her eye. She was there only as an intermediary. She had two millionaire "customers" who, not realizing that she was paid 10 per cent of everything they bought, heaped her with gifts in gratitude for her skimming the cream of the collections for them. One was a neurotic multimillionairess who literally covered all her friends and even the wives of her tradesmen with jewels, furs, and costly gowns. The beneficiaries had the nerve to ask the house for a muff or a hat to match, or if the indefatigable doner offered them a certain beaded evening gown, to exchange it for four less expensive ones. Of course, the 10 per cent allotted to the intermediary cost the house nothing, since it was added to the already fabulous price paid by this overgenerous woman. She gave so easily that her chauffeur had the habit of making sure whether she was still wearing all her jewels when he picked her up after the evenings during which she had too much to drink.

The baroness' second millionairess was much less interesting now that she no longer occupied the center of the American political stage. But although she was much less generous than the first and not really elegant any more, it was still flattering to be her "couture scout."

The first twelve models followed each other very smoothly, but at the thirteenth, when it was time for the first mannequin to reappear, there was a hole. Madame Estelle panicked, she pushed a button which lit a light on the other side of the curtain. Whew! Out came Amalia in "Rouault," a deep red mohair costume with sable at the hem.

Amalia's technique was entirely different from Daphne's. She walked slowly, turned regretfully, gazed into the reporters' eyes, almost fell at their knees, leaned against the wall, as if drunk with her own beauty. While Daphne was as cool and precise as a computer programmed for ultimate elegance, Amalia, on the other hand, made you want to reach out and

186

touch her. She was sexy in spite of her slenderness, a disturbing black panther.

The six temporary mannequins, hired for these three days, were superb. There were two English girls, an Israeli, a Swede, and two Americans. Marie-Victoire admired them as a connoisseur. What ease, what professionalism. No one would have believed they had tried on their gowns only once before the rehearsal. They really earned the fees that they asked. Even the "Greco" ensemble, which made that idiot Véronique look as if she'd fallen into a dish of pistachio-and-raspberry ice cream, looked marvelous on Daisy, who sailed into the salon with the assurance of one of Her Gracious Majesty's liners passing the Statue of Liberty. As for Alan's little friend, who was replacing Ingara, she too was perfect.

Adelaide now came out of the dressing room in Jean-Loup's almost transparent black angora jersey dress. It was plain that she was absolutely naked underneath—even her pubic hair was outlined by the bias fabric—for this dress was actually much more revealing than the completely transparent mousseline of past years.

Madame Estelle announced "'Boldini,' number eighteen," in a clearly disapproving voice. Balmain, where she'd worked before, known as the last existing couturier of royalty, would never have permitted such a garment. But applause and exclamations broke out and she thought: No doubt about it, all they care about these days is naked women.

Adrien, on the other side of the curtain, hated to admit it, but up to this point, the only applause had been for Jean-Loup's creations. He turned toward him and gave him a half-hearted "Bravo!!" Coolly, the younger man made a belly-dance movement and let out a "Whoopee!" so loud that everybody around went "Shhh!" What would the salons think if they heard Sioux war whoops coming from the dressing room?

187

Madame Durand smiled at the ceiling; no need for a decision about this model either!

Edwina Callianis sighed: Only ten years ago! . . .

There was a rustle from the *Elle* staff, but they reminded themselves how much of the magazine's advertising came from girdle and brassiere manufacturers. On the other hand, they might find a way of selling space to some plastic-surgery clinics, health farms, and saunas.

Monsieur Dabadie didn't think he ought to mention this one to the lady readers of *Le Figaro* and held his pen suspended over his notebook.

Madame Suzette, who specialized in a clientele of "starlets," immediately thought of Josiane King, who was trying to make her way in the cabarets, as much with her beautiful body as with her thread of a voice. Her lover of the moment was a movie producer and would be delighted to give his pals a good look at the pretty pair of buttocks he enjoyed in bed.

Baroness de Stock was frightened: Adrien must have gone crazy or have had a sunstroke; her dear millionairesses would certainly go back to their beloved Lanvin.

Madame Annie shivered, thinking of what a horrible spectacle the skeletal body of her dying client would make in this pitiless jersey.

Chavanaux, who had not been back to the Folies-Bergère since he was eighteen, surprised himself by smiling lewdly as his grandfather must have when he went to the Moulin Rouge to see the can-can dancers. If he had been wearing a mustache, he would have twirled it.

The reporters from *Time* magazine, who had planned to write an article called, "Are the couturiers all masochists? They're undressing women instead of dressing them!" noted the number of this dress which would be photographed along with all the transparent dresses from the other houses. Their titled photographer felt strangely attracted by Adelaide's lovely little body and made a note not to have the dress modeled by any other mannequin.

A famous sociologist, sent by the *Ladies' Home Journal,* wrote quite seriously that bias fabrics, outlining the mannequins' breasts and buttocks as they did, revealed modern woman's libido, which she simultaneously expressed and suppressed.

Madame Sylvette raised her voice to call for silence and announced the next gown: the first formal evening gown. It was a long sheath of thick pale pink crepe, cut on the bias, with neckline and wrists trimmed in white mink. Topsy, one of the English girls, pink and white herself, wore it perfectly, and the name, "Boucher" fitted this bonbon well.

An adorable dress in black velvet trimmed with a big white satin bow, "Holbein," a style which had always been Adrien's greatest success, still brought a few handclaps. But out-of-this-world embroideries, supple lamés, evening wraps worthy of the Russian court left the reporters cold. Christiane Helouis ostentatiously closed her notebook. The readers of *France-Soir* were more interested in what to wear at the Club Méditerranée or the local Whiskey-à-GoGo than at the next ball at the Farnese Palace.

When "David" appeared, a gold lace ball gown entirely covered with jewels and worn under a gold tulle cape, Marie-Victoire was waiting for a wonderstruck "Ah!" and was completely put out of countenance by the thick silence. At last she admitted: This time it's a failure, the notices won't be good.

Edwina Callianis immediately calculated: If she could get into this dress, Adrien would surely lend it to her for the April in Paris Ball, and even if she paid half price for other dresses, if she didn't have to pay for this one she would have made a considerable saving.

Some reporters wrote: "It appears that Monsieur Lecouture has spent his life at the court of Iran and thinks in terms of coronation ceremonies."

Christiane, dazzled, touched the gown as it went past, to be sure she wasn't dreaming and this wasn't a fairy tale.

Chavanaux knit his brows. It certainly wasn't worth spending 5,600 francs on embroidery at Jean Guy Vermont if you didn't even get any applause from *Family Weekly*.

In the dressing room, Adrien grew more and more nervous. Ordinarily polite, he shouted at the hairdressers: "You put so much false hair braids on the mannequins' heads that they looked like Gorgons! Monsieur Alexandre must think my collection is a *bal de têtes!*"

Jean-Loup thought: Papa's mad! But I told him that slums, dirt, and bums are more fashionable than Buckingham Palace these days. The richer you are, the less you want to look that way this year. Even if *Women's Wear* writes only about ritzy clothes. The millionaire's first rule is: go barefoot on your yacht. He'll never understand that young people want to be "amusing" first and foremost. Poor old thing, let's try to look sympathetic and give him our condolences.

Daphne had tears in her eyes. They were pigs not to applaud such a beautiful dress! Coming back to the dressing room, she squeezed Adrien's arm affectionately, but he shook her off. He had no interest in pity; what he longed for was a few greenish smiles of envy, like the ones he used to get.

From her place on the staircase, Marie-Victoire saw an assistant saleswoman animatedly explaining something to Chavanaux who was moving toward a seated lady in the second salon. Another one sketching the models, she told herself. I hope the lavatory session won't begin again. She was remembering a painful incident when she had literally had to snatch pages covered with drawings from the hands of a Dutchwoman, who, knowing she had been caught, had run to tear them up in the toilets. She really was a reporter but her brother made leather clothing. She sent him all the latest models on the day of the showings and he came out with his little collection in the latest style two weeks after Paris did. The classic designs were also mass-produced a year in advance, and as salaries in Holland were low, he had customers all over the world buying Paris designs at prices that defied all competition.

In all the houses, members of the staff were seated around in the salons to keep an eye on the journalists and buyers. At one time these spies even wore hats and gloves so as to look like guests. Ideas from haute couture were systematically stolen, and while it was impossible to stop all of the thefts, at least the amateurs could be discouraged. The result was predictable: The one who steals a scarf from a counter for the first time in his life is arrested, while the international gang which deals in millions gets off scot-free.

Chavanaux held a pile of papers in his hand on which there were in fact drawings. All he could do was take the lady's name as she left and cross her off the invitation lists. If he had really wanted to frighten her, he could have called the police, but few houses went to this length.

The Princess, very much troubled, made a sign to Marie-Victoire that she was wanted on the telephone. The latter knew that she would never have disturbed her before the end of the showing except for some very serious reason. She got up and made her way to the Princess.

"Madame, I'm sorry to bother you. It's about your daughter. It seems she's been in an accident and the hospital is calling."

Marie-Victoire ran to the telephone in the entrance hall. "Hello, Madame Forval here."

"Faure, intern in surgery at the Hôtel-Dieu. I'm sorry to have to give you bad news; your daughter was just admitted to the hospital for an emergency operation."

"My God, what's happened to her? An automobile accident?"

"No, madame, but it's very urgent. Can we do what is necessary?"

"Of course. I'll be there."

"Thank you, madame." And he hung up.

Marie-Victoire, very pale, turned to the Princess. "Make my excuses to the reporters. Ask Monsieur Adrien and Monsieur Harside to take care of it. Clothilde has had an accident, and I must run to the hospital. Have Maurice get out my car while I get my bag."

Without even her usual glance in the mirror before going out, Marie-Victoire hurried down the stairs and waited a few minutes, which seemed to her like hours, for Maurice to bring her car.

The trip from the Place de la Concorde with the stop lights at the quais was torture. Luckily she could drive quickly after that. If it wasn't an auto accident, what was it? And why was Clothilde in Paris instead of Normandie? She suddenly realized that her daughter had turned into a stranger, that she no longer knew anything about her, that the flesh of her flesh was as remote from her as last Saturday's little bride.

Notre Dame; the Hôtel-Dieu is to the left, she remembered. How am I going to get in there? She left her car in the first space she found. Never mind the ticket. She ran to the desk.

"Someone just telephoned me that my daughter was having an emergency operation. Where must I go?"

"What name?"

"Clothilde Forval."

"What time was she admitted?"

"I have no idea."

"Same old thing!"

Taking his time, the man in the dirty white coat ran his finger down the page of the big register.

"Oh, yes, here it is. Emergencies are down there. Check with the supervisor."

Marie-Victoire went in the direction indicated, horrified by this strange world. Every morning police buses full of derelicts in the last stages of alcoholism were brought to the Hôtel-Dieu. In the corridor several of them were stretched out on benches, with knapsacks filled with their wordly goods beside them. An old woman had fallen on the floor and vomited a red pulp, the sight of which ought to have cured a regiment of legionnaires of drinking alcohol.

My own daughter with these human rejects; it isn't possible! thought Marie-Victoire. At the emergency room, she asked a nurse where she could find Mademoiselle Clothilde Forval. The nurse directed her to the office of the Supervisor of Nurses. The supervisor was a middle-aged woman with a harsh manner and abrupt speech who examined the visitor unsympathetically. She took in her elegant dress, and the coral-and-diamond brooch.

"Are you Madame Forval?"

"Yes, an intern telephoned me that it was necessary to perform an emergency operation on my daughter, but he didn't tell me what it was. Where is she? Is it serious?"

"She is in the operating room; I can't tell you anything, but she wasn't very pretty when she got there."

"My God, have pity on me, don't you see I'm worried to death?"

Marie-Victoire, who often provoked this kind of hostility in women, suddenly remembered that her father-in-law was an important figure in public health.

"My daughter is Professor Forval's granddaughter."

At this the sergeant in skirts softened up immediately. "Dr. Faure will speak to you as soon as he has finished operating. Sit here while you wait."

From the little office she could see a large room filled with men and women waiting to be examined. Injured or sick, some of them seemed to be in comas. There was some attempt to isolate the most desperate cases by half partitions, but they could still be heard groaning or retching. A very young girl, unconscious, was being taken into the operating room, and the supervisor, with the best of intentions, said to Marie-Victoire:

"If that isn't sad! She was on the sidewalk and a car went out of control and cut her leg off just below the knee. Poor little thing, they put her leg beside her on the stretcher."

My God, thought Marie-Victoire, I hope she doesn't say that to prepare me for the same kind of horror! She never perspired, even in the worst heat, but now she felt a sweat of anguish form a drop between her breasts, and this unfamiliar sensation sharpened her discomfort.

The nurse left her alone and went to spread the news that Forval's granddaughter had been operated on and it would be a good idea to put her in a private room instead of the ward. The only bed they could find was in a semi-private room already occupied by another young woman.

The operating room doors finally opened and Marie-Victoire had difficulty in recognizing Clothilde, green and lifeless

194

on the stretcher, her head thrown back, a gag in her mouth, and a blood-transfusion bottle hanging over her.

"My God, she's dead!"

"No, madame, she'll come out of it, but we got her just in time."

"What happened to her?"

She walked beside the stretcher, looking at the young surgeon who studied her a moment before answering. Evidently satisfied that she was not a silly woman, he told her the truth:

"The poor kid was butchered by some practical nurse or girl friend, in any case certainly not by a professional. It was too late for a curettage; we had to go in quickly, and unfortunately it was out of the question to leave a uterus like that. There was peritonitis and septicemia in the pelvis. Ten years ago, it would have been hopeless. We even thought we might have to use dialysis, she was so toxic, but it's not necessary now. Still and all, she was pretty far gone and this afternoon it would have been too late."

It is having cases like this from time to time that keeps doctors' morale up. Their professional life is less exciting than television serials or paperback novels suggest and they don't often win victories over death. This young man looked extremely pleased with himself and it was plain that he would do all he could for the patient he had brought back to life.

"I can never thank you enough, monsieur."

Marie-Victoire suspected that this young man was not the boss, but she knew that in hospital usage, heads of units were called monsieur rather than Doctor.

"You know that she is Professor Forval's granddaughter. For family reasons I'm sure you'll understand, I'd prefer that he didn't hear about this."

"Privileged information, madame."

They arrived at the room where Clothilde was lying, still unconscious, in a metal bed whose white paint was flaking off. The sheets were coarse and wrinkled, but the room had a big window and the occupant of the second bed a pleasant open face.

"When will she wake up?"

"In about an hour . . ." He hesitated a moment: "Don't tell her right away that she won't be able to have children. She might not be able to take it; she must have gone through a very bad time and you'll have to be very patient with her. I'll make an exception and let you stay with her, though it isn't visiting hours."

Marie-Victoire sat on the metal chair and stared fixedly at the needle in her daughter's arm. She was overwhelmed by what she had just learned. My little girl, my baby, just yesterday she came to me for comfort when she had the slightest bump: now, in this serious situation, she didn't trust me. It's terrible, it's all my fault, I'm a bad mother. I love her so much, yet I caused her unhappiness by my negligence. Not to be able to have children is a terrible handicap for a woman. Who knows if she will even get married now? I've spoiled my child's life. And to think that during the time she was in agony, I was in Oliver's arms. I'll never forgive myself.

She told herself these things without thinking how trite they were: remorse seldom has any literary value.

Marie-Victoire had always laughed at her more egotistical and frivolous friends who overflowed with sentimentality and devotion to their grandchildren. She maintained that young couples should get along on their own or wait until they were rich enough to be able to pay a nurse to take care of their

196

children; that there was no reason for sacrificing a comfortable middle age for ungrateful youth, etc.

The idea that this problem would never arise for her now dumfounded her. This baby who would not be born, and whom her child had carried, suddenly took on tremendous importance: she was sure that it would have been beautiful and gifted. She saw herself in a gray lace dress in the first row of a crowded Carnegie Hall applauding a little boy in short trousers, who played exquisite melodies on a piano, or making a graceful curtsy to the King of Sweden on the arm of the youngest winner of the Nobel Prize. She said to herself: We could have revived the name of Baussigue (for in her fantasy there was no question that this child could have been anything but a boy). Papa would have been so happy. She even went so far as to think that she would not have had to share this child with any other grandmother, and imagined herself as a sort of sublimated Auntie Mame. Having learned to get along without a husband herself, she did not think of it as a catastrophe to raise a child alone, and Clothilde misjudged her if she thought that a bastard would have distressed her. Many middle-class women who had to choose between a dishonored daughter or no grandchild at all would have preferred the second solution. Marie-Victoire would have chosen the first.

A groan from Clothilde brought her back to reality. She took her daughter's hand, and Clothilde returned the pressure feebly. Though Marie-Victoire had managed not to cry before, this contact broke her down; great tears ran down her cheeks as she was overwhelmed with pity. Clothilde opened her eyes and saw her mother smiling at her through tears which she was trying to wipe away surreptitiously.

"My darling, my darling!"

197

"I feel awful . . ." her eyes fell on the transfusion bottle. "Where am I?"

"In the hospital. Everything is going to be all right."

Clothilde closed her eyes again, but did not let go her mother's hand. A little color was returning to her cheeks.

"I'm thirsty."

Marie-Victoire did not know whether she ought to give her anything to drink, so she released her hand and went into the corridor to ask. A very young woman in a most becoming white cap came with a bottle of Evian water and held it for Clothilde to drink.

"I'm going to give her a sedative."

Quickly she uncovered Clothilde and gave her an injection. Marie-Victoire had never been able to watch injections, and she turned her eyes away, but not before she glimpsed the rough hospital gown spotted with blood.

"Now she must rest. You can come back later in the afternoon perhaps."

Marie-Victoire didn't dare argue and the young woman in the next bed, seeing that she looked very much upset, said to her kindly:

"If anything is wrong, I'll call the nurse, she's very nice."

Marie-Victoire looked at her for the first time and smiled.

"How kind you are! Thank you."

Outside Notre Dame she found her car with a ticket under the windshield wiper, and this ordinary nuisance comforted her. Come now, life goes on as usual. It would take at least an atomic bomb dropped on Notre Dame to keep traffic cops from passing out their paper butterflies. . . . She was so near home that she went there to change her clothes to suit the gravity of the occasion and to put some toilet articles, a nightgown, and eau de Cologne for Clothilde in a little suitcase. What was she to tell everyone? She began with Thérèse:

"Mademoiselle Clothilde has had a burst appendix with peritonitis and had to be taken to the emergency ward of the hospital. Fortunately she's all right but it was a very close call, and Mademoiselle will be there for at least a week."

She went back to Place Vendôme and had to tell the story at least twenty times, for the first person who heard it hurried to spread the news and give herself importance thereby. Immediately, to show the boss that she really cared about her trouble, the next person informed hurried to her, hoping to hear about it at greater length and to lord it over her colleagues in her turn. The saleswomen adored this kind of tragedy, and in their rest room, the one who could tell the most dreadful story of peritonitis came out on top. Their memories went back to 1910, when surgery was still in its infancy, and a whole legion of peritonitis deaths were resurrected and their ghosts walked in Place Vendôme. Employers who never have personal troubles are not very sympathetic, and Marie-Victoire was immediately raised five points in their affections.

Knowing the true value of these friendly demonstrations, Marie-Victoire could not help thinking: How much greater my success would be if they knew the truth!

All the reporters had left and Alan, after having shown real concern, told her about the end of the collection.

"They said it was charming, elegant, stunning, very nice."

"That means we're done for! You know that anything less than 'sublime' is the equivalent of 'dreadful'!"

"Humm. I must admit that the only compliments that seemed sincere were for Jean-Loup's models. He took bows at the door—Adrien didn't want to appear."

"I hope you didn't give him any encouragement. With the Americans, especially, he'd better not start thinking he's cock of the walk!"

"I have to admit that I translated for him. You know, if they talk about the collection, it will only be because of him. They love new talents in America."

"That's true, but it would be nice if they could remember the old ones too. When I think of how Mainbocher was called Remember-the-Mainbocher! But in New York it's better if they talk about your past than not at all. Adrien was wrong not to come out, when I asked him to take my place. What did you say to the reporters about my absence?"

"The truth: that your daughter had just been taken to the hospital and we didn't know what for."

"Lord, they're all so considerate! I'll be overwhelmed with telephone calls: I must warn the switchboard. No one has decided which models will be photographed yet?"

"Yes, yes. *Harper's Bazaar* is hesitating between 113 and 127, the gray suit with white mink and the navy blue trimmed in red fox. It seems that fur-trimmed suits this season are coming back in fashion."

"Aha, the very ones I changed! Adrien will be furious."

"*Marie Claire* liked Adrien's last cape very much, and *Jours de France* like Jean-Loup's lamé dress. They talked about using it for the Christmas cover. *Jasmin* loved the black jersey dress."

"Of course, it's sexier than bare breasts and we've seen so many of those lately that we're bored with them. And *Elle?* What did they say?"

"Not much."

"And Eugenia Sheppard?"

"Not a word."

"So all that does not smell good. In any case, this time we

can't have dinner together and wait for the papers to come out as we usually do. I have to go back to the hospital. I hope you don't mind."

"I've already canceled the table."

Passing the dressing room, Marie-Victoire stopped for a moment. Madame Suzanne had known Clothilde since she was a little thing; it would be nice to give her the news herself.

The house mannequins, in girdles and brassieres, were finishing a plate of *petits fours* brought by a new headwaiter from Potel and Chabot, who was excited by being admitted to a mannequins' dressing room for the first time. He left very much disappointed, announcing to his comrades that he much preferred his own little woman who had enough flesh on her to keep you from getting bruised. In France temporary mannequins are called flying mannequins. They justified their descriptive adjective by moving on immediately to Grès, whose collection was being shown at lunchtime. They would be back at three for the showing for buyers. Madame Suzanne was mending a belt and got up when she saw Marie-Victoire.

"I heard about Mademoiselle Clothilde's trouble. These days peritonitis is nothing if it's caught in time. But you must have been terribly frightened, madame. With all the misfortunes of these last few days, you've been very courageous, and I'd like to tell you how much I admire you."

"Thank you, Suzanne, you're a great comfort."

"And I want to offer you my sympathy too, madame," said Daphne, putting down her teapot.

"Thank you, little one. Do you know why Monsieur Adrien didn't want to make an appearance after the collection? It wasn't very polite. Even Cardin comes out and takes a bow like an actor."

"No, he said he wasn't feeling well. He must be in the studio. I don't think things went the way he'd hoped."

"I think you're right, though I missed the end. I'll go up to see him."

"He didn't want to see me."

"You know how it is, Daphne, everyone prefers compliments to condolences."

"But his collection is wonderful!"

"Yes, but it doesn't suit the times."

"But, madame, don't you prefer his designs to Jean-Loup's yourself?"

"For my personal wear, yes."

Daphne didn't answer. She didn't admit the slightest criticism, even tacit, of her god. Marie-Victoire didn't realize that by her minor reservation she had become one of Daphne's numerous personal enemies. The mannequin turned her back on her employer and, after refilling her cup with black tea, sat down in her chair with her feet up.

To tell the truth, Marie-Victoire had other concerns more pressing than the states of mind of her designer and manne-quins, but in spite of that, she went to the studio and entered without knocking,

"Well, my dear, Daphne tells me you aren't feeling well, so I've come to see how you are."

"A slight headache; it will pass. I was told that Clothilde is in the hospital. I hope it isn't serious."

"Serious enough. She had acute peritonitis."

"Poor lamb. I'll send flowers to cheer her up."

"The Hôtel-Dieu isn't exactly a chic clinic in Neuilly, you know."

"You're not going to leave her there?"

"Why not? She's getting wonderful care. She'd be dead if it wasn't for the doctor who operated on her." Unconsciously she

202

touched the wood of Adrien's desk. "By the way, I think you'll understand why I don't feel much like having our usual dinner together. I hope you won't hold it against me if I break with tradition for once, but I think that, aside from my worry about Clothilde, Ingara's ghost would be at the table."

"I'm sorry for the circumstances for canceling, but I must admit that I'm relieved the dinner isn't taking place."

"Come, come, the collection may not have been an overwhelming success, but you'll see, the European buyers will adore it. Try to suspend judgment for a few hours. Actually, they're more important than the papers. I'll leave you to rest a little; I just have time to arrange the buyers' places in the salon."

She gave him a friendly little pat on the shoulder and left, rather disappointed. She would have preferred a good cry which she would have been able to comfort—but if he didn't want sympathy, too bad. Anyway, she was the one who really needed it today.

Adrien lay back on the cushions with his eyes closed, thinking: every woman is a nurse at heart. How disgusting they were with their soft gestures and velvety voices when you only felt like screaming! If you weren't careful they would wrap you in a blanket and rock you like an impotent baby. Only idiots could really be taken in by that angel-of-mercy act. What they really want is to tie you down with their so-called tenderness and if you aren't careful they'll reduce you to the state of the nut in the chocolate. Poor Marie-Victoire, I'm probably not being fair. The fact is that if the collection is a failure it will hurt her as much as it will me and maybe more. After all, it's her money. But she'd still like to coddle me, like Daphne. They're all alike! Also, I'm relieved not to have to see Jean-Loup this evening, he's had too big a triumph. What a beautiful animal, you want to stroke him, but you're always afraid he'll bite!

The words "beautiful animal" immediately brought up images which accelerated his pulse and made him need to see the beautiful boy. When he was honest with himself, he recognized what he felt for Jean-Loup was not respect but an anguished physical need for his presence. He knew that some day he would lose him and that his withdrawal symptoms would be as agonizing as a cocaine addict's.

Until he met Jean-Loup, Adrien had never felt for anyone this frenzied need to possess. His desires and passions were more likely to be for inanimate objects. Aesthetics were so important to him that he could not bear it, for example, if his toilet paper didn't match his bathroom walls. That was why he got on so well with Hubert, for they both had the same perfect eye for detail. They had been happy together as a well-matched old husband and wife, but they had never felt for each other any of the turbulent emotions that Adrien had experienced lately with Jean-Loup. On their anniversaries they gave each other things they both wanted for their place and their fondest memories were of the finds they had made together rather than of their honeymoon nights.

Adrien's attention was so centered on himself that when a car backfired unexpectedly in the street, he sucked in his stomach with a guilty look, sure that the noise had come from inside him. On the whole, he could have easily have been classified as a miser for he had never given anything willingly until now, when he thought of nothing but how he could please his young lover.

This was the moment that Hubert chose to call on the telephone: "I haven't seen you so I haven't been able to congratulate you."

"Don't waste your breath. It was a failure."

"What makes you think so?"

"Yes, old cock, it really looks like the time to change my line. It's funny, but that decision looks less like a tragedy than I'd ever have believed. For more than twenty years I've lived for nothing but couture, twenty years when a badly set sleeve could keep me awake nights, when I read *Women's Wear* with more interest than the political news, when the discovery of a new fabric excited me more than going to the moon or an earthquake in Peru—and twenty years when I've judged everybody by the more or less elegant way they dressed. Twenty years when perfection of cut, suppleness of fabrics took the place of religion for me. I never thought I'd be able to say good-by to it all with a light heart."

"Oh look here, Adrien, with your talent, you mustn't dream of it!"

"Yes, I must. Some people are insane about their bodies, like La Callianis; they have no idea of good taste and they fall for the most horrible get-ups; all they want is to be noticed. In Jean-Loup's coat she'll look like a monkey on a wheel organ, as my grandmother used to say. How could she imagine I'd designed such a thing? And then there are the ones with no courage at all, who dress like everyone else. How many women are there left in the world who dare to be elegant? A dozen in America, three or four in France, a few more in Italy and Spain. They are always the same ones and they aren't young any more. Marie-Victoire doesn't really want me, and if she wants to start a ready-to-wear operation, she is quite capable of adapting a good salable collection herself—it was the suits she changed around that *Harper's Bazaar* liked. When couture was really couture, elaborate, sophisticated, architectural, like Balenciaga's, for example, it was not becoming for the very young. So now elegance has become synonymous with maturity, but as they all want to prolong youth as long as possible, this is the result! No use holding out against it. I'm going to have a long talk with Marie-Victoire. It isn't going to be easy for anyone but at least I can go into another profession which interests me. I am going to shave now, and then I'll feel better. See you this evening then. Won't you be glad to have me working with you?"

"Of course."

At the peak of the firm's success, it had been necessary to reserve the first showing after the press showing for American buyers, Europeans not being invited until the following morning. Reporters of minor importance were also admitted, but no individual customers except the most important or glamorous could see the collection for two weeks. But the Americans were becoming fewer and fewer so, to avoid having half-filled salons, Europeans were now invited to the first showing.

Almost everyone had his seat reserved by his agent a week in advance. However, if the collection received bad notices, they didn't come and didn't even bother to make excuses.

Usually Marie-Victoire let the Princess give the empty places to society women, actresses, or even second-day buyers. But on the first day, it was better not to risk annoying anyone, for, like the reporters, the buyers were very touchy about what seats they were given. So Marie-Victoire "made up" her salon herself twice a year. From the list of reservations, the Princess prepared little cards which she brought to Marie-Victoire. Some houses had a regiment of solid-core regulars ready to pay a double or even triple security, the minimum security being for two people.

"Let's see now," said Marie-Victoire, "where is Bergdorf Goodman?"

In all the houses this was the store which, with I. Magnin, was always given the best seats, for their prestige was more important than the number of models they bought. Between

Bergdorf Goodman and Orbach's, for example, though the second bought more models than the first, the buyers from Bergdorf still had the right to the places of honor, for the store represented high fashion and Orbach's, volume sales. An individual buyer had never been known to be angry at finding her dress remade to measure by Bergdorf at the same price as in Paris, but some would cancel their orders if they found out their dress had been bought by Orbach's or Alexander's, because they would be sure of seeing thousands of copies all over the United States.

Bergdorf Goodman's cards placed on its usual seats, Marie-Victoire arranged the pile of others. The big manufacturers didn't like being seated beside each other. So between each of them she inserted some prestigious European, like Jean Liétart, the top couturier of Brussels, her favorite buyer, or Paul Daunay of Geneva. She spread the cards out in front of her as if she were playing solitaire.

Lord & Taylor couldn't be seated next to Korvette. Good, let's put the Pedrinis in there. With their 60,000-franc contract, even if they resold everything as patterns, they were entitled to some respect. Ben Shaw? He didn't buy anything, but he was a dear and very important: put him in front. Wallis of London? Hmm. It's amazing how well they copy, it would almost pay me to take the plane and buy my models there. Here, let's put them with the sun in their eyes and this Bonn house next to them. Pumpernicke? We can tear this up, he certainly won't come.

Marie-Victoire continued to combine temperamental United States customers with European ones, thinking quite rightly that, for the time being, Dutch, Danes, or Norwegians wouldn't be friendly enough with Germans to exchange patterns. By the next generation, she foresaw, they would have to be watched.

"Monsieur Oliver Mayer" . . . the little card gave her a

shock. She reddened like a poorly adjusted color television and her heart beat quicker. Her first impulse was to look at herself in one of the big salon mirrors. She had put on her chestnut-colored dress with the big red scarf again, and she looked rather tired. To think I had forgotten he was to come at lunchtime: I must ask the Princess what happened.

"Yes, madame, I'm sorry, I haven't had time to tell you! Mr. Mayer said he would be back to see the collection at three o'clock, and that's why I made the card."

"Thank you."

She put down the little card with a thoughtful air. All I have to do is think of him to feel paralyzed! That's ridiculous, but I may as well admit it, no one ever affected me this way before.

The Princess, looking delighted, added: "I don't understand it at all: all the Americans are telephoning to confirm their reservations. With the reaction we had this morning, it's quite unexpected."

The arrangements for the showing were almost the same as in the morning. However, it was Chavanaux who stood at the bottom of the staircase to get signatures on the promises to purchase, or even the 3,000 francs in cash, for an unknown European client. Alan Harside stood beside him to greet the press. Marie-Victoire, her work done, gave her plan of the salon to the Princess who would thereby know where to seat the customers.

Now the first guests began to come up the staircase and, thank God, and thanks to the reporters of the least important papers who were not admitted this morning, the crowd was large enough to be very flattering to the house. Oliver Mayer arrived with Bonwit Teller's representative. He had practically kidnaped him from his hotel, promising that he would see "a really distinguished collection" without paying any security. Oliver knew him well enough to know that he would feel

208

obliged to buy something, and hoped that his coming would influence many others who were hesitating. He asked Chavanaux to warn Marie-Victoire. He didn't want any awkwardness to spoil his plan and when she appeared he murmured quickly to her:

"Let him in without a security; I'll be responsible."

Marie-Victoire, who had always wanted to have Bonwit Teller, but had never been able to get them to come because they preferred the avant-garde houses, made a sign to Chavanaux to put away his papers and extended herself to be extremely friendly, while asking herself, Lord, where shall I put them?

An important Zurich house had been seated opposite Bergdorf Goodman. Too bad! She quickly removed their card to put it in a less favorable corner.

Soon it was necessary to add a row of chairs while Mayer shook everybody's hand, as if he were already master of the house. He had been on the telephone since morning and had rallied all his supporters among the buyers. *Thread Needle News* and *Le Figaro* would not be out until the next day and the comments in the French evening papers were not very important: so they must get as many Americans as possible to come today.

Marie-Victoire was growing aware that without him there would have been only half the number of people there, and she squeezed his hand a little timidly in passing. It's funny, she smiled to herself, what childish gestures you make when you're in love.

The saleswomen chattered in pidgin English and fawned on their customers. They felt important and elated. The unexpected success went to their heads, and they already were beginning to say that buyers would have to come tomorrow morning at dawn so that they could take care of their orders. The well-organized buyers immediately gave their lists of models so as to find them ready on a rack when they came and lose as little time as possible. Besides looking over the collection from which they had to choose which garment's cut would give them a maximum of ideas, they also had to buy fabric and trimmings. Those who only stayed a week worked from eight in the morning until midnight.

On signing their order, they received a list of all the makings of the model, including the thread with which it was sewn, but they didn't get the pattern until a month later when they were back in their own country, to prevent earlier copying. If they wished to copy the garment in every detail, they had to order the same fabric, the same lining, the same interfacing, the same buttons, the same belt, or the same trimming from the suppliers, figuring how many pieces they would sell in advance.

At exactly three o'clock, Marie-Victoire signaled that the showing could begin. As in the morning, she would watch the show from the fifth step of her staircase.

The audience was silent. The more important the buyer, the less he made notes on details, for he always had an assistant or one of his agent's employees to record the details of each number. He only had to note which model he wanted to see again. On the other hand, the small houses, eager to get the maximum for their security, frantically noted every detail, and there was a young Milanese woman in the second row who wrote as much as a whole novel without ever looking at her notebook, her eyes riveted to the mannequins and her mouth open so as not to lose a crumb. If a mannequin saw a buyer drawing, she immediately made a sign and there were spies in strategic places to watch the salons carefully.

The first applause was for the gray suit trimmed with white mink which had won all the votes, from *Harper's Bazaar* to

Herr Pumpernicke's. This would be the "Ford" of the season. It would be seen from Helsinki to Sydney, often trimmed with rabbit and bastardized by all sorts of changes, but still looking like a distant cousin to the original. The buyers' perspective and the reporters' was diametrically opposed. As to the customers', it was often the most conservative of the three. To please the very young customers and not to look old-fashioned, the big stores all over the world bought a few eccentric models, but most of their stock was made up of classic models which changed only in detail from one year to the next, except when a couturier like Dior had had the power to change fashion radically in a single season: but this could not happen today; it had taken two years to adopt long skirts, and then giving in to general resistance, couturiers shortened them by the third season.

The second successful model was a red crepe dress which had a cutout at the waist showing a bit of skin. There were crepes at all prices, and anyone who owned the pattern for such a dress could make a model for 125 francs. By the same token, the embroidered gold dress scarcely got a glance from experienced buyers who saw at once they could never make it up in ersatz materials. On the other hand The Ebony Club, which organized fashion shows for charity all over America, would buy the model because of its sumptuousness.

The applause which greeted the appearance of the bridal gown wasn't exactly delirious, but it was enough to bring a smile to Adrien's pale, drawn face.

Marie-Victoire bowed to numerous people: to Elieth Roux and Nancy White, the buyers from Bergdorf Goodman; and to the buyers of the other big stores, many of whom called her by her first name. She gestured to Adrien to come to the rescue and shot an impatient look at the saleswomen to let them know that it was time to come to their customers. Like all born saleswomen she loved nothing more than this charged atmosphere, more exciting than a bottle of champagne.

A Canadian buyer, a faithful customer, took her arm. "My dear, I really liked this collection very much. If you want, I'll buy the gray suit or the red dress like everyone else. But I think it would be better if you'd seriously consider doing a boutique collection. We'd be very much interested, because the style would be quite different from what we've had before, and it would be marvelous publicity for you."

"By all means, I'll come talk to you about it in November. Please feel free not to buy anything for now. I won't hold it against you."

Ben Sholt, financier for the biggest manufacturers in New York, approached Marie-Victoire and kissed her on both cheeks. "Were the black jersey dress and the silver lamé one both designed by Adrien's assistant? June Weir pointed them out to me."

"She certainly doesn't miss much! Yes, his name is Jean-Loup and I think he is quite gifted. He's a rather bad-mannered kid, but he'll get over it."

"He wants to come to the U.S.A. and asked me for an appointment. I wouldn't want to steal him if you're fond of him."

"My dear, I'm grateful for your consideration. May I give you my answer before you leave?"

"Of course, I'll be in Monte Carlo at the Hotel de Paris for a week starting next Sunday. That will leave you almost two weeks to think it over. Telephone me early in the morning. Don't forget to call me in New York when you get there. Bye-bye, darling, take care."

Marie-Victoire turned to three striking American men, one very blond, who looked as if he had just come out of a fashion magazine. These were the Vogue pattern buyers and they represented important business for the house for not only did they buy four or five pieces both in cloth and in paper, but they also paid a royalty on all patterns sold, which over the seasons could go as high as twenty thousand dollars.

In France, people always think that American women buy everything ready-made, from frozen foods to clothing, which they throw away so as not to have to mend it. In fact, many women dress themselves from patterns, and they are often the most elegant ones.

Since these buyers knew exactly what they wanted, and were perfectly proper and precise, Marie-Victoire liked to take care of them herself. They asked her if they could make their choice immediately, and she agreed enthusiastically.

Oliver approached her. "Well, that wasn't bad at all!"

"You're a love. It was mostly thanks to you. I don't think it will be a record season, but there are really quite a few buyers."

"You'll have dinner with me this evening? I don't know what has happened to your daughter. When I came at lunchtime you had left for the hospital. What can I do for you?"

"Nothing at the moment. I have to go back to see my daughter at six o'clock, but wait for me at the house, I'll telephone Thérèse. I have a great many very serious things to talk about with you. We'll have dinner at my house. I'm dead tired."

"Good. Until later, then."

Marie-Victoire made a sign to Christiane to come help her, gave her the list of models to bring from the dressing room for Vogue patterns, and asked another little second saleswoman to roll a clothing rack into the almost empty main salon. When the models were brought, she left the buyers to arrive at a decision.

If all the customers were like them, she said to herself, this would be the ideal profession. She went back through the first salon where the Amsterdam buyers had had ten dresses brought out to buy two paper patterns. They talked freely among themselves since they thought that no one could understand their difficult language. One of them, the tailor no doubt, measured the pleats of a skirt with a pencil, felt the fabrics, noted the placement of darts in a notebook, while his boss asked the exhausted saleswoman for more and more models to get her out of the salon.

This kind of buyer never had a list prepared in advance and sometimes even invented a number to gain time to be able to study the models already brought out. Nor did they show the slightest impatience if a model already selected by another buyer could not be found. The more time they could spend examining details, the happier they were. But they were no worse than most of the buyers, who openly copied as many garments as possible and bought as few. Marie-Victoire, always annoyed by these proceedings, leaned over the tailor's notebook but unfortunately could not see any drawing. She had to be content with saying in English: "Take your time."

She returned to her dear Vogue patterns. They asked her if two similar dresses could be shown again on two mannequins so that they could compare them and decide on one or the other. She went to the dressing room herself to be sure that it didn't take too long, and fifteen minutes later the order was signed, the last instructions were given on which photos were to be taken the next day, and the last amiabilities exchanged.

Between times, Marie-Victoire had been able to negotiate most of a sale of an evening gown to Bergdorf Goodman and was thus assured of having at least one model in the Fashion Group showing at the beginning of September. For the prestige of the house it would have been catastrophic not to appear there. Evidently since Alexander's had closed its line-for-line department, the Import Show had fewer and fewer genuine purchased models and the couturiers sent garments there at their own expense. More and more this became a sacrifice

rather than good business. The day when all the couturiers decided that it was no longer profitable to sell their
models to the Seventh Avenue manufacturers and that they
would execute their ideas themselves, Parisian haute couture
would cease to exist in the form it had had for the past fifty
years.

It was five-thirty, and since none of the remaining buyers
were important ones, Marie-Victoire left them in the hands of
their saleswomen and went up to get her bag and the little
suitcase she had prepared for Clothilde. The telephone rang
and she picked it up automatically, a little surprised to hear
Mitzi's voice.

"How did you happen to get through to me directly?"

"Does that mean you wouldn't have spoken to me?"

"No, no, of course not, but it isn't usual that just anybody
gets through to me. I'm in a great hurry, I'm on my way out."

"I only want to tell you how sorry I am about your mannequin, and also about the Princess Herminie; you seemed so
pleased to be making her trousseau!"

What a rotten bitch, Marie-Victoire swore to herself, she
must be delighted. "I thought you were at Cap Martin."

"But I am, darling, that's where I'm calling you from. I went
to Saint-Tropez yesterday, and I heard something which might
just interest you."

All right, sighed Marie-Victoire, what bad news has she got
to offer this time?

"I heard that things are much worse between Liliane and
Vachez." Vachez was the manager of a great couture house,
and Liliane was the directrice of it. "The poor darling, you know
how fond I am of her, I feel just terrible for her."

"How does that concern me?"

"Maybe she'd like to change houses; she has a fabulous
clientele, she'd be very good for you. You know, it's in-cre-di-
ble, Vachez told her she looked as if she were a hundred when

she'd just had her face lifted! I might add that to make up for his insults she's absolutely surrounded by boy friends, and even girl friends, so of course she looks rather tired."

"Listen, Mitzi, I'm sure you want to be helpful, but if this is the kind of story you tell about people you're fond of, I don't dare think what you must say about the ones you hate. Your Liliane is a very nice attractive woman. I've met her several times. Let her take care of her own business. I'm not looking for a manager and I certainly don't want to get someone who will discover she has literary talents some day and tell about how all the customers wear dirty brassieres."

"You know I only told you about it as a favor. Everyone is saying you're going to close."

"My dear, before you celebrate, I think that if I did it would hurt you and your little friends worse than me. If ever I sell my house, I'll get a great deal of money, while you won't be able to borrow dresses or have your coats relined free any more. Thanks for calling, have a nice vacation—darling!"

And Marie-Victoire hung up the telephone with a loud, liberating bang. . . . That snake, that camel, that horrible harpy! I would like to kick her, scratch her, put her through a meat grinder! To take her anger out on someone, she called the operator: "Since when do you allow calls to come through to me without announcing them?"

"Oh, madame, I'm so sorry. That lady was calling long distance. She said that she was a personal friend and that it was urgent."

Marie-Victoire, realizing that the operator, whom she was really fond of, was near tears, repented. "Come, come, I'll forgive you, but don't do it again even if the caller says he's the President of the Republic."

The hospital corridors were empty of the morning derelicts. A few convalescents dressed in dark blue Public Welfare robes

216

were shuffling up and down. Marie-Victoire was ashamed of the pretty little suitcase, of her simple, well-cut dress, of her beautiful hair, of her feet that didn't hurt, and of her look of good health which she couldn't hide from these miserable human beings. In all the clinics where she had visited sick friends, the corridors had been filled with an overflow of flowers and with well-to-do visitors. All kinds of miseries were on display here. The inequality between rich and poor is most conspicuous in the ills humanity suffers from, for the rich can hide themselves away to die while the poor have to do it in public. She remembered her mother's discreet death, and her grandparents'. She shivered as she thought that she might have been that woman before her, crying as she walked away, supported by sympathetic but uninvolved neighbors, ashamed of making a scene. All healthy people should be made to visit hospitals once a month: they would complain less of their supposed misfortunes. What a lesson in serenity could be learned here, she thought.

Clothilde still had the IV bottle hanging above her, the needle stuck in her vein. She now was very flushed and breathing quickly. Marie-Victoire looked at the temperature chart at the foot of the bed: 103°.

Clothilde's neighbor said: "The doctor came by and said that it was to be expected. She'll be better tomorrow."

Marie-Victoire sat on the chair and taking out the eau de Cologne, dampened a cloth with it. She passed it gently over Clothilde's forehead. Clothilde opened her eyes and sketched a smile before closing them. She groaned in her troubled sleep and murmured bits of sentences. Marie-Victoire leaned over to try to guess what they were: "Papa, Papa, don't fire, I love you, I'll take care of you, it's silly to die!"

Her mother understood immediately. Only one person in the world was vile enough to have told Clothilde about this tragedy and that was her aunt! What a vicious woman! She hated me from the day we announced our engagement and she finally found a way to hurt me as much as possible. Now I understand why Clothilde has been so distant recently. God knows what poison that wicked witch has poured into her ears! I'll have to get to the bottom of it and find out just what she did tell her. I can't let my child believe I drove her father to suicide.

Marie-Victoire shivered at the idea of having to explain her father's sexual behavior to her daughter and she knew that in spite of her desire to defend her own innocence to Clothilde, she could never be able to bring herself to such confidences.

Marie-Victoire's compresses on Clothilde's aching head were no use, for she kept on groaning. Now she called out: "Pierre, Pierre, please, have pity on me!"

Marie-Victoire was horrified. What agony had her daughter lived through without her knowledge? Tomorrow she would go to Rue de la Huchette to see if Monsieur Feuillot was still there and try to find out what happened. She opened Clothilde's bag and took a key from it.

Finally Clothilde breathed a little more slowly and stopped muttering. Her mother went to find the pleasant nurse to ask if someone couldn't stay beside her through the night. She would pay, of course. In her place she found a swarthy little woman, wrinkled as a prune, and she sighed with relief when she heard her accent. With a smile she said to her:

"You're from the Midi, so am I. What part do you come from?"

"From Fayence. And you? You don't have a southern accent."

"Yes, I was raised in Paris, but my father was born in Baussigue. That's ten kilometers from your home."

"Oh, I know it very well. You live in the château?"

"Yes."

This impressed her much more than Professor Forval whom the day nurse had told her about. "We'll take good care of your little lamb. The intern on duty is very nice. You have nothing to worry about."

Reassured by the knowledge that she was dealing with a compatriot from the Midi, Marie-Victoire left feeling better about Clothilde's health, but with a heavy heart because of what she had learned. At the door she ran into a young blond girl whom she had met once or twice at the Quai de Béthune.

"Aren't you Agnès, Clothilde's friend? Do you recognize me?"

"Of course, madame. How is she?"

"She's delirious, but they say that's to be expected. Since you've come, you must know what's been going on. Please tell me what you know about it."

"I tried to call you this morning, but your line was always busy. I think Clothilde called Saturday morning too but couldn't get you before she decided to go to that horrible midwife. You must tell the telephone company that your telephone is out of order."

"No, it was off the hook and I didn't know it."

"That's bad luck. Luckily, I finally went to Rue de la Huchette this morning. The poor thing, she wasn't a pretty sight!"

"A few hours more and they wouldn't have been able to save her. Do you know that they had to remove the whole infected uterus and she'll never be able to have a child? The doctor is afraid it will be a terrible shock when she finds out, and if I knew what happened to her I might be able to soften the blow. I don't care who committed this butchery. What I want to know is, who is the man who is responsible and why didn't Clothilde think of marrying him?"

Agnès wasn't sure what she should do, but this woman

219

seemed sincere, and it was really a tragedy that Clothilde could no longer have a child, so she might as well speak up.

"Madame, Clothilde was very much in love with a friend of ours who is very political; because of this he has some rigid ideas about marriage, he thinks it's pointless."

"So is he the one who made her have an abortion?"

"Not at all. He told her that if she had it, he'd never see her again. He thinks women can raise their children alone and that anyway in a few years children will be taken care of by educational communes, the way they are in Israel."

"My God, then why didn't she tell me? If she didn't want this child, I would have taken her to Switzerland or even New York! If she wanted to keep it, I'd have arranged that too. What is a little scandal compared to this tragedy?"

"She must not have thought you'd be so understanding."

"What a pity! The people we know the least are the very ones we love the best. So you think this boy will never marry her?"

"Definitely not. He just asked me about her and told me that he wouldn't even come to see her. I don't think he dares show himself again. He must feel remorse, though. There's nothing like it for turning men into cowards."

"That's dreadful! If Clothilde loves him, we must get him back."

Agnès didn't reply. She never would have imagined that a woman, decorated with the Legion of Honor, clothed in costly garments, who openly exploited the working class to dress super-rich dollies, could be capable of putting love above social considerations. Her own parents, both civil servants in the Social Security Administration, hadn't such broad views. Agnès had left home because her mother never stopped telling her that love and fresh water were very nice for six months, and that she'd been a fool not to marry the Lavalotte boy, who was a department head at twenty-five and had a very promising future in Penal Administration. A supercop, for God's sake! Agnès shivered just to think of it. To live out her days with the Chief Warden of French Prisons! Besides he was fat and had a thick white skin. Her mother must be crazy! She had slammed the door behind her and since then had lived with a well-tanned boy friend and given private lessons in mathematics, at which she was very good.

"As for loving him, she loves him all right. But just the same I don't think she's ready to share a militant political life with him. And he makes no secret of the fact that his sole passion and aim is revolution, and you can't live with a man like that if you aren't burning with the same fire. They're loners by definition, at least the ones who are honest with themselves. And if Pierre isn't easy to live with, he really is sincere."

"Still, I have to talk to him."

"Well, you can try, but he's pretty tough."

"You saved my daughter's life. I can never thank you enough. What can I do for you?"

"Nothing at all, madame, Clothilde is a great girl and I'm very fond of her. I just happened to get there in time. I'd done the same for a stranger."

"Look! How would you like a dress?"

"A dress like yours? Oh no, I wouldn't have any place to wear it."

"Well then, a warm coat for winter?"

"No, madame, I have my windbreaker and warm sweaters, that's plenty. Honestly, I don't need anything, but it's very nice of you."

Marie-Victoire saw that she was going about it in the wrong way, that this generation was not interested in the things that she used to dream about when she was young. But she was stubborn, and insisted.

221

"Are you going away during your vacation?"

"My boy friend and I are thinking of hitchhiking to Saint-Tropez tomorrow. He has a friend who has promised us jobs as beach boy and waitress in Pamplona."

"When Clothilde can travel, I think I'll take her to Baussigue for her convalescence. That's our family place. It's only seventy kilometers from Saint-Tropez. Here is the telephone number. Bring your friend and come to visit us whenever you like. There are ten rooms in the house, you are welcome to them and it will entertain Clothilde. You'll see; there are practically no 'tourists' in our village"—she put the word in quotation marks as if she were mentioning some disease—"we built a swimming pool last year. My father is a dear, and the cook is marvelous, if you don't mind garlic. And if you need money, you can pick raspberries, and jasmine too, but you have to get up at four o'clock to do it!"

"That sounds great. I won't say no. We'll call Clothilde in a couple of weeks."

"May I kiss you?"

"Of course. You're a real doll—oh! I shouldn't have said that!"

"Ha! I'm used to the language and you're a doll too. Anyway, we'll be seeing you soon."

Quai de Béthune was just across the Seine from the Hôtel-Dieu, but even so, it was seven o'clock before Marie-Victoire got home. Thérèse, hearing the door, hurried to greet her mistress.

"Monsieur Mayer is on the terrace, I gave him a drink so he wouldn't be impatient."

And he must have given you a nice tip to make you look so happy, old girl, Marie-Victoire guessed, noticing that Thérèse had gotten out the Chivas bottle.

"Will you hold it against me if I leave you for another ten minutes?" she said to Oliver. "Long enough for a quick bath. I'm dead tired. Thérèse will serve dinner at eight."

"No, of course not. I'm beginning to understand what you said to me about the view this morning; the apse of Notre Dame is really marvelous!"

Marie-Victoire smiled without answering and went to run her bath. While it was filling she chose a negligee of orange lamé threaded with gold, cut like a loose caftan, in which she knew she looked her best. Fifteen minutes later she reappeared on the terrace wearing very little make-up, with her hair down, and smelling of soap and toilet water.

"Ah! I needed that. The hospital is horrible."

"How is your daughter, and what is the matter with her?"

The peritonitis story was good enough for strangers, but since there was no danger of Thérèse understanding a conversation in English, Marie-Victoire felt relieved to be able to tell the truth to someone finally. But she didn't know where to begin. Oliver took her silence for hesitation.

"I want to know all about it from the beginning. I'm sure there are things you haven't told anyone."

"How did you guess?"

"I could have made a fortune as a psychoanalyst."

"It's true; when I'm in your arms I feel both as secure as in a bomb shelter and defenseless as a newborn baby."

"That's an important compliment. So tell me what sort of adolescence and marriage you had. We'll speak of your daughter afterward."

She had poured two generous glasses of Chivas, and with no hesitation, she began to tell everything, including the disappointment of her marriage, her husband's suicide, and her own success in business. She accused herself of not having paid enough attention to her daughter lately, of having been busy both with the business and with her affair with him, of having allowed the moment slip when everything could still have been taken care of. Helped by emotion and whiskey, she ended in tears over what had happened. "Clothilde," she added between sobs, "even tried to telephone me Saturday morning when the telephone was off the hook."

Oliver had only nodded his head or murmured encouragement during her recital. He asked what Clothilde was studying. But when he had asked questions, he listened to the answers without adding anything. Most listeners are not really interested in anything but their own problems, or take advantage of confidences to offer the fruits of their great wisdom.

He understood that Marie-Victoire had opened herself to him even more fully than she had the previous evening, and he knew he must be the only person in the world to have possessed her in this way, body and soul. It made him feel both very proud and immensely tender. After dinner, seeing that she was exhausted, he took her in his arms, undressed her, helped her put on her nightgown, and laid her on her bed as he would have a child. He kissed her tear-swollen eyelids.

"Sleep well, darling. All this mess will be cleared up."

She dared not object. He had given her more than any other human being, and, content, she was asleep in five minutes.

Adrien, Jean-Loup, three mannequins, the Princess, and Chavanaux decided to go to Adrien's studio to see the news on television as they always did after a collection. To see these films alone at home would be too depressing. At the end of the television news there were two short sequences on the most important couturiers of the day. This began with Lanvin and touched on all the others in turn. Daphne, who had gone

224

on a trip for the Chambre Syndicale with Frédérique, Lanvin's top mannequin, asked in a low voice how that house could stand such a tart . . . especially when she was at least thirty-five, if not more! Adrien, looking at the Lanvin coat, said: "I did that four years ago!" The Princess: "Even with her stringbean figure, that mannequin looks like a pumpkin. Imagine Madame Durand in it!" Everyone burst out laughing, to grow serious again when Adrien appeared in the screen. Daphne: "You really are photogenic!" It was true that Adrien looked like a diplomat in a '60s Hollywood film. He made a graceful statement that he had memorized on women's love of elegance and the influence of French good taste on the whole world, that good taste made out of glorious recipes from the past and refined taste. The only thing missing was the "Marseillaise" in the background. Everyone cried "Bravo!" Amalia thought she had looked divine, because she was a natural optimist. Daphne, on the other hand, remarked: "That dress breaks in the back, I shouldn't have turned around."

Meantime, it was Lanvin's associates' turn to make fun of Adrien: "He's so pompous he could be hired at the Élysées tomorrow as chief of protocol."

But all in all, everyone was very pleased at seeing themselves, or just hearing the name of his or her house mentioned on the little screen. If a factory would put its best workers on television instead of giving bonuses it would have a wide following, for the attraction of being seen by multitudes is irresistible.

"We can't just separate now," Daphne begged. "It's horrible about Ingara . . . but we really must wait for the papers to come out. I suggest we go to dinner in some little bistro and each pay for himself."

"Very good idea," the rest chorused, comforted at the

thought they wouldn't have to be alone on the evening of the collection.

"I know a marvelous one in the Rue des Canettes," Amalia cried.

"Do you know the phone number?"

"Yes, I'll call them now. Let's see, how many of us are there? Adrien, Jean-Loup, Daphne, Monsieur Chavanaux, the Princess, Véronique, and myself. And since Madame isn't here, will anyone mind if I ask my boy friend to come along?"

"Of course not."

Without Marie-Victoire's presence, the venture turned into a kind of picnic. While waiting for the hors d'oeuvres, they began to tell stories, for like all people who work in the same business, they only cared about their own little world. For the benefit of Amalia's boy friend, a handsome young man, an executive in a hosiery factory and dressed in a style he approved of, Adrien regained his enthusiasm and told the story of the lady arriving at Dior with a very decrepit husband. She settled him in an arm chair and, in a perfectly audible voice, ordered a mourning hat: "He won't last more than a week," she remarked, pointing to the unfortunate fellow scornfully, "and don't worry, he's deaf as a post."

Then each one had his own story to tell, usually unkind, all classics in the annals of couture. There was the one about the tailor, exasperated by the insatiable demands of a very ugly client, who burst out: "Madame, God didn't create a miracle when He made you, so you can't expect me to do my job better than He did His!"

Then there was the story of the same tailor, who was extremely nervous, and snipped the wire to the hearing aid of a lady who never listened anyway, after a moment she complained because no one was talking to her any more! And the one about the customer who loved trips and parties so much that she concealed her husband's death on the twenty-eighth of December until the first of January so as to wear a special evening gown she had ordered for New Year's Eve!

Finally, after several glasses of wine, the Princess emerged from her habitual reserve and cleverly imitated the saleswomen's conversations, which were always the same: the best way to cook fish . . . illness and death of some acquaintance . . . the magnificence of their prewar customers. She related how they had recently been discussing the marriage of one of them at fifty-eight to a seventy-year-old widower whom she'd met at dawn in the market after living alone for forty years. Would it be better to buy her a television set for a wedding present? Or a table service so that she could receive her dozen new grandchildren properly? What these ladies were really dying to know was whether the marriage would be consummated or not.

Then the Princess told about Madame Nicole's latest tragedy. She was known to divide her affection between a fat cat and some pigeons which had nested on her balcony. This good soul's dream was to make peace between these natural enemies. Unfortunately, scarcely a week passed when the cat didn't pull feathers off one of her beloved pigeons, in spite of the moral lectures she gave him every morning.

"Don't tell that in front of Daphne," Adrien teased, "you know that the great love of her life is Crou-Croune and the idea that a cat could eat her birdie would break her heart."

"Really, you never miss a chance to say something mean!" retorted the poor bird lover.

Chavanaux looked at his watch. He could never get over Daphne's idiotic attraction to Adrien, nor her total scorn for himself.

"I think someone could go to Le Drugstore. The papers must have been delivered by now."

The criticism in the papers was as expected. *Figaro,* in apparently neutral terms, spoke of the frozen elegance and customary good taste of the collection and deplored the three or four sexy gowns which seemed out of place in such a cathedral of haute couture.

"An article like that," said Adrien, "could only attract the Mother Superior of a very aristocratic order which was thinking of changing its habit. It's a subtle put-down."

Nevertheless he was pleased that Dabadie hadn't liked Jean-Loup's dresses.

Eugenia Sheppard in the international *Herald Tribune* was less tactful and barely avoided calling Adrien a has-been. The only dresses she liked in the collection were the clinging gowns designed by a young man whom Madame Forval had better give a more important place in her house if she didn't want to end up dressing nothing but dowager duchesses. She mentioned Princess Herminie's accident and ended by saying that in our times dressing prominent women or taking advantage of the publicity created by the death of a mannequin was no longer enough to influence fashion, for fashion today belongs to the streets.

Even Jean-Loup was troubled when he read this article and said to Adrien: "She's really too much . . . I am wondering if her compliments for me don't conceal poisoned barbs too."

"No, not at all; she's right," Adrien replied thoughtfully. "Look at the people here: these boys and girls who touch each other more from habit than desire. All the hair; all the necklaces made of iron, zinc, copper or shells around their necks; the tanned skin; the bare feet; the dull eyes; and the ambitionless souls. Look at them walking around Saint-Germain-des-Prés, looking for a crash pad, using marijuana to take the place of comfort. They are as stupefied in Amsterdam as they are in Paris and New York and Tokyo. Even Victorian education with its taboos wasn't as stupid as that! Do you remember how blasé the men on the beaches of Saint-Tropez were last summer looking at all those naked breasts! And then think how heroes in novels of 1900 went into ecstasies over an exposed ankle! Even Adam and Eve got sick of a Paradise where everything was free in less time than it takes to say: ouf! Man is so constructed that he loves only what he is forbidden to do, and coming back to our beloved profession, an elaborate costume and complicated rites practiced by a chosen few makes those who don't participate want to be members of the club. Tell women they can dress as they please and it won't interest them any more. On the other hand, if *Elle* or *McCall's* this year said: With a green dress of this length, worn with red boots and a violet bow in your hair, you will represent perfect chic, they would feel reassured, even if what they really wanted was a white tunic. They love the idea of suffering to be in fashion. It wasn't so long ago they confined their waists in corsets and their feet in pointed shoes. A woman must be either very intelligent or very rich to feel comfortable with originality; the masses prefer to be led, even if they have to give up their comfort. Real haute couture would dress every woman to suit her mood, her figure, and her income. You can't find that in a supermarket. Coming back to you, you must send flowers to Eugenia tomorrow. And go kneel at her feet so that she'll introduce you to Seventh Avenue. In America success comes quickly. You must take advantage of it. They have discovered sex in the past ten years and it will go on fascinating them for another three or four years. When you've made your fortune, you can always retire to Torremolinos."

And with a bitter little smile, Adrien added: "I say, there's

Alan with a group of lady journalists. Go to Régine with him. It will surely be on the Maison Forval expense account. It's part of the image an ambitious young designer must present. I'm going home to bed."

Chapter VII

When she awakened Wednesday morning, Marie-Victoire didn't know where she was. However, the room was the same as always. Popoff was stretching and yawning loudly, the tea cart squeaked a little, Thérèse was wearing her stony face, and the sky was gray. *Le Figaro* was there, a hostile sentinel beside a pretty teapot and, seeing it, Marie-Victoire remembered that it was the day after the collection . . . and that reading about it was going to be painful. Ordinarily she saw the papers the evening before with everyone else and it was less disagreeable. Let's see. Well, well, Dear Dabadie doesn't like Jean-Loup's dresses . . . "cathedral of haute couture," oh dear! Might as well call it a mausoleum! I'd very much like to know what the Americans have to say. If I sent Thérèse to get the international *Herald Tribune* and the New York *Times* she could walk Popoff too. I'm going to be quite late at Place Vendôme. I want to put my thoughts in order. It's time to make some decisions. My God, I'm tired! She let her head fall back on the pillows, but the thought of Clothilde wiped out all the problems of haute couture. She called the hospital; she was told that Mademoiselle Forval had passed a good night, her temperature was normal and she was sleeping. Yes, her mother could come to see her at lunchtime.

No sooner had she hung up than the telephone rang.

"Darling, how did you sleep?"

"Like a log."

"How is Clothilde?"

"Much better, it seems."

"I'm going to have to go back to Dallas for a few days. I'll be leaving tomorrow at noon. Will I see you this evening?"

"Of course."

"Let's have dinner at your place again, if that's all right. We have a lot to talk about."

"Delighted. See you later, then."

Just hearing his voice on the telephone made her feel both alert and languid. All emotions seem to meet in the stomach: it expands with joy or contracts with fear. There is no such thing as happiness without a good digestion. This idea led her directly to think about dinner. She was sorry not to have time to make one of her own specialties for she knew that cooking for one's beloved always takes on the air of a sacrament. And all kinds of dishes she would have liked to cook for him passed before her eyes. But today she would have to be satisfied with going to Fauchon and bring home some cold meat. Well, she said to herself, that's a good idea and I'll buy some nice fruit for Clothilde at the same time. I'll go there on my way to the hospital.

Even in the most difficult circumstances, Marie-Victoire never lost her sense of organization. At the time of her husband's death, her sister-in-law had often told the malicious story of how the young widow's immediate preoccupation had been to have a chic black outfit made to wear at the funeral.

Now I must telephone my father. He must know what has happened to his granddaughter. The connection was quickly made, and there was his familiar, warm voice.

"Hello, darling, I'm very glad to hear from you. Is business going well?"

"So-so. You'll see the review in *Le Figaro*."

"Everyone watched your Adrien on television. Why didn't you do the talking? He's much too pretentious, he acts like an ambassador in an operetta."

Marie-Victoire smiled. Her father, though tolerant, had never been able to stand Adrien.

"That isn't important. I'm calling you mostly to tell you that Clothilde is very ill. I've been very worried; she had a severe attack of appendicitis and peritonitis set in. There was an emergency operation yesterday."

"Good Lord, that's very serious! Are you sure that she's better now?"

"Yes, she received excellent treatment, but she'll have to be in the hospital for ten days."

"All right then, I'm coming. You won't have much time to spend with her, but I'll be able to stay with her all day. When she's feeling better I'll bring her back here: Nounou and I will soon have her on her feet."

Marie-Victoire had not thought that her father would be able to come to Paris, but the idea of having him near delighted her. She would feel less alone, especially since Oliver would be gone.

"But you hate Paris. Isn't that too much to ask of you?"

"What's a few drops of rain compared with the pleasure of being with the two of you? And especially to be of some use

233

to you. I'll take the eleven o'clock plane from Nice tomorrow. Can you meet me at Orly?"

"Yes, especially since I have to take an American friend there at the same hour. But are you sure it won't tire you?"

"Don't be silly, my dear. I'd hate to have to live out my life up there in the smog, but a short visit will be a nice change. Our poor priest, my usual scrabble partner, is really failing. He can't even digest garlic, the poor old fellow!"

Like all healthy old men, Nicolas de Baussigue couldn't help mocking his contemporaries' infirmities and had only scorn for the ones who were so weak as to allow themselves to die, like his wife.

"Well, I'll be delighted to see you, I've had a great many problems to wrestle with lately, and I could use a man in my life!"

"Oh dear! Seventy years old next month is a little too old for you!"

"I adore you and you're marvelous. We'll have a big party for your birthday. See you tomorrow, I'm looking forward to it."

"May God bless you, my darling."

Thérèse came in with the American papers at that moment and an excited Popoff.

"Thérèse, we must get Mademoiselle's bedroom and bath ready. Monsieur le Comte is arriving tomorrow. When she comes back from the hospital I'll let her have mine and sleep on the living room couch."

Thérèse's face lit up. "Monsieur le Comte! Oh, I am glad!"

"Monsieur Mayer is coming again this evening. I'll buy the dinner, just make a salad and bring some champagne up from the cellar. Monsieur Mayer is going to be my partner and we have to talk business."

An eloquent silence welcomed this last sentence, and

Marie-Victoire bit her lips. . . . Honestly! I really don't need to give her any explanations!

"I have a lot to do this morning. Can you iron my black linen suit, please?"

"Yes, madame."

Suddenly, Marie-Victoire felt an irresistible desire to meet the young man who had hurt her daughter so much. The previous morning, she had relegated him to a place behind a screen of thoughts which necessarily took priority. Now, these had been dealt with. How wonderful if she could make him change his mind and drag him off to the hospital with his promise in her pocket! She had the key to the little apartment in her bag and she decided to go there. She would behave as if Clothilde had asked her to bring something from there.

In fifteen minutes she was ready, and leaving the Austin with Popoff in it not far from the Rue de la Huchette she asked the concierge for Monsieur Feuillot and climbed the four flights, panting a little. She took a deep breath on the landing, and, key in hand, hesitated for a moment before opening the door, but curiosity overcame good manners and she went in, slamming the door after her. A disheveled form rose from the bed covers and a hoarse voice articulated:

"Who are you?"

"Excuse me for coming in on you like this, monsieur, I thought the place was empty. Are you Monsieur Feuillot?"

"Yes, madame."

She noted the "Madame" in passing. Revolutionary though he may be, she thought, he's still only twenty-five and I impress him.

"I'm Madame Forval, and Clothilde has asked me to bring her some things."

Pierre was now fully awake and furious at being surprised

in such a humiliating position. He always slept without his pajama trousers and he couldn't get up in front of this woman.

"Would you be kind enough to step outside for five minutes so that I can dress?"

"Of course. Call me when you're presentable."

He slipped on his blue jeans, a pullover, and moccasins, but didn't comb his magnificent hair, which was as curly as a girl's and tangled from sleep. In spite of his beard, he still looked like a child, and Marie-Victoire couldn't help smiling at him when he opened the door.

"I'm sure you'll be able to help me find two or three things."

He grew slightly pale. For three days he had not been able to get rid of the picture of a bloodless Clothilde carried off like a package by the ambulance aides. Without her constant enfolding love he felt naked and shivering, a little like a bather who comes out of the water when a cloud is passing over the sun.

He usually spent the month of August morosely in his family's house, because he had no money to go elsewhere, but he could not stand the idea of going back there this year. He had been changed by Clothilde's presence without being quite conscious of it. For the first time he became aware of what a mediocre, banal life his family lived. Instead of telling himself that if he had wanted to, he could have lived with that sweet and intelligent girl and that he probably had lost a rare chance at happiness, he had become harder than ever. The memory of his family's intellectual bankruptcy only made him congratulate himself on not having become enmeshed in the warm net of bourgeois comfort. He remembered with particular horror his parents' sacred television. They swallowed anything, he thought, with about as much critical spirit as mass-produced chickens. Ah! the time when Marx said that

236

religion was the opium of the people was long past; now TV was their drug, taking the place of Bible, newspaper, theatre, and conscience.

"Do you know just what Clothilde wants or should I give you everything?"

Marie-Victoire was a little embarrassed and all she could think of was: "Doesn't she have a little pillow to put under her neck?"

Without answering, he turned his back and climbed on a stool to reach some things stowed over the cupboard. Marie-Victoire saw some trousers and a leather jacket on hangers, also a woman's peignoir hanging emptily against the wall. Who can express the sadness of abandoned clothing? On the shelf there was a pair of sheets, three shirts, and two slips. Her heart contracted as she thought how her daughter's dream had been to live in such barrenness.

He must have brought her extraordinary intellectual richness to give her such a scorn of material goods. He must be marvelous, she thought, examining him in detail as only a woman accustomed to looking for flaws in clothing knows how to do. And she let a silence fall between them.

Feeling her eyes on him, he got down from the stool with a little pillow whose embroidered and beribboned case made it look in the austere room like a butterfly in a parking lot.

"Yes," said Marie-Victoire, "Clothilde is like me, she can't read without this kind of cushion under her neck."

He held it awkwardly in big hands with long fingers and well-kept nails. My word, she thought, he has beautiful hands. All in all, if you care for the prophet type, he's really something; he looks like a younger version of all those pictures of Christ. It was a striking resemblance: he had the same reddish hair, the same beard. Hard to believe he wasn't aware of it himself. . . .

He held out the little cushion, looking her in the eye for the first time: "How is she?"

"As well as can be expected. I think I'll be able to take her to the South when she can travel. Her grandfather is coming tomorrow to keep her company while she gets better, since unfortunately I don't have much free time for her. And I hope that her friend, Agnès, will be able to come to the château to keep her company."

"I see. There she'll be, saved by the happy consumer society she thought she had escaped. . . ." And sneering: "You may escape your fate, but never your family!"

"Don't you think it's better than being dead? I think even a militant communist mother would prefer to see her daughter married to the worst bourgeois boss than in her grave. Another hour and she couldn't have been saved. Do you know that she can never have a child and this could be the tragedy of her life?"

"I didn't want this. When she realized I couldn't and wouldn't marry her, she told me she preferred to get rid of the child. I threatened to leave her to make her change her mind. I even took my suitcase with me. I thought that would make her think it over but I purposely 'forgot' some laundry so I would have an excuse to be able to continue the argument. But when I did come back, it was all over, and she was dying."

"I know all that and I'll never forgive myself for not being available when she tried to talk to me about it. I never would have let her commit this madness, especially under such conditions. You know, I have paid dearly for the knowledge that very often children are a woman's only consolation in a bad marriage. But why does anybody marry except because everybody else does? And with what that 'everybody' makes of the institution, would be much better to abstain from it."

238

Pierre could not conceal his surprise at what he had taken for an elegant tool of the capitalist system: "You're really amazing!"

"Don't think, though, that if I share your views on marriage, I agree with the rest. To begin with, your total condemnation of abortion doesn't go with your hatred of the consumer society. Because in order to consume, the greatest possible number of consumers are needed. So, the more people you'd suppress, the better the society would work, isn't that true? If abortion were legal and openly practiced in hospitals, there would be fewer accidents like this one. Confess that you have a military interest too: you need soldiers—excuse me, militants!"

Pierre ignored Marie-Victoire's barb. He was suddenly full of assurance again. Marie-Victoire had returned him to his element: dialectic. Inwardly, he smiled. Clothilde reasoned more soundly but with less fire. What hordes of people were anesthetized by the bourgeoisie! Worse than epidemics in the Middle Ages!

"I recognize that abortion is a hyperpolitical weapon. The administration uses it to make sure of the women's vote when they appear to accept it, or that of the Catholic masses when they disapprove of it. They really play games with free will!"

"You said it, not I. Then what decision is more important to a couple than whether or not they are going to reproduce? Through lack of education, or of information, at this very moment, in spite of the pill, more than 50 per cent of all pregnancies are accidents—unfortunate result of Saturday night fun and games."

"Of course, but it is also a form of freedom to choose not to kill one's own child, even if its arrival will upset your personal life. To do as one wishes, one must be adult, and in spite of

239

appearances, Clothilde is not. That's what we want, a society of adults."

"Yes, yes, I've read that: down with the father myth. I agree, but unfortunately the way you've chosen only plays into the reactionaries' hands."

Pierre cut Marie-Victoire off in mid-speech. "That's the reaction of a frightened bourgeoisie to any change or transformation or evolution. It was Christ who said, 'Cursed be the lukewarm.' "

Marie-Victoire, bent on convincing her opponent, had forgotten with whom she was arguing. She had the disturbing sensation that this was the first time in years she had had a real dialogue with anyone.

"Perhaps," she said softly. "But unfortunately violence attracts violence. In underdeveloped countries each time you start a revolution that goes wrong it's for the benefit of colonels or generals who take the power you've helped to create! Every time I go to America, I tremble when I see the increase in crime and the backlash it is causing. Obviously sensational reporting exaggerates the Mafia, drugged hippies, armed Puerto Ricans, and pro-white or pro-black fanatics. But it's the crushing mass of honest ordinary Americans who will bring about a dictatorship without really wanting it."

Pierre cut her off again. "A dictatorship, or, I hope, a real revolution. We know now that it has to start in the U.S.A. Europe is too old and too tired. For good or evil, all revolutions, sexual, industrial, or otherwise come from there now."

In a lightly ironic tone, Marie-Victoire said: "What makes me wonder is that in the countries where there has been revolution, life doesn't seem to have improved. I'll withhold judgment, since I haven't actually been to most, and because I instinctively distrust all propagandists, whether press attachés or special envoys. But the growing number of refugees from Cuba and East Berlin and Central Europe means something, surely. Admit that we don't hear of French refugees, except for a handful of millionaires who want to escape taxes and go to Geneva."

They had both sat down. Pierre had asked her permission to make coffee, because he couldn't argue, he said, before he'd had his morning fix. She accepted the cup he offered and complimented him on its quality.

"Revolution aside, what are you doing?"

"I'm about to finish my doctorate in law this year. If I find some little job which will make a living, I'll try to take the examination for the faculty. But you need another doctorate and three more years of study. If not, I can go into politics right away, there's plenty to do there."

"I shall never understand why unions refuse to settle with their bosses and prefer a bad strike to a good compromise."

"I'm afraid it would take too long to explain it to you. . . ."

". . . unless you're honest enough to admit that when workers share management with bosses, the militant unionists will have to join the Salvation Army, or, vulgarly speaking, tend to their own knitting!"

Pierre lifted his coffee cup, then set it down again.

"Who ever told you we agreed with the union position, especially in France? We know very well how little we can count on their promises about wage increases. It's too easy, madame, to put things in different bags and divide them into black and white according to your own convictions. Nowadays, one can be on the left and struggling against the syndicates, that's what's called being a leftist or an extremist!"

Marie-Victoire raised a thumb.

"Agreed, agreed, I still have a lot to learn about revolutionary doctrine. But at my firm, at my modest level, no one has ever gone on strike and in good years I've had as many

241

as two hundred fifty workers. Some of them laugh behind my back and call me paternalistic, but over the years the atmosphere has always been excellent because I've always given ten centimes an hour more than my competitors so as to get the best workers. I've never refused a necessary leave of absence or a loan in case of illness, and I close the house between Christmas and New Year's, for example, and work some Saturdays after to compensate, which the union leaders would never allow. And I've been able to provide very cheap vacations for my workers by renting an enormous châlet near Chamonix for the ones who want to go to the mountains during that period."

"That's not progress. The general rule should be respected without favoritism in business and there is no reason why the best workers should earn ten centimes more than the less good ones. Workers shouldn't depend on one boss's good will any more than they should be the victims of the ill will of the bad one."

"So the good should pay for the bad and it's no use being more intelligent or working harder than the worst moron or slacker?"

"Exactly."

"Very well, I'll have to cut my staff to an absolute minimum. If you and your kind had your way, it would become impossible to find skilled workers anyway. If this is a picture of our rosy future, I'm glad I'm not twenty years old."

She does not understand a thing, but she isn't completely stupid nor quite hopeless, not as bad as my parents anyway. We can almost communicate.

As if she had heard what he was thinking, Marie-Victoire added: "All that would be unimportant if there were some communication between human beings, but it's as though each person goes round his own little personal track and meetings

242

can only end in collisions. I want so much to avoid the same tragedy for Clothilde that I experienced myself. My husband committed suicide, although I loved him very much, and there was nothing I could do for him."

"I didn't know."

"Clothilde only found out about it just before your separation—I'm sure it was from her own aunt. It must have been a terrible shock for her. The proof of it is that she didn't even tell you about it! The discovery seems to have alienated her from me, and I know I'll have a hard time getting her confidence again. I hope she'll understand that my love is unconditional. In fact, I was all ready to be a doting grandmother. But God didn't want it for me!"

Pierre couldn't help reaching for her hand at the sight of her twisted smile.

"I'm sorry . . ." he said awkwardly, and repeated ". . . yes, I really am sorry. Tell Clothilde, if she can still stand to hear my name."

Marie-Victoire, with a tilt of her chin, retorted: "My dear, I haven't mentioned it to her, but the women in our family are faithful."

Pierre smiled slightly: "Did Clothilde really ask you to come this morning? That surprises me."

"No, she didn't. I'll admit it now, I took the key from her handbag. I knew your name and address because of a bill from the Bazar de l'Hôtel-de-Ville that I saw. I hoped there might be a way to bring the two of you together in spite of everything that has separated you."

"Really? For a moment, I thought you'd come to kill me! You wouldn't have run any risk because any jury would have acquitted you. I can see the headlines now: FAMOUS COUTU-RIÈRE KILLS NOTORIOUS LEFTIST SEDUCER OF UNDERAGE DAUGHTER."

243

"You don't think one dead child is enough? If it would bring my daughter happiness, I'd rather see her live with you unmarried than see her sobbing on your grave. I hate all death, even dead flowers, and especially dead loves. I only want one thing in the world: to see my child happy! Not only had I no intention of killing you, but I hoped to bring you back to her."

"I'm sorry, madame, I'm not the right one to give her that kind of happiness. My politics and my beliefs are more important to me than anything else. No woman, and especially not a woman in love, could stand that. Besides, does she still want me?"

"I'm very disappointed. I hoped to change your mind, but now I see it's better if she doesn't see you again."

"Clothilde won't always be so stubborn; she'll come to realize how much you love her, I'm sure. I hope with all my heart she finds a husband who is more normal than I am. And I'm sorry too that I didn't meet you sooner."

"That's life, young man. You'll find that everything always comes too late . . . even revolutions. Probably that's why there are five fortunetellers for every clergyman in this world."

Pierre agreed, and, bowing slightly, took the hand that Marie-Victoire extended to him quite naturally. She blushed with pleasure at this impulsive homage, and concluded:

"Whatever anyone says, we are all points on the same continuous line; parallels, curves, or circles belong to the realm of higher mathematics. A little good will and memory should be enough to make the old understand the younger generation. And if the young were finally recognized as valuable by their elders, they would not feel obliged to treat them like rubbish and might profit by their experience."

"I see that you dream of Utopia too, madame, but I thank you just the same. Don't you want to take the little pillow?"

244

"No, I think it would be better not to let Clothilde know I was here."

"I think so too."

In the Place Vendôme, some of the European buyers were still crowded around the racks, but there wasn't the same keen sense of competition which had marked the great days. Marie-Victoire saw Jean Liétart from Brussels making him selection.

"Jean, my dear, how is your wife? Did she come with you? Why isn't she here? You know we'd never ask for a security for her! We'd almost be willing to give her clothes to have her wearing them, she's so elegant! Ah, I see you're hesitating over one of Adrien's assistant's dresses. Just between the two of us, what did you think of the collection?"

"It's a good classical collection. I'm looking for evening gowns in particular. Brussels has become more elegant than Paris, people give more parties, and all the society women have several formal evening dresses."

"You're right, people aren't ashamed of being rich in Belgium. It's a long time since I've been to Brussels; I really must take a little trip there. I adore Belgium and the Belgians too."

"I thank you on their behalf. We would be delighted to have you visit us, and I've just laid down some excellent Bordeaux."

"Oh, you're trying to tempt my palate! I remember your father's port vividly! I'll telephone you; I have to go to New York too. Anyway, give my kindest regards to Armelle. I'll leave you to choose in peace. Besides, I see they want me. See you soon!"

Madame Annie had brought in a new customer from West Berlin whom she wanted to introduce to her employer. He was a blond, very tall, thin, and elegant; he spoke English with almost no accent, and was much too young to have been in the war.

245

"I like your collection very much, madame; it will suit my clientele very well—sensible but elegant."

"Thank you very much, monsieur, it's always a pleasure to hear sincere compliments."

"I'd like to discuss making an arrangement with you which would allow me to buy thirty patterns at a reduced price. Of course, we would pay a royalty on all the models we reproduced. I've got the same contract with two other Paris houses and you could get all the information about it from them."

Marie-Victoire was attracted by this boy's distinguished look.

"I don't object to the idea. I'll tell my manager so that he can discuss details with you. Delighted to have met you. See you soon."

She saw Alan climbing the stairs four at a time.

"You look as if you didn't sleep very well."

"I was at Régine and Castel until four in the morning with the girls from the New York *Times,* English *Vogue* and *Jasmin.* We'll have the cover on *Jasmin.*"

"Jean-Loup's black dress, of course?"

"Of course! He was with us last night and his 'charm-boy' act went over big. He is much easier to sell than Adrien."

"I always thought you two were made for each other."

"Is that a compliment?"

"No, not really. By the way, did you meet Ingara's fiancé?"

"No, he was not at the Ritz. The police had found him before *France-Soir*'s publication."

"Good for them, though I would have loved seeing you with a black eye or a broken jaw—you're too lucky!"

"I've just come from the Hôtel-Dieu. I took some flowers to Clothilde, but she was asleep and they wouldn't let me in."

"That's sweet of you. I'm going over there soon. In a few days she'll want to see you."

"I don't know if I'll be able to go back. In fact, I didn't want to tell you so soon and so unceremoniously, but just so you'll be the first to know, I'm going back to Akron. I've decided to take my place in the factory; my father has just had a slight heart attack and he needs rest."

"Well, I must say this is sudden. When was it you were talking to me about taking over my firm?"

"It's true! I'm sorry."

"Don't be sorry. In spite of our different ideas on the moral limits of publicity, I would have been very sorry to have to dismiss you. I'm glad you're the one who took the initiative. When will you be leaving?"

"When the papers are through taking pictures. Anyway, I'll be keeping my apartment; the rent isn't high and I'd be sorry to get rid of it. I'll come to Paris often, and if I get married, it will be more convenient than a hotel."

Marie-Victoire hated to see a man console himself too quickly, though she knew Clothilde would never have married him. She resented his cheerfulness as if it were a personal insult, preferring to think of him as an unhappy lover.

"I see you're full of projects. But don't forget that the life of the president of a big business in America is busier than that of a public relations man in Paris. We'll surely be seeing each other before you leave; we'll have a big farewell dinner, but now I must go to the hospital."

Alan watched her disappearing and for a few seconds a shadow of sadness fell across his handsome, toothpaste-ad face.

As Marie-Victoire planned her dinner at Fauchon she could not help thinking of Alan. What could have happened to change his mind so drastically? Their argument over Ingara? Surely not, for he firmly believed that the end always justifies the means. My relationship with Mayer? He must suppose I'll sell to Big Mills. Then he'll have nothing more to do in Paris.

I wonder if it's only that— In the hospital corridor, she ran into the little nurse whose eyes were like two black olives.

"Ah, good morning, madame, you're going to be very happy, your little girl is much better. It's too bad, this morning her fiancé couldn't see her because she was asleep, but I gave him all the news about her. And then I fixed the flowers. The room is full of them."

Marie-Victoire immediately understood who the "fiancé" was.

"Would you mind telling me just what you told him?"

"Well, I didn't exactly pat him on the back, since he was the one who got her into this condition. I didn't handle him with kid gloves—I let him know she couldn't have any children. What clumsy oafs these Americans are! I hope I didn't make a mistake?"

"No, not at all. In a sense, you've even done my daughter a favor. Look, I've brought you a bottle of my toilet water. Do you know this kind?"

"I've smelled it in stores, but it's too expensive for me. Thank you very much, I'm delighted."

So this was probably the reason for the handsome Alan's flight! Marie-Victoire realized bitterly; he always knows how to get people to talk! Anyway, I can't imagine Clothilde winding up in Akron, Ohio, even out of desperation and disappointment. But she mustn't think he left because of her or she'll be upset by it! My God, how hard it will be to make her gay again!

In front of the door of Clothilde's room Marie-Victoire hesitated, seeing six people, four children, an old woman and a gentleman with a sinister look surrounding her roommate's bed. Then she made up her mind and came in, greeted them, and found her daughter smiling at her.

"How do you feel this morning, darling?"

248

"Much better, I slept very well."

"Don't all these people disturb you?" whispered Marie-Victoire.

"No, it's funny, I never realized there were people like that. That lady is very nice, but her husband—did you notice him?"

"The kind of man who has only to put his trousers on the bed and zoom, twins are produced nine months after! Skinny little dark fellows like that, watch out for them!"

Clothilde laughed: "Exactly. It's easy to understand how she got the fifth. Her husband is very Catholic and forbids her to take the pill. The poor thing, the hospital is a wonderful vacation for her."

"I have good news: Grandpa is arriving tomorrow to keep you company."

"That's lovely! This hospital life is strange: you're well taken care of but at the same time, it feels like being in prison and abandoned by the outside world. Suddenly the family seems more important than you thought it would."

"In other words, you never thought you could be so glad to see me?"

"Perhaps . . ." and to mitigate the cruelty of the thought, she took her mother's hand and squeezed it.

"Also, I invited your friend Agnès and her young man to come to Baussigue and cheer you up when you're better. I don't suppose that she and her friend have too much money, so it will make a nice vacation for them. After all, she saved your life."

"I don't know if Grandfather will appreciate that kind of friends very much!"

"Grandfather and I are much less bourgeois than you think. Besides, all we want is for you to be happy and I promise you that from this day forth I'm going to try to do everything I can to make you so."

"You don't know what a job you've taken on!" and tears rose in her eyes.

"My darling, when you finally can believe that you are the most precious thing in the world to me, I think you will be able to accept the unavoidable conflicts between the generations more easily. When you're better, we'll have a serious talk and I'll tell about my own disappointments—perhaps they can help you to bear yours. You can tell me about your own or not, depending on what you feel like doing; we all have things we'd rather not speak of. I understand that very well. For the moment, all you have to do is get well as quickly as possible so that we can leave for Baussigue. Most of all, I don't want you to feel guilty toward me in any way. You are my daughter and I love you, and it's as simple as that."

She could not keep the tears from her own eyes as she said this, and Clothilde squeezed her hand and pulled her arm gently so that her mother leaned over to hug her.

"Why do we have to be so miserable before we can talk to one another?"

"Oh dear! It's because what seems so important at the moment so often hides the essential from us. And then there's that false restraint which keeps us from showing our emotions the way people used to and from talking seriously about any problems except financial ones, or, in a pinch, politics."

"Don't talk to me about politics, I'm sick of it."

"You can be sure I won't. I have enough to do myself without looking out for the rest of the world."

The roommate's little family were plainly aching to leave. The overburdened father muttered that he had promised the "kids" to take them to the "Tuileries" for a ride on the donkeys. The

250

youngest was bored with rummaging in his grandmother's bag and now wanted to explore Marie-Victoire's. The older sister, who looked like a little old woman and took her role very seriously, stopped him, and he began to yell. The middle two, who never let go of each other, were saying: "The donkeys, the donkeys!" over and over and stamping their feet, and the grandmother took advantage of the occasion to say a cool good-by to her daughter-in-law. She was obviously a cranky, authoritarian woman, quite sure of her rights and of which road led to heaven. "Dreadful woman," murmured Marie-Victoire, "she probably doesn't miss a day at mass but she's quite able to ignore Christian charity, a real caricature of a mother-in-law."

In fact, when the little group left, it was as if a window had been opened in a room full of cigar smoke, and the roommate turned to Marie-Victoire with a big smile.

"I hope you're happy that your daughter is so much better. She looks quite different from the way she did yesterday. And see all her beautiful flowers!"

"Yes, madame, you're very kind, and I'm happy that you can enjoy them too. By the way, darling, I don't know if Alan will be able to come back to see you, he told me this morning he's going home to Akron. It seems his father has had a heart attack so Alan has decided to take his place in the factory."

"I'm not surprised. In spite of all his talk about breaking with tradition, there's no one more conservative than Alan. I'll bet that a year from now he'll be married to a very pretty and very rich girl—some pink-and-white beauty with long legs. He'll become a pillar of his church and of the Republican party and she will be president of the Junior League. He'll play golf on Saturday and Sunday, have two martinis every evening before dinner, and play baseball with Alan Harside III. All that he'll keep from his stay in Paris will be a knowledge of wines and a reputation for good taste which will make people consult him about charity balls. I see it all quite plainly. He's very nice, but I would never have married him. He asked me. Did you know?"

"I suspected it."

"You would have liked it, wouldn't you?"

"Before Ingara's death, maybe, but not afterward."

"What do you mean? Ingara, your beautiful Swedish mannequin, is dead? Wasn't she going to get married?"

"Yes, she committed suicide when her fiancé realized she was ten years older than he."

"The poor thing! All you need is to be very sick to realize that there's nothing as valuable as life. Nothing is worth losing that for . . . !" and she waved her hand at the pale blue sky where a few white clouds were floating, ". . . or that," and she pointed to the beautiful fruits from Fauchon.

"Darling, how happy I am to hear these words! Whether you like it or not, you are getting to be more like me: not to love life simply shows a lack of imagination!"

"And what had Alan to do with the suicide?"

"He had nothing to do with the suicide. But to get a good front-page story he gave the pathetic little letter that Ingara had written me to the newspapers. He thought it was good publicity, but I thought I'd die of shame to see that unfortunate girl's tragedy used in such a way. It's true, you haven't seen any papers. Princess Herminie was badly injured in an automobile accident yesterday too."

"My God, how awful!"

"Yes. It's been a ghastly series. Hard to believe. Now you're tired, my darling. I'm going to leave you. This evening I'll bring you some magazines. Have you read *Gone With the Wind?*"

"That old thing!"

"In your weakened condition, it's just the thing. You'll see; it's marvelous!"

"If you say so."

For the time being Clothilde was ready to do whatever her mother wanted, for she was tired of struggling with a life she had found too complicated.

At Place Vendôme, the Princess told Marie-Victoire that Chavanaux and Adrien had asked to speak to her when she got back.

"Good, tell Monsieur Chavanaux he can come up first."

Two minutes later, Chavanaux arrived with a file under his arm.

"Madame, I've prepared the contract with that Berlin house and I'd like you to look it over."

"Three years? That's too much. I can't commit myself for more than one season."

"Do you intend to close?"

"I didn't say that, but things aren't going well enough for me to make such a long-term commitment."

"I telephoned the other houses; it's a very profitable deal and they're all delighted with it."

"So much the better, but I'll only sign a contract with an option to renew in six months."

"You don't trust me enough to let me know your plans?"

"I can't let you know what I don't know myself."

"Haute couture by itself isn't viable any more, and you know it."

"I also know that it takes enormous capital to start a luxury boutique, and I don't even know if it's that that I want."

"But you'll have the money. Big Mills of Indiana is offering you a high price, aren't they?"

"But God knows what they want to do with the house. No,

253

I don't want to sell my name without keeping control of the way it's used."

"Under those conditions, I don't think you'll get far and I'd better offer you my resignation."

"If you've found a job that suits you better than couture, I think you're doing the right thing. You have to believe in what you're selling if you're going to have any success at all, and I know that you really have a contempt for the rag business. But you can depend on me for an excellent reference. Where are you thinking of going?"

"How do you know that I have a place to go?"

"My dear man, you're not one to give up the substance for the shadow, even if the substance seems to you to be going sour. For once I'm paying you a compliment!"

"Yes, I can't say that you've overwhelmed me with them."

"That's true and I've been wrong. That's probably the only thing that keeps people going, just the way the wind pushes sails. But don't hold it against me, dear Chavanaux. In spite of all your very real virtues, you don't have quite enough imagination for me."

"Obviously I'm not as glamorous as Alan!"

"Alan is going back to his American household gods. You're wrong to feel jealous of him. If I had to choose between his brilliant plumage and your mournful neckties, I think I'd prefer your stern apparatus of an office manager coated with solid principles. If only human beings didn't feel they had to present an image of themselves, either too far out, or too conservative, white or black! I only like mixtures. If you prefer, you needn't stay on after Saint Catherine's Day; six months' notice would only hold you up if you're in a hurry to go elsewhere."

"Thanks."

Chavanaux left, deeply mortified that Marie-Victoire had

254

accepted his resignation so readily. Human nature is like that; when one is leaving a place, one hopes it will collapse like a house of cards as soon as one is out the door. The idea of not being indispensable is hard to accept.

Poor Chavanaux, Marie-Victoire thought, he was about as suited to couture as I am to becoming an astronaut. And he always annoyed me, even though I liked him. He was like those big family heirlooms handed down from generation to generation which you'd like very much to be rid of, but which you finally bequeath to your grandchildren. He would have made a marvelous civil servant. Well, now let's see what Adrien has to say. Not the same breed of cat, that one!

He arrived, dressed as usual, in perfect taste. He must have spent hours, she reflected, assembling the tweed suit, the pale yellow shirt, the chestnut brown socks and that chestnut brown tie with the yellow dots. The memory of Oliver's casual elegance gave her a little stab of the heart. That's the first time that I've noticed the unattractive side of being perfectly dressed. You've really gone through some changes, old girl, as Clothilde would say. . . .

"Well, my dear, how are you? You've seen the records of purchase for the day? I just saw them. Thank God for the Belgians, the Dutch, the Germans, and even the provincial French! Without them, and with only the Americans to count on, we'd have to close up. It's strange, the prestige they still have here. It must be *Women's Wear Daily*'s brainwashing. Commercially speaking, they'll be less important to us than the Scandinavian countries in the end. It's crazy how long these myths hang on: with only two night clubs worthy of the name, Paris is still Gay Paris and the American buyer is a Maecenas even if he only buys one model to make up into ten."

"I haven't read *Women's Wear Daily* for a year. It makes me feel as if I'd been walking through nettles, I don't know anything more irritating than that paper. It ruins my sleep. I've come to talk about the future to you."

"Go to it."

"The fact is that I've had enough of this business. Hubert and I are thinking of going into decorating and we're leaving for Milan next week to contact the Italian manufacturers, who are much better than the French at the moment."

"What, you're letting me down?"

"No, surely not when we've found a very good young designer to take my place. I've heard rumors of the sale of your house to an American."

"It isn't settled yet."

"No, but might as well be."

"My dear Adrien, shall I forget what you just said so that you can collect your severance pay, which will be considerable in your case? A year's salary! Have you thought about that?"

"I never doubted for a moment that you would behave perfectly, and that's why I haven't lied to you. On the contrary, I want to relieve any remorse you might feel, for I know that you are a real friend and that the idea of throwing me out must have tortured you. After all, we've had a wonderful association and it's not your fault that the form of elegance we both believe in is dead. It isn't enough to be personally satisfied with a creation, it must please the public too; I suppose that it's the same for all artists. There will still be great couturiers who set fashion, and it will still come from Paris, but little by little custom dressmaking will disappear. If we had a boutique, when I had a good idea I really don't know what I'd do with it: make up the garment in a rich fabric and sell it to four women, or reduce the price and see thousands of copies walking around. Besides, the day when a couturier no longer likes

256

the current styles, he's ready for the Costume Museum. It will give me a new lease on life to change my profession."

"I hope you'll wait until the end of the season anyway. I'd like you to make me a whole wardrobe, and one for Clothilde before you leave. No use saying elegance is out of style. When you've worn haute couture clothing all your life, you can't get used to rags from these so-called with-it boutiques. I'd rather look like a little old lady in a well-cut dress than a young gypsy who left her caravan before she finished dressing. I find these amusing dresses all very well for Saint-Tropez or at home, but not for the street!"

"It will seem sad to be dressing you for the last time, but I'll try to design such beautiful clothes that they'll be timeless. I was afraid you'd jump at the chance to have Jean-Loup make his sexy dresses for you. Aren't you thinking of replacing me with him?"

"My dear, give me time to catch my breath. Alan is going back to the U.S.A., you tell me you're leaving, and Chavanaux hands me his resignation. You must admit that that's a lot of things to happen in one afternoon. I really don't know what I'm going to do, and besides, it doesn't entirely depend on me. If I were given to paranoia, seeing everyone leave this way might make me feel as if I have a contagious disease."

"Your buyer, is it the Monsieur Mayer who brought us Bonwit Teller?"

"Well, yes and no. For the moment there's only Big Mills of Indiana, and he's on their board of directors. If I sold them the firm, I'd have the consolation of getting a good deal of money, but I wouldn't have anything to do with the business and I can't get used to the idea. I've also been very worried about Clothilde; if I kept control of the house she might develop the perfume line and even add cosmetics. She has studied chemistry just for that purpose."

257

"How is she feeling?"

Adrien realized with horror that he had been so absorbed in his own concerns that he had forgotten to ask after Clothilde.

"Much better, thanks, but she is still very weak." Marie-Victoire looked at him for a moment: "Really, without you there's no reason not to give up haute couture! But think of La Callianis! She'll be heartbroken: no more sensational gowns, that will be a hard blow for her!"

"That's some consolation!" and Adrien smiled, for he knew Marie-Victoire's antipathy for his protégée.

"Don't tease me, I'm not that impractical. But all these darling ladies who think haute couture is a charitable institution—when there are nothing but boutiques, where will they go for their evening gowns? Just to see that happen I'd almost be glad to close! When I think of the nerve of some of them and the state in which they return the things I've loaned them—dirty, torn, without even a word of excuse or some flowers with a thank-you note—I'm still furious! The better known they were, the worse they were. Not to mention all the hangers-on drawn to couture in the hope of gleaning some garment or accessory here or there by acting as intermediary. How many little jobs will disappear? Between them and the whiny old saleswomen, I'd surely be better off selling nothing but ready-to-wear!"

"Of course, I'll be at your disposal to help with the conversion of the firm, if that's the way you decide to go. There are all kinds of ready-to-wear. Perhaps you'd like to manufacture for yourself, with your own designer."

"I really don't know yet. In the past five days the sky has fallen on my head. It's no help to be a natural optimist. Events have been too much for me. See Chavanaux. I think there are papers to be drawn up. And I shall go see my friend Paul Malot, he always gives me good advice. Oh my! It's six o'clock already and I promised Clothilde to go to the hospital to bring

258

her something to read! If you like we can have lunch together next week before you leave for Milan. Maybe by that time I'll have put my head in order; right now it's spinning."

Outside the door, Adrien felt very melancholy. Suddenly he realized that he had felt the maximum of attachment and warmth of which he was capable for this woman, and he felt the same regret he would have at finishing an engrossing book. These have been my best years and they are ending now, he sighed, feeling sorry for himself, and he hurried home to Neuilly as quickly as possible so that Hubert could console him.

Marie-Victoire's head was literally empty. She went through all the necessary motions of parking her car and finding the hospital room like an automaton. She stayed only a little while with her daughter, who said: "You really look tired, my poor Mama." Then she hurried back to the Quai de Béthune to plunge into her favorite element: the warm water of her bath. Thérèse came and knocked on the bathroom door:

"Monsieur Mayer is here."

"All right, give him a whiskey on the terrace. I'll be there."

Looking at all her cosmetic jars, she decided that she didn't have the necessary energy to do her face properly, and merely put on a bit of powder and a light lipstick. Mechanically she chose the same housecoat she had worn the day before.

"Oliver, dear, I need a pick-me-up. This evening I feel completely drained. In the course of the day my public relations man, my manager, and my designer, have all resigned; I've tried to reconcile my daughter and her lover; I've been to the hospital twice to see her, and on top of all that I've done the necessary bowing and scraping with the buyers."

"Sit down and tell me all about it."

"This is becoming a habit."

"I hope so!"

He gave her some whiskey the way she liked it, this time without asking how much ice or water.

"All right, so begin at the beginning, I believe in order. I went to the little apartment my daughter shares with that boy, and I found him in bed."

"With another girl?"

"No, no, don't turn Gallic so quickly!"

"You had the key?"

"Mmm. Yes, I took it from Clothilde's bag."

"Well, I see there are times when you dispense with your scruples."

"If I'd brought back a repentant lover to her bedside it would have been well worth the indelicacy of taking a key from a handbag, wouldn't it? You don't get much in this life by sitting on your behind."

"And your charm didn't work?"

"I guess not, but I'm glad I met him. He's most attractive: a kind of visionary, as beautiful as a Christ. I can't blame my daughter for having loved him. What happened would have been even sadder if the object of her affections had been without physical and spiritual qualifications as a husband or a bed partner. At least she will have known a real man, and not every woman can say the same."

Oliver smiled. "A real man," he said. "If more of them existed would there be a women's liberation movement? Isn't that just what every woman wants? It's the disappointment of not having one that makes them aggressive. And the more they become so, the more men run from them. . . . No wonder there are so many homosexuals. . . . But let's get back to business. So that was the first upset of the morning."

"Yes. After that, Alan came to tell me he had decided to go back to Akron. At the time I was very surprised because only three or four days ago—I don't know what I'm doing any

260

more, so many things have happened to me in such a short time—he offered to buy my business. Obviously with the tacit but primary condition that he would marry Clothilde. But when I went to the hospital I found out that he had accidently discovered that she hadn't been hospitalized for peritonitis but for an abortion, and that she could no longer have a child. This news made him run like a rabbit. I had the impression that he would have rather swum home than stay here."

"Well, I'm not surprised. The Harside factory needs an heir. What else?"

"Well, my manager never really liked couture and he's found a similar position in cosmetics. Besides, everyone thinks I'm going to close: it's natural he should have looked for another job. As for Adrien, he has felt himself becoming dated for several seasons and instead of becoming a has-been he's decided to retire—which is very sensible. Actually, all these resignations are going to make my decision easier."

"You're selling to Big Mills and I shall marry a rich wife!"

"Of course that's the temptation. Unfortunately there is my daughter."

"Well, she can come to the United States, to my cosmetic factory, or, if she likes, to the university to finish her studies and do whatever she decides."

"And live with us, and try to change into an American. . . . No, it really wouldn't work!"

"Do you think she would hesitate an instant about sacrificing your life if she found happiness with someone?"

"No, but that's the difference between parents and children."

"Admit you don't want to live in Dallas!"

"It's not just Dallas: it's no worse than any other city; it's being president of this club and secretary of that one, showing off my diamonds at the opera on dressy evenings—I hate opera music!—I like only the Baroque—going on pigeon shoots when

261

I think it's a cruel sport, putting up with men and women who smell of gin and get more maudlin every minute, not seeing the Seine when I wake up! No, I couldn't stand all that alone. Because you would leave at eight o'clock every morning and come back at seven, and our social position would oblige us to see people every day. In two months we'd be like all the others: two strangers living under the same roof. My love, let's be reasonable. If we had a common business I would stay in Paris to take care of it, you would come here often, and I could go there too on the pretext of seeing my daughter, for I think the idea of sending her to America to study chemistry in a university is a very good one. As long as you wish, we can start over again on a boat, the way we did in the spring, to live another fairy tale in a distant land. If we lived apart, our bodies would have time to hunger for one another, and we wouldn't run the risk of growing tired of each other."

Oliver, who had perfected a foolproof technique for escaping the clutches of hundreds of sirens who were avid for present social position and future alimony, had to admire the wisdom of this woman who, though completely under his spell, still knew how to preserve her dignity.

"You know how easy divorce is in America, but acknowledged mistresses are not so common."

"Very well, then, we'll go to Mexico or the Caribbean; I've always dreamed of going there. I'd like to travel very much."

He smiled. "We'll talk about it another time."

"I hope the Lord will give me the strength to resist you at least on this point."

"What an odd Lord you believe in if he approves of fornication without marriage."

"God is French, as we all know."

"And your business, how do you see it changing, since

262

whether you like it or not, couture is deserting you before you leave it?"

"First, I'd thought of starting a specialized shop for evening clothes. That way I can leave suits and woolens alone and not compete with Courrèges, Ungaro, and all the sports houses. One day, as I was passing IBM, I had an idea for electronic machines which would find the ideal model for each woman and give her a pattern to her measure just by pushing a button. Finally, I'm wondering if it's still enthralling working for a happy few. It should certainly be more rewarding to create elegance for a crowd that for a vanishing so-called elite. A luxury boutique might be the only thing I'm capable of handling, but giving notions of elegance to millions might bring more happiness and cash. But we may not be ready for that yet. No, I admit it, for the first time in my life, I feel discouraged. I believe I'll just close the haute couture part of the firm up in November at the end of the season."

As she said this, her French accent was stronger than usual. He took her hand: "Darling, I can afford to invest in a losing business if that's what would really make you happy, but it would only postpone failure. You were made for haute couture, but you'd never survive a year in the ready-to-wear jungle, specialized or not. That's a totally different field, run by manufacturers who have no artistic scruples. If the public has bad taste, well, they'll give it to them for their money! Their gospel is the cash register and they don't mind making every woman in the world look like a scarecrow if it will make them a profit.

"I think you're right not to sell your name to Big Mills if you want to keep your perfume. And that's where I can help. With your name, which stands for elegance, funds to finance a hard advertising push, and factories already set up to make good cosmetics, there's a 90 per cent chance of success with

263

a big beauty-products operation. When Clothilde is better, come to Dallas with her. There's nothing like work to make a girl of her age forget a broken romance. And who knows, she may be a real businesswoman!"

"I succeeded myself."

"I know, my darling. But while you may be the ideal French businesswoman, let me tell you you don't come up to the ankle of the American ones! If you like, I can introduce you to some specimens who will give you goose flesh. I mean that as a compliment. I'm happy that you've arrived at the decision not to sell. Maybe you could become a great asset as a fashion consultant in our mail-order business too. But I won't stop hoping that when Clothilde marries, you'll agree to do the same."

"Maybe. There's nothing in the world as intoxicating as succeeding alone, but when things aren't going so well, you feel lonely. Let me think about it some more. I love you too much to decide too quickly. The day I say yes to you, there mustn't be trace of regret or apprehension in my mind."

"So let's live in sin, since that's what your religion recommends. Your damned Thérèse just went out. I heard the door slam."

This time, as if she had much to be forgiven, it was she, with his help, who strove to make him perfectly happy; and she discovered with surprise that this was a game which could be learned at any age. When he left her at six the next morning, she had just enough strength to promise him that she would be at the Ritz at ten-thirty to drive him to Orly.

During the drive they avoided speaking of business. Oliver merely promised to give her negative response to Big Mills. His lawyer had a correspondent in Paris who would get in touch with Paul Malot. He promised to come back in two weeks and take her on a little Mediterranean cruise again. Would she like to go to Sardinia? OK, Sardinia then. Before separating in front of customs, she ostentatiously kissed him on the lips as if they were an old married couple, and murmured:

"I belong to you more than if we had been married in front of a mayor, my priest, and your rabbi. I would like to give you something, but first promise not to laugh at me."

"I promise."

She took a pair of black wooden castanets out of her purse, the kind available in any Spanish gift shop.

"What's that?"

"I bought them at the Palma airport last time, right after you left. I couldn't stand not to have something to remind me of our wonderful stay and . . . it was all I could find."

During her explanation, she had been separating the two halves of the castanets.

"Take one; I'll keep the other—and be glad it wasn't a bronze Eiffel Tower! It's wood, so it should bring us luck."

"What a child you are under that façade of the sophisticated woman!"

"Don't tell anybody; this is just for you. Promise me you'll always keep the half?"

"Always."

"I love you; take care of yourself; telephone me."

Before he disappeared into the left-hand corridor, he turned to give her a big wave as if to say: I'm still here! But the few yards which separated them already seemed as wide as the Atlantic to her. Would she have had the strength to go away from him that way?

It would be five minutes before the arrival of the Nice plane, and she went toward the gate which had been announced for it. She saw her father immediately, for in spite

265

of his age he was the handsomest passenger. A wave of tenderness overwhelmed her.

How well he looks, what a presence! Like a mixture of Vittorio De Sica and Henry Fonda. And, as usual, she noticed the details of what he was wearing. The shoulders of his old navy blue blazer are too big, I must buy him another. How elegant he would be with a wine velvet evening jacket; I'm going to have to persuade him. I feel like spoiling him. . . .

"Papa, you look marvelous. . . . I'm so glad to see you!"

"And I to see you! But let me look at you: you're radiant. I was afraid you'd be too tired, and here you are more beautiful than ever! You must be in love!"

"What an eye you have, I can't hide anything from you!"

"Well, we'll talk about that later. First tell me about Clothilde. How is she?"

"Much better."

"I didn't understand about this peritonitis very well. It seems impossible these days."

"I didn't want to upset you on the phone, and besides there was no use setting the whole village talking. I suspect that the good Titine listens to our conversations through the switchboard. Clothilde's illness was much more serious than I told you. She had just gone through a terrible experience for such a young girl. She will be marked by it for life, because she won't be able to have children."

Marie-Victoire could not keep her voice from trembling, and her father took her arm.

"That's dreadful, why did you hide it from me?"

"What could I do? I must be more old-fashioned than I seem. I didn't like to admit even to you, or perhaps above all to you, that my own daughter didn't trust me enough and had an abortion by the first butcher she could find."

"Couldn't she marry the boy?"

266

"It seems he's some sort of visionary"—she used the same word she had used in speaking to Oliver of him—"a Maoist or something. I don't understand these subtleties, to me it's all the same, fascist or communist. He doesn't believe in marriage, but it must be said in his favor that he was against abortion too and he warned her that he would never see her again if she got rid of the child. Clothilde believed we couldn't have stood having a bastard in the family, when in fact I'd a thousand times rather be a grandmother under those circumstances than be deprived of that joy forever."

"I agree! We are descendants of a bastard son of Good King René. For our time, the bastard of a revolutionary would be almost as illustrious, and he could have revived the name! What a tragic story! That will complicate the job of finding her a good husband. It's only natural for a man to want children by the woman he loves."

"How right you are! You remember the young American, Alan Harside, my public relations man? He was in Baussigue for three days at Easter."

"Yes, very well. He was handsome and seemed polite, but too ambitious. I don't really care much for that sort."

"Right, you saw through him. Well, the minute he found out that Clothilde would not be able to have children, he told me he was returning to the U.S.A., though three days earlier he had wanted to buy my firm and my daughter."

"It's really time rich people found out they can't buy everything. Would Clothilde have married him?"

"Never."

"So good riddance. Tell me about yourself. It's true, my darling, I've never seen you so blooming, you must tell me everything. If you knew how I worried about you struggling alone, and how I would have liked to have helped you; I can admit it to you now, I always detested that young man you married. The first time I saw him I'd gladly have strangled him. I believe that if I'd found your mother dancing the tango with an Argentine gigolo it would have made me less unhappy than seeing you when you came down to Sainte Maxime with him. When he came back from Germany, it was still worse, and I was sure he had become impotent. But how could I say it to you? I'd never have dared, and your mother, whom I talked to about it, didn't dare either. How stupid we were then! As a judge I've heard stories that would make your hair stand on end, but at that time they weren't told so freely or with such scientific detachment as they are today, especially in the home."

Marie-Victoire interrupted him: "Have you much luggage?"

"No, just my big tan suitcase."

"Oh Lord! I know that one, it weighs a ton. Fortunately the car is near."

As soon as they were settled in the Austin, her father continued: "I can tell you now, you have always been my most precious possession. I fell in love with your mother's beauty and we were happy for a few months, but we had no tastes in common . . ." and like a final verdict: "What she liked most was hunting, and how proud she was of being a good shot! With you, I have always had a perfect communion of minds. But I'm not complaining, we had a happy enough marriage; in spite of her taste for blood sports she was a good woman, and with her strong sense of duty and her good education she helped me a great deal in my career. Now I miss her. . . . After a certain age it is better to be married to someone who isn't perfect than to be alone, and I have worried about you being alone for such a long time. Today I thank heaven for giving me the joy of seeing you happy before I die. I've prayed a great deal for that; you are beautiful and intelligent. It wasn't possible that a man, a real one, wouldn't see it. I very much want to know the one who has finally made you glow like this. . . . I hope you are going to marry him."

"Unfortunately, it's not so simple! He is Jewish, he—"

Her father interrupted her: "I was afraid you were going to say he was married. But Jewish, I hope that isn't stopping you. Our family has never been anti-Semitic, that's the reaction of middle-class men who are furious at having shrewd competition."

". . . He has been married too, but that's nothing! What is more serious is that he lives in Dallas and is younger than I am. You don't know America. It's both wonderful and frightening too, and unfortunately I think I'm too old to adapt to it. If I could live away from the cities and never see anyone but the simple, generous people who make up most of the country, it would be easy. But Oliver is the head of a big business, and the so-called society he's obliged to be part of is even less attractive than what we have here under that name. People don't realize how compartmentalized American society is. In Europe the aristocracy is always surrounded by artists and intellectuals. There, that catalytic element doesn't exist, so it seems as if everyone is classified in drawers in an enormous filing cabinet. Multimillionaires at the top and the poor at the bottom, as they are everywhere . . . but besides that, financiers with financiers, intellectuals with intellectuals, blacks with blacks, Jews with Jews, the "beautiful people" with the decorators and designers from Seventh Avenue . . . and politicians all warm and cozy in Washington."

"But if you love him as you seem to, can't you get around all that? And he, what does he think?"

"He's offered to marry me several times. He is very American and doesn't realize yet how important this is to me"—she pointed to the Île de la Cité which they were approaching from the quai opposite—"even if it's only that!"

"It's true that this is very beautiful. It's a long time since I've seen it! Can't we stop for a moment? I used to love to walk beside the Seine. But aren't you being a bit silly? There are plenty of beautiful landscapes in America. Besides, when you're rich you don't have to stay home, and Texas can't be as bad as all that!"

"Yes, the country, and some of the cities, but Dallas! I have the feeling that the good Lord gave it oil to make people forget its ugly face . . . like girls with dowries big enough to make the world forget they're cross-eyed or have piano legs!"

"You know, when a woman is lucky enough to find a man who has the effect on her that this one seems to have on you, she doesn't give him up for a landscape."

"True, but don't you think that happiness evaporates quickly in a place one hates? And that desire lasts much longer if it isn't too easily fulfilled? If I were to go over there, how long would my wonderful nights make up for my empty days? I hate the forced activities of most rich Americans. Of course, I could still work, I might even become fashion consultant for a big mail-order business. That's certainly what I'd be most interested in. He can look after the cosmetic business himself with Clothilde, if she cares to. After all, dressing people well is the only thing I know thoroughly and I have made myself a good name in that field. But I haven't agreed yet. Sometimes I think I'd rather make jam in Baussigue and look after my child."

"You've been telling me for years that haute couture was dying, but all the same, won't you miss it?"

"I don't know any more. Right now, a strictly haute couture operation is such a losing proposition that it becomes no more than a publicity gimmick to sell stockings, ties, shoes, girdles, and especially perfume. It's an extinct profession. You really can say: 'The collection is over.' That's what we've come

270

to, and to a great extent it's publicity that's killed it. After all it's a legend to say that perfumes cannot live without the haute couture. Look at Madame Rochas, when her husband died she closed the couture and since then her perfumes have been much more successful."

"So, my dear, surely this is the moment to give up business and marry this man."

"You're probably right, he has become much more important to me than all the reasons against him that I just gave you, including American life and business. No, the real obstacle is Clothilde. She counts more in my life than he does, at least in a different way. I feel responsible for her while I depend on him. If I had been younger I surely would not have thought this way, and I don't say that the day when she's found herself a good husband I won't finally let myself relax in the arms of a strong man instead of going on alone. But for the moment she needs me too much."

"I don't think that one need sacrifice one's own life for that of one's children, my dear; they always need their parents much less than the latter hope. But I can understand your feeling that you mustn't show too much happiness when your child has just passed through such a bad time. However, time will take care of that."

"Perhaps. Anyhow, right now it really doesn't seem right to get married before she does. Besides, if Oliver can wait, won't that be the best proof that I'm not mistaken about him?"

"I hope I'll have the happiness of seeing both you and your daughter happy before I die. . . ." And to hide his emotion: "How do you intend to change your firm if you want to give up haute couture? And what are you going to do with your staff?"

"That's the worst part of it. Fortunately, my manager offered me his resignation yesterday. Obviously, my biggest

271

worry was Adrien, but yesterday he too told me that he wanted to go into the decorating business with Hubert. So really the only person whom I'll be sad to lose is big Suzanne. You know, the dressing-room supervisor; you saw her when we showed the collection in Nice. But I think I can help her start a dry-cleaning business, that's always been her idea. Here we are. Let me carry that suitcase. That leather is very handsome, but it's much too heavy."

While waiting for the creaky little elevator to come back down from the fifth floor, she went on:

"Oliver also offered to take Clothilde into one of his factories. If she would agree to live in America for a while, that might change her mood and give me a good excuse to go there more often."

"You don't know what you want! Now you want to go there more often, when you just told me that it was impossible to live there."

She laughed. "It's true. As long as you know that you don't have to stay there, it's an exciting, generous country, where anything can happen. I adore going there to visit, but it's a country for the young. Clothilde will love it. And if she married an American that would change the problem too."

"My darling, I think you will always fall on your feet. All I ask is that you never sell Baussigue. Clothilde will adopt a child, perhaps, or else marry a widower or a divorcé with children . . ."

Opening the door of the elevator which finally had arrived at the ground floor, Marie-Victoire interrupted: "I think your priest will keel over if we both marry divorcés!"

"Before then he will be replaced with a more accommodating type in blue jeans who'd be in tune with the times. Anyway, I've never been able to believe that God cares about such nonsense. There is really only one thing that should count: to do the least possible harm to one's neighbor—make love not war!"

"You're turning into a hippie! Clothilde won't believe it! You really are marvelous and I adore you."

Opening the door wide, Thérèse welcomed them with one of her rare smiles: "What a pleasure to have Monsieur le Comte here! See, even Popoff is beside himself!"

After luncheon, Nicolas de Baussigue decided to go and see his granddaughter at once. He stopped at a florist shop and chose a bouquet in yellow, white, and blue, carefully selecting flowers whose scent was not too strong. Old gentlemen often think of details which escape those in the so-called prime of life. Seeing him come into the room, Clothilde blushed, and her grandfather, leaning to kiss her, said: "Don't feel ashamed. Your mother told me all about it. All we want now is to see you happy. Let's never speak of all this again. You know, life is really wonderful and it's no big thing to make a mistake at twenty. Let me look at you. How beautiful you are too. I really have had three lovely women in my life."

"But you're handsome too, Grandfather, and so nice . . . everyone loves you."

"So, we're the best!"

And they burst out laughing together. He added:

"Tell me, speaking of the best, we must keep your mother from making a mistake. Do you know this Oliver Mayer?"

"I've seen him once or twice. He's very attractive."

"With your views, I was afraid you'd say he's a horrible Yankee."

"No, Alan was a horrible Yankee, but this one looks like a real man, strong and tender . . ."

"Well! Quite a recommendation! Has your mother spoken to you lately?"

"No."

273

"That's what I thought. She refuses to be happy while you are unhappy."

"Why? Does he want to marry her?"

"Yes, but she refused when she was dying to."

"That's ridiculous. Doesn't she think I have enough with my own regrets and my own mess without adding remorse over her?"

"Now, now, don't get upset. She also feels remorse over you. She reproaches herself for not having been there when you needed her."

"You can hardly reproach her for not staying by the telephone to be there when I called. Besides, I was the one who drifted away from her after my aunt told me about Papa's suicide. That really was a shock though, you know!"

"Yes, that was a tragedy, but he came back from prison camp very ill, and he was never right for your mother. We tried to change her mind, but when one has lived four years remembering an ideal love, one can't imagine that one's fiancé has changed into an old man."

"You didn't like him either. But fathers never like their sons-in-law, do they?"

"That's not true; I feel an enormous sympathy for this American without even knowing him."

". . . because your daughter isn't twenty any more."

"Perhaps, but that isn't the real problem. If you don't push her into this man's arms, she will end up alone and never get over having let her last chance at happiness get away. Haute couture took the place of a lover for her, but it's leaving her now. Adrien wants to become a decorator, her manager wants to do something else, business isn't too good, and will be worse if no one will invest more capital in the firm. Do you know that she spoke to me of making jam in Baussigue? Can

274

you see her as the kind of lady who does good works and is out of work, as our good friend Renée Brock would say? At the end of two months she would be snapping at everyone like a caged monkey. We must put a stop to that and you're the only one who can, just because you're the one she feels guilty about."

"And you, won't she listen to you?"

"No more than you'll listen to her, or I listened to my parents. On the other hand, if she said to me: you must sell this vineyard and put another bathroom in the château, I would immediately take her advice. It's wrong to consider parent-child relationships as unchangeable. Just because you've taught your children everything they know doesn't mean you remain a teacher all your life. On the contrary, as soon as they are adults, it's up to them to decide for us."

"So you consider me an adult and think it's up to me to take things in hand. That comes as rather a blow, when I'm feeling so exhausted."

"In a month you won't feel that way, that's the miracle of youth. You must tell your mother that you would adore to live in America and urge her to accept the fashion consultant job for that big mail-order business. You might even tell her how you want to get to know that American better so that you can give your blessing to their marriage. You ought to go to Sardinia with them . . ."

"Now you're going too far!"

"Not at all, I want happiness for my daughter, and the only way she'll get it is to be at peace with her own child. Besides, if this Oliver is as nice as he seems to be, he'll be grateful for your help and you'll find the paternal affection you've always missed."

"I think you're right. Besides, I would like to try a new

world. It's lucky you came, I would never have thought of that by myself!"

"You'll see, sometimes old people are good for something!"

That late afternoon in the Place Vendôme nothing interesting was happening, and after greeting some buyers from Nice, Marie-Victoire suddenly had a desire to be out of doors in the golden haze of a summer evening. She had listened, nodding, to the complaints of some nice ladies, owners of one of the best firms on the Côte d'Azur, who were lamenting the aging of their clientele. She had laughed openly at their description of some of their customers, freshly powdered, beautifully coiffed old ladies, dressed in white or pink—rich mummies, regularly taken out of a padded refrigerator by the inevitable companion who humbly picked up their crumbs. Light-colored mink abounded on those shores, they said, but there was also drab ermine and carefully mended fur neckpieces, and the lace suits and spike heels that had given fifteen years of good and loyal service.

It was true, all widows on the Côte d'Azur or in Florida weren't rich, thought Marie-Victoire as she backed the car out of the garage. And for the first time in her life she was struck by that dreadful word: widow. She was one too! Surprise overcame her and made her brake unconsciously. A taxi driver, forced to do the same so as not to run into her, cried: "Stupid bitch . . . you'd be better off at home, knitting!" Popoff barked and showed his teeth as the taxi passed them.

"You'll take care of me . . . you're a good dog. . . ." A morbid thought came to her . . . a widow with only her dog to defend her . . . how awful. How could she not have seen it sooner!

Oliver, strength; Oliver, tenderness; Oliver, security; Oliver, bliss. Oliver, the great, the sublime, *the man* . . . Saint Oliver, pray for me . . . even if I have to live in Dallas, Texas, all year round!

And suddenly Notre Dame became quite gray, just a soulless pile of ancient stones. Paris without a man was only another city!